OFFICERS AND GENTLEMEN

For duty, for honour, for love

Bound by honour and family ties, three brave men fought for their lives in France…

Now, back in the drawing rooms of England, they face a new battle as three beautiful women lay siege to their scarred hearts!

PROTECTED BY THE MAJOR
January 2014

DRAWN TO LORD RAVENSCAR
February 2014

COURTED BY THE CAPTAIN
Already available

AUTHOR NOTE

This is the second of the Ravenscar cousins' trilogy. Hallam helped Adam when their cousin Mark Ravenscar was murdered. Now that they have caught the culprit Adam and Jenny are married and Hal turns his mind to his own problems. He has never been able to forget Madeline, the girl he asked to wed him before he joined the army. She turned him down to marry a wealthy lord, but now he has discovered that she is desperately unhappy. Should he forgive her for the pain she caused him and help her in her time of need?

I hope my readers will enjoy this second book. The third is coming soon.

Love to you all.

PROTECTED
BY THE MAJOR

Anne Herries

Published in Great Britain 2014
by Mills & Boon, an imprint of Harlequin (UK) Limited,
Eton House, 18-24 Paradise Road, Richmond, Surrey, TW9 1SR

© 2014 Anne Herries

ISBN: 978 0 263 90932 6

Harlequin (UK) Limited's policy is to use papers that are natural, renewable and recyclable products and made from wood grown in sustainable forests. The logging and manufacturing processes conform to the legal environmental regulations of the country of origin.

Printed and bound in Spain
by Blackprint CPI, Barcelona

Anne Herries lives in Cambridgeshire, where she is fond of watching wildlife and spoils the birds and squirrels that are frequent visitors to her garden. Anne loves to write about the beauty of nature, and sometimes puts a little into her books, although they are mostly about love and romance. She writes for her own enjoyment, and to give pleasure to her readers. Anne is a winner of the Romantic Novelists' Association Romance Prize. She invites readers to contact her on her website: www.lindasole.co.uk

Previous novels by the same author:

I would like to dedicate this,
the second of the cousins' trilogy, to my editors
at HM&B past and present for all the help
they have given me over the years.

Prologue

'Please do not do this,' the handsome young cavalry officer begged, catching at the girl's arm as she started to walk away. 'If you marry him you will break my heart and I know he cannot make you happy, Madeline.'

She blinked back her tears as she looked at him, her green eyes misty and filled with an appeal that caught at his heart. She was lovely, with her long, naturally wavy hair brushing her shoulders and her soft mouth that had always smiled for him. In her eyes he saw the love she had once declared beneath this very apple tree, but her words were cold and dismissive.

'I pray you let go of my arm, sir. I have accepted the count's proposal of marriage and the contract is signed. There is nothing I can do.'

'Come away with me now,' he said, breathing deeply as the wintry sunlight caught the red-gold of her hair. 'If you are my wife, he can do nothing to prevent it. I know you love me…you swore it to me only last summer.'

'In the summer things were different.' She turned her beautiful face from him. 'You do not understand, Hallam. It was all arranged and I…I am happy with my promise. The count is rich and will give me all the things I…require. Besides, I do not love you.'

'You swore you would always love me. We kissed to seal our promise to each other and I was to speak to your father when I returned.'

'You were away too long,' she said, and her face was proud, cold and withdrawn. 'And you have no money, Hallam. How can you expect me to share your poverty? If your father had not lost all his money gambling or…' She pulled away from him, her face turned from his so that he could not read her expression. 'I should not even have come to meet you. My father will be furious. Please go away now, Hallam…and do not bother me again with your unwanted attentions.'

This time Hallam released his grip on her

arm. 'Bother you with my attentions? No, indeed, Miss Morris, I shall not. I believed your protestations of love and your lying smiles, but I was a fool. Run back to your father and your bridegroom-to-be and I wish you joy of him.'

He turned and strode away, leaving her standing beneath the apple tree where they had promised undying love just a few short months earlier. Madeline stared after him, her pale face turned to stone and the tears slowly slipping down her cheeks.

She longed with all her heart to call him back, but it was too late. She'd had no choice but to send him away, for her father had signed the contract despite her pleas to wait for Hallam's return.

'Even if he comes it will not serve,' Sir Matthew said to his only daughter. 'I am ruined, Maddie, and Lethbridge holds my notes. Would you see your mother and sister thrown on the parish—and me in my grave? I could not live with the shame if Lethbridge took everything. You are my only hope.'

'But I do not love him!'

'Foolish child,' her father said. 'Marriage and love have nothing to say to each other. Marry Lethbridge and live in the style you were meant to live, and, when you have given him his heir, he will probably tire of you and leave you to sleep alone. Perhaps then you may look elsewhere for love if you are discreet.'

'Papa!' Madeline stared at him in horror. She knew that it was often the case that both men and women looked for love outside marriage, but she had wanted something different. She had hoped for love—but how could she deny her father when he would be ruined if she refused the count's offer? 'Very well… if it is your wish.'

'My dear good girl,' her father said and kissed her brow. 'I knew you would not let me down.'

Madeline had had no choice, but pride would not let her tell Hallam that she had been the victim of emotional blackmail. She knew that he would not have understood that she must do her duty. No, it was best if he thought her heartless, but it had broken her heart to see the pain and disappointment in his eyes.

'Oh, Hallam,' she whispered as she turned to walk back through the meadows to her father's house. 'Oh, Hallam, I loved you so…'

But she must put away all thought of

love and do her duty. Madeline knew that
the count was a jealous man and she sensed
that he might be cruel if he were thwarted.
She must try to make him a good wife, even
though she was dead inside.

Chapter One

Hallam Ravenscar, now a major in His Majesty's Own elite cavalry regiment, and the recipient of some half-a-dozen medals for gallantry on the field, straightened an imaginary crease in his immaculate coat of blue superfine and placed a diamond stickpin in the soft folds of his cravat. His short dark hair was brushed casually into a fashionable style and he looked the complete man about town, his eyes grey with a look of steel in them. Having returned to England after Napoleon was finally defeated to the shocking tragedy of his cousin Mark's murder, he had played his part in the unmasking of an evil rogue. He was now in London to see his man of business and to purchase a wedding gift for his cousin Captain Adam Miller to Miss Jenny Hastings.

A half-sigh left his lips for he had been urged by his lawyers and agents to consider marrying an heiress, too. Indeed, it must be marriage or the more drastic step of selling his late father's estate, which was at present burdened with insupportable debt. His father had been a lifelong gambler and after the death of the wife he'd adored, he had plunged deeper and deeper into the abyss.

Hallam had been fighting for his life in France when his father succumbed to a virulent fever and it was only on his return to England that he truly understood what awaited him.

'You have little choice, sir,' Mr Hatton, his father's lawyer, told him. 'Had your father lived he must have sold most of the estate but since his death I have had hard work of it to keep the bank from foreclosing. It would be better to sell than let them simply take the estate. That way you might save something.'

Hallam knew that he was close to ruin. He had the small estate his maternal grandfather had left to him, but that was little more than a large farmhouse and some one hundred acres, most of which was let to tenants. Together with his pay, it had brought him sufficient income to sustain him as a cavalry officer, but was hardly enough to support a wife and family in style, unless he could find another source of income. Adam had invited him to come in as a partner with a wine-importing business, and Hallam had agreed. He would need to sell his commission and that would bring sufficient funds for a modest investment—but what of the future?

His lawyer had made no bones about it. 'Your mother was the youngest daughter of an earl, Major Ravenscar, and your father the younger son of an old and respected family. You do not at present have a title to offer, but I think you might find that the daughter of a rich merchant would welcome an offer.'

'Good grief, you want me to sell myself?'

Hallam had greeted the suggestion with horror and disgust, but in truth he could see very little alternative. He might make a fortune with Adam, but that was well into the future. In the meantime he had two choices, neither of which appealed.

Damn it! He would not think about the problem of his estate tonight. He was engaged to meet some friends to dine, and from there they would go on to a card party at the house of Lord Devenish. He understood there would be some dancing after the musical recital for those that cared for it—nothing lavish, just a few couples standing up in the gallery.

He picked up his swordstick and hat, gave himself another depreciating look and left his lodgings to keep the appointment. It was years since Hal had thought of marriage, being content to flirt mildly with charming young ladies and enjoy a friendly relationship with an obliging widow while on service in Spain and France.

How could he even consider marriage when his heart had never completely healed? Madeline had dealt his heart and his pride a severe blow. While the pain had subsided gradually, and a harder, stronger man had been forged in the fires of battle, Hal had never felt anything stronger than affection for the lady who had so kindly tended his wounds and given generously of herself.

Had he wished to marry for comfort's sake, he could not have done better than to wed Mrs Sarah Bowman, for she had been a soldier's wife and would have been willing to follow the drum—but Hal did not wish for a wife. How could he marry when his heart was dead? Madeline had killed it when she married her count for his money.

It was ridiculous to think of Madeline. She had long forgotten him—and was probably content in her marriage with several children at her skirts.

The picture gave him pain and he put it from his mind. He must forget Madeline and move on. Perhaps it would be better to take his lawyer's advice and seek out the daughter of a wealthy Cit, who would be grateful to offer her father's money in return for a home and a place in society.

His lips curled with distaste at the idea, but he would not be the first or the last to seek a solution to his money problems in this way.

If the worst came to the worst, he would consider it, but for the moment he would look for other ways to pay his debts.

Lord Devenish's rooms were overflowing with guests, all of them enjoying the fine champagne and other wines, which waiters offered them constantly as they circulated with trays. Hal accepted a glass and sipped it, moving through the crowded rooms and stopping now and then to talk to people he knew. He was hailed as a hero by many, welcomed home and greeted warmly. His bravery had been mentioned in dispatches and everyone was eager to congratulate him, asking how long he intended to stay in London and offering invitations to all manner of events.

'The Regent told me you were an outstanding officer,' Lord Devenish told him as he clapped him on the shoulder and welcomed him to the house. 'Knew your father well, m'boy—and regretted what happened at the end. If you need any advice or help you know where to come.'

'Thank you, sir,' Hallam said and smiled. 'I do not suppose you know of an heiress in desperate need of a husband?'

He meant it as a jest, to turn off the offer of help, but his host looked grave and then light dawned in his eyes. 'As it happens I do, Hallam my dear fellow. Her father is indebted to me for various matters of business I put in his way and told me he would like to see his girl settled with a decent fellow. He made it plain that he doesn't look for money, but a good family and the entry into society is what is hoped for. Would you like me to arrange a meeting?'

'Oh, I hardly think it necessary just yet,' Hal said lightly. 'It would be a last resort, sir.'

'Well, I can't vouch for the girl's looks or manners, never seen her—but I'll ask them to a supper party and send you an invitation. Make up your mind when you've seen her.'

Hallam thanked him and passed on as some newcomers arrived. He had spoken lightly, but his host had taken him seriously—but he would not think of a marriage of convenience just yet.

As the rooms filled up, the ladies took their seats for the musical recital, but most of the men moved into the card room, where several tables had been set up in readiness. Hal was invited to join a hand of whist for modest stakes and accepted. He was a skilled player and won as often as he lost. Provided he stayed within the limits he'd set himself for his lifestyle, he did not consider it wrong to gamble a little. Unlike his father, he never played the dice or faro, though he enjoyed a game of skill.

His luck was mixed that evening for he won the first hand with his partner, lost the second and third, then won the fourth, which meant he rose from the tables for supper in no worse case than he had been when he sat down.

Making his way into the supper room, he

helped himself to a small pastry and ate it, sipped some wine, then made his way out to the terrace to smoke a cigar. A lady was about to enter the supper room and for a moment he stood in her way. He apologised and glanced at her face, feeling shocked as he saw the beautiful sophisticated lady whose path he'd blocked. Her hair was piled high upon her head, one long ringlet falling on to a white shoulder, her gown cut daringly low to show off the sweet valley between milky-white breasts. So far different from the girl he'd known was she that he spoke without thinking.

'Madeline…good grief! I should not have known you.'

For a moment she seemed too stunned to answer, then a look of sadness swept into her eyes. 'I dare say you think me much changed, for I am older.'

'No, no, you are beautiful,' he said, recovering. 'You have become a great lady, Madeline.'

'It is the gown,' she said and a half-smile was on her lips. 'I had heard you were home— and I was sad to hear of Mark's death. You must have felt it deeply. You were always close as young men.'

'We became even closer for we served together in France,' he said. 'How are you? You look very well.'

'I am quite well,' she said. 'I am glad to have seen you. Please excuse me, sir. I went out for some air and my husband will look for me.'

Hal stood to one side, allowing her to pass. For a moment as he'd looked at her the years had slipped away and he'd forgotten their parting, forgotten the pain she had so carelessly inflicted. Now he had remembered and he felt the bitterness sweep over him.

She was obviously content with her life and her marriage, and why should she not be? The diamond necklace she was wearing must have cost a king's ransom. He was a damned fool even to think of her. She had made her own life and he must make his. Perhaps he should move on in his life, make a marriage of convenience, as Madeline had.

He walked about the terrace, smoking his cheroot and then threw it into the bushes. He would speak to Devenish, ask him to arrange that supper party soon. If the heiress were presentable and—more importantly—agreeable, he might as well take the easy way out and marry her.

* * *

Madeline entered the hot, overcrowded rooms and realised she could not bear it another moment. Her throat was tight with emotion and she felt close to tears. How unfortunate to bump into Hal like that! He had been much in her thoughts these past weeks, since Lethbridge had told her about Mark Ravenscar's murder. She had longed to write to Hal and tell him how sad she was, but it would not have been permitted. Indeed, she dare not for fear of what her husband might think or do.

Lethbridge was unpredictable in his moods. When she pleased him, he would buy her a new jewel or a stylish gown such as the one she was wearing this evening, but he was often jealous and if she appeared to enjoy the company of a gentleman too much he would come to her room last thing at night and rage at her. Sometimes he would punish her.

When they first married, she had tried to be a good wife to him, welcoming him to their bed with a smile, but he was a cruel man and he had taken her without thought for her pleasure, subjecting her to things that shocked her innocence, as if she were a whore rather than an innocent girl. It was a long time since she had been able to smile at him or do anything but freeze when he touched her.

A little shudder went through her for her husband had been in an odd mood of late. Their relationship had been deteriorating for some time, because of their unfortunate situation. Lethbridge needed a son to succeed him, but Madeline doubted it would ever happen. Her husband blamed her, though what she could do about it when he'd ceased to visit her bed long since she did not know. When he did come to her it was to punish her rather than make love to her.

She blinked hard, blocking out the tears that threatened. She would not pity herself simply because she'd seen Hallam—been so close to him that she might have touched him, had she dared. Pain ravaged her, but she struggled to keep an appearance of calm. No one must be allowed to see her distress. Pride was all she had left. She did not ask for pity. Indeed, she would not allow it. She had married for the sake of her family and nothing had changed. Nothing could ever change while…

No, she would not think of that now. She had the beginnings of an unpleasant headache and all she wanted was to go home. In her own room she could give way to the tears that might bring some relief to her distress.

She stopped a passing footman and asked for her carriage to be brought round.

Only when she was being helped inside did she ask for her husband to be told that she had retired with a headache. The last thing she needed was to drag Lethbridge from his cards to accompany her home. He would be angry either way, but tonight she needed a little solitude.

Seeing Hallam so unexpectedly and at such close quarters had brought home her wretchedness. She must hope that Lethbridge would play late and be too tired or too drunk to bother with her when he returned. In the morning she would have recovered sufficiently to face him, but if he questioned her tonight she was not sure she could hide her despair.

Fortunately, Madeline's husband had enjoyed a successful evening at the tables and had ignored the message that his wife had gone home because of a headache. Rising from the tables at three in the morning with his pockets filled with the guineas he'd won from his companions, he'd called for his carriage, which Madeline had had the forethought to send back for his convenience. Conveyed to his home in a mellow mood, he did not bother with visiting his wife's room, but drank a glass of brandy after his valet had undressed him and went to bed to smile over the evening's play and sleep through until late the next morning.

Madeline was up and dressed and about to go out when her husband entered her room in his dressing robe. He looked at her from narrowed eyes.

'Is your headache better, madam?'

'Yes, sir, I thank you,' she said. 'Forgive me for leaving early. It was shockingly bad and I did not wish to disturb you.'

'Just as well for I could not have left the play,' he said. 'My luck was in and I won several hundred guineas.'

'I am sure that is very pleasing, sir.'

'It pleases me,' Lethbridge said, a slightly sour twist to his mouth. 'As you are aware, Madeline, I have little else to please me in my life.'

She lifted her head proudly, a nerve twitching at her temple despite all her determination to show no feeling of any kind. He was looking at her in such a way and she steeled herself for what must come next.

'Madeline, must you always treat me so coldly? Is it unreasonable of me to want a child? I've given you so much.'

'Forgive me, I cannot love you.' She raised her head, cold and proud as a marble statue, and heard him suck in his breath.

She tensed as he moved towards her, her body suddenly rigid as he reached out to take her in his arms. An icy coldness swept through her and she stood perfectly still as he held her crushed against him, his mouth on hers. He tried to force her mouth open with his tongue, but she could not open to him. Every nerve in her body rejected him, even though she did not say or make any attempt to repel his caress as his hand moved over her breast. She could not prevent him touching her, but neither could she respond for he had killed her young eager warmth with his cruelty and his vile treatment of her body, making the most intimate of acts a bestial ordeal rather than a pleasure.

Lethbridge swore and flung away from her. 'You do not refuse me, but you make it impossible for me. You are frigid, madam, an iceberg. Your father cheated me and so did you, for you told me you would obey me in all things.'

Madeline looked at him, seeing him from a distance. She had learned long ago to shut out his cruel words and to stop herself feeling anything. She could not help herself, for the first few weeks of their marriage when he'd claimed her as his bride had shocked and distressed her so much that the only way she could cope was to lie still and think of something else as he forced himself on her. Lethbridge called her cold and perhaps she was—but she really could not bear his touch unless she closed her mind to what was happening.

'I am sorry. I cannot be what you want me to be. I would if I could, but it is impossible. Why will you not divorce me and take another wife who can give you all you want?'

'Because I want you,' he said, his mouth hard with anger. 'I was deceived in you, Madeline. I thought you a warm lovely girl who would welcome me to her bed and give me an heir.'

'Forgive me, I have tried…'

'Oh, yes, you try. With that look of martyrdom on your face. It is enough to make any man shrivel. Damn you, madam! You have cheated me and I shall not stand for it.'

'I have already asked you to let me go. What more can I do?'

'You could act like a woman instead of a damned ice queen,' he muttered. 'Where were you sneaking out to when I came in?'

'I have an appointment with my dress-maker.'

His eyes narrowed in fury. 'Go and spend more of my money then, but remember there will be a reckoning one day. You will accompany me to dine with friends this evening— and I want no more excuses, no headaches. Do you understand me, madam? I want a child and I shall come to your bed tonight without fail. Be prepared to accept me.'

'When have I refused?' she asked, and as he flung away in disgust she took the opportunity to move towards the door. 'I must not keep the horses standing, sir. Please excuse me, I shall see you this evening.'

Lethbridge was a bully when angry, though he'd been kind enough in his way at the beginning of their marriage. It was her fault, Madeline knew. Her fault that his attempts to be a man in her bed had begun to fail soon after their wedding. Her husband said it was her frigidity that had made him impotent and she believed him. Yet her dislike of being touched by him was so great that she could not bring herself to accept him with smiles or sweet words. She had tried, but as soon as he touched her intimately, she froze.

If only he would divorce her and take another wife.

If only she had never married him.

Bitter tears stung her eyes as she thought of what might have been. Seeing Hal the previous evening, remembering the sweetness of his kisses before she'd sent him away, had made her see her life for what it was—an empty shell. If only she could go back to that day…if only she could have been Hal's wife…

Hal dressed with care that evening. Lord Devenish had arranged the supper party to which both Hal and Miss Helen Carstairs were invited together with perhaps fifty others. The introduction was to be casual, for as Devenish said, if too much were made of it and Hal did not care to continue it would be an insult to the young lady.

Hal would never wish to cause a young

lady distress and he believed Miss Carstairs to be no more than eighteen; the daughter of a Cit who had ambitions, for his only child was no less deserving of respect than a lady of high degree.

Two weeks had passed since the ball and Hal had begun to recover from his brief meeting with Madeline. He'd been stunned by the change in her, amazed by her beauty and reminded of the pain she'd caused. But he had his feelings under control now and was giving serious consideration to the idea of marrying for convenience.

If Miss Carstairs were an agreeable girl and not a complete antidote, he would arrange to meet her again and discover if they were suited. And he would not compare her with Madeline.

Madeline sighed as she looked at the gown her husband had asked her to wear that evening. It was a pretty shade of green, fashionable and made of the finest silk, but once again the neckline was far too low for her taste. Given her own way, she would have worn a tulle fichu with the gown to cover herself for modesty, but if she did Lethbridge would more than likely tear it away. However, she would wear a stole and cover herself a little whenever she could.

They had been invited to a supper party at Lord Devenish's house, an evening of cards and pleasant conversation with some music. There would be no dancing this evening, but that did not disappoint her for she was seldom permitted to dance, unless Lethbridge chose to bestow the privilege on one of his friends, which seldom gave her pleasure.

She wished that she might plead a headache and stay home, for she would have rather gone to bed with a book to read, but her husband would have been furious with her again. His recent visit to her bed had once again ended in failure and at the moment he was treating her with icy indifference.

She found herself thinking once again of the man she'd loved as a young girl. It had shocked her to see Hal the other night, but since then she had looked for him in vain. If she could just speak to him, see his beloved face…explain why she had been forced to marry Lethbridge…but it was all too late.

Tears caught in her throat. Of what use was it to think of a time when she'd been happy? She was married to a cruel man and nothing could change that, as she knew too well.

Lethbridge was waiting for her in the hall when she went down, glancing impatiently at the long-case clock in the hall, as if he thought she were deliberately making him wait.

'Can you never be on time?' he demanded. 'I do not wish to be late, Madeline. Come along for it does not suit me to be caught in a queue of carriages.'

She sighed, but made no reply. Since this was a small supper party by the standards of high society they were unlikely to have to queue outside the house and would possibly be some of the first to arrive. Why he was so impatient she could not know for he normally preferred to arrive later in the evening.

However, she went silently ahead of him and out to the waiting carriage. It was, she supposed, unlikely that she would meet Hal this evening for it was a small affair and she was not even sure that he was still in town.

Miss Carstairs was a pretty fresh-faced young woman with a lively mind. Having been introduced to her by his host, Hal stayed to talk to her for a few minutes, asking her how she went on in town and whether she was enjoying herself.

'I live in Hampstead, sir,' she told him in an unaffected manner that did her great credit, 'but if you mean am I enjoying this supper party the answer is I think so. I am not sure why I should have been invited for I am certain most of the company is above my touch, but Papa was keen to come. I believe he has business with Lord Devenish.'

'Yes, I dare say,' Hal said. He smiled, feeling relieved that her father had said nothing to his daughter of a possible match with one of the guests. She seemed a pleasant girl and he had taken a favourable opinion of her when he moved on to greet other guests.

Hal could not flatter himself that she had been more pleased to meet him than any of the other gentlemen present and for himself there was at the moment no more than a mild appreciation of her open manner. He would need to meet her several more times before he could even consider the idea of asking her to marry him.

Unsure of his feelings on the matter, he moved forwards into a large drawing room where several ladies were seated at a table. They had cards, wine and sweet biscuits before them, but seemed more interested in talking than in actually playing cards. The serious players, usually gentlemen, would be found in the card room where several tables would be set up for their convenience.

He was about to pass through when he heard laughter and, glancing towards the table, saw that Madeline was one of the ladies seated in the group. Her beauty was dazzling and his breath caught in his throat. She looked up and saw him and for a moment he thought he saw pleasure in her eyes, but in the next instant it had gone. She inclined her head to acknowledge him, but her expression remained calm, even withdrawn.

Hal walked on towards the card room. He felt a tumble of emotions inside, torn between dismissing Madeline and making himself known to Mr Henry Carstairs with a view to courting his daughter.

It was what he should do, what the wealthy merchant had hoped for when he brought his daughter to this supper party. Yet even as he told himself that the girl would make an excellent wife, he knew he could not do it.

Miss Carstairs did not deserve to be treated so ill. If he married her when his heart was still so affected by a look from Madeline's green eyes, he would be doing her a disservice.

If he courted Miss Carstairs he might arouse feelings in her—feelings that might be crushed if he could not love her as he ought.

It had been a stupid notion. To marry for money was wrong and he would not subject any woman to that pain.

He must find another solution to his problems and he must forget Madeline. It was time he returned to the country.

Lethbridge rose from the card table after having lost heavily to the man sitting opposite him. Two weeks had passed since Lord Devenish's ball, where he had won nearly a thousand guineas from Rochdale, but this evening he had lost more than three times as much. It was unlike him to lose, but the situation had been forced on him for Rochdale held the bank at faro and insisted on replacing the cards every hand, which made it impossible for them to be marked. He would have left the table before he became so badly dipped had the marquis not goaded him into remaining.

'I believe I am in debt to you for several thousand pounds,' Lethbridge said, trying to hide his anger, as much with himself for being a fool as the other man, for faro was not his game. 'I shall have to beg your indulgence for a few days—say next week, when I shall have the funds to repay you.'

'No hurry,' Rochdale said and smiled in a way that annoyed Lethbridge. Accustomed to winning large sums himself, he did not care for being a substantial loser. 'We may come to some other arrangement. But we should play again and you may recoup your losses.'

'I do not play if I cannot pay.' Lethbridge scowled at the thinly veiled insult. 'I shall sell some bonds and pay you next Thursday—and certainly I am ready to play whenever you choose. It is not my habit to lose.'

'No, I have noticed it,' Rochdale said, an unpleasant smirk on his face. 'Shall we meet again on Thursday next at the club and try our luck again?'

'Delighted,' Lethbridge said between his teeth. 'But I prefer whist or piquet next time.'

'Certainly, whichever you choose, Lethbridge.'

Walking away from him, the count balled his hands at his sides. Something pricked at him, something that made him suspect that the marquis knew the reason why Lethbridge normally won most evenings at the tables.

He couldn't know for certain. Lethbridge

was so careful. No one had ever questioned his luck, because he made a point of losing now and then. Most of the gentlemen he played with were half-foxed or too careless with the money they had so much of that they could afford to lose a few hundred guineas or even a thousand on occasion. He took care never to win huge pots, just enough to maintain his way of life—and he'd been forced to cheat because he himself had been cheated, not at the tables, but in a business venture that had failed, losing him some thirty thousand pounds. The ships he'd invested in had been unworthy and had sunk in heavy seas carrying a cargo that would have doubled his investment, but like a fool he had not raised insurance and that meant he'd lost all his money rather than just a part.

His family seat was intact for the moment, though it was heavily mortgaged, but he had expensive tastes—one of which was his wife. Her beauty pleased him and he liked to see her wearing valuable jewels and costly gowns…even though she was unresponsive to his advances. Why must she be so cold to him? He glowered at his thoughts for he honestly could not understand what he'd done, not realising that his habit of coming to bed the worse for drink, his coarse manners in the bedroom and his selfish way of taking what he wanted without considering her needs had turned her from a sweet gentle child into the cold woman whose icy stare could make him incapable of performing as a man ought.

With his mistress he indulged in all the base acts that pleased and aroused him, but with Madeline he could not manage to perform the simple act that might give him an heir.

Damn the woman! He was not certain why he put up with her. It would serve her right if he gave her the divorce she wanted. He could throw her out without a penny, for he'd never given her the settlement she'd been entitled to on marriage although it was hers by right, having been left to her by an uncle. Lethbridge suspected that if she had any way of supporting herself she would leave him and that would not suit him. He liked other men to envy him and he knew that Madeline was much admired. If he gave his wife her freedom, she would no doubt marry again, and quite possibly to a man even richer than he had been before a few unwise investments had made inroads into his fortune.

No, he would not let her go like that. He

would force her to accept him. He would get an heir on her somehow.

Madeline walked into her bedchamber a week after the supper party at Lord Devenish's house. They had attended one of the most prestigious balls of the Season, but she had danced only once with her husband, after which she had been forced to sit with the matrons and watch the young unmarried girls enjoying themselves while he repaired to the card room. She enjoyed the music and the conversation of her friends, but her feet tapped and she longed to dance. However, she had not dared accept the only offer she'd received, even though the gentleman was a friend of her husband's. She would have suffered for it had she been reckless enough to dance without his permission.

And the only man she'd wished to dance with had not been there. She'd looked for him in the crowded room, but had not seen him.

'I wish for a word with you, madam.'

Madeline breathed deeply as her husband followed her into the room. From the harsh expression on his face, she feared that she had displeased him yet again.

'Is something wrong, my lord? Have I displeased you?'

'Have you?' he asked, eyes narrowed. He reached out and grabbed her by her upper arms, his fingers digging hard into her tender flesh. 'You look guilty, Madeline. What have you done?'

'Nothing.' She lifted her head proudly. 'I am tired, sir. I should like to be allowed to retire.'

'And what of my wishes or needs?' he demanded, his mouth thin and spiteful as he tightened his hold. 'Will you never do your duty as a wife ought?'

'Forgive me, Lethbridge. Have you forgot this is my monthly cycle?'

'It is always some excuse with you—a headache or your feminine cycle. Is there someone else?' He moved in closer, his face dark with suspicion. 'Is that the reason you are so cold to me? If I discover you have betrayed me...'

'How could I when you have me watched all the time? You know it is not so, sir.'

He pinched her arm. 'I want a son, madam. You will give me one or I shall know what to do.'

'I am at your disposal, sir. You may do with me as you wish.'

'Damn you,' he muttered and let her go so abruptly that she almost stumbled. 'I came to remind you it is Adam Miller's wedding next week. You will wear the blue gown I bought you—and I want no long faces in front of my friends, nor will I accept a headache as an excuse for not attending.'

'Very well,' Madeline said, lifting her head to look at him once more. 'May I retire now, my lord? I am really very tired.'

'Do as you please,' he said. 'You are a cold cat, Madeline. I shall spend the night with my mistress. She gave me a son…why can you not be as obliging?'

'I only wish I might have a child,' she said with such a ring of sincerity that his skin flushed a dark red, then he turned and left without another word.

Maddie rang for her maid, standing silently as she undressed her. She held her tears back until she was alone, but then, in the silence of the night, she wept.

Her life was so hopeless and the memory of Hal and what might have been served only to make her weep more.

Emerging from her milliner's shop into a wet morning some days later, Madeline re-

gretted having sent her coachman on an er-
rand. She had intended to walk home, for it
was but a few streets, and she had dispensed
with the man's services, preferring to enjoy a
little fresh air. Now the rain had made it uncomfortable and she stood in the shelter of
the doorway, looking hopefully at the sky. It
looked to be easing off and, unless she called
for a hackney, she had no choice but to walk
home. She took little notice of the covered
chaise that had just drawn up at the kerb.

About to walk past it, she halted as someone let down the window and looked out at
her.

'May I give you a lift home, Lady Lethbridge?'

'Sir?' Madeline stared at the gentleman
in surprise. She was not on intimate terms
with the Marquis of Rochdale and the idea
of sharing a carriage with him was far
from appealing. She knew little of him, but
had been told that he was not a man to be
trusted, though she was aware that her husband played cards with him. 'I thank you
for your thoughtfulness, my lord—but I am
merely going in here.'

She turned into a small shop that sold
gloves and laces and spent some minutes

looking through them. The marquis drove off almost immediately and after a moment the rain had stopped enough for her to venture back outside.

The rain had almost stopped now and, by walking swiftly, she was home before it could fall again. She thought no more of the marquis's invitation or of her refusal.

Chapter Two

'You should not wear a sleeveless gown,' Madeline's maid said as she brought the pale-blue silk dress that morning. 'It will show the bruises on your arm, my lady.'

'It is the gown my husband purchased for me to wear at the wedding of his friend's daughter. I have a new hat to wear with it, which is most becoming,' Madeline replied. 'You must powder the bruises on my upper arms and my breast, and I will wear a fichu of lace in the bodice of my gown and a stole to cover my arms. Perhaps no one will notice.'

'Perhaps,' Sally said and frowned. 'Why does he do these things, my lady—and when he knows you will be seen in public?'

Madeline bit her lip, blinking back the

tears that hovered. She'd steadfastly refused to weep when her husband punished her for not receiving his attentions with the enthusiasm he demanded of her. He'd called her a block of ice when he'd visited her bed the previous night and his hands had gripped her arms so hard as he shook her that his fingers left dark bruises. Sometimes he hit her in other places, but was usually careful to abuse a part of her body that was not on show when she was in company.

'You are an unfeeling wretch,' he'd shouted at her, when he'd come to her room. 'Damn you! I've given you everything you could possibly desire: carriages and horses, jewels, clothes and a house in London. What more do you want?'

Madeline had not answered him at once, because what could she say? Her silence infuriated him and he'd shaken her. She had tried to apologise, but that only made him angrier. He blamed his failure in the marriage bed on her coldness, her icy indifference to his love making, and perhaps she was to blame, for a husband was entitled to some warmth from his wife. It was not that she ever struggled or refused, but she could not be the whore he desired.

'I want nothing you can give me,' she answered proudly. 'If I am not satisfactory, I pray you divorce me. Give me my freedom and take another wife.'

'And have the whole of society laughing at me?' His eyes narrowed and he'd grabbed her by her arms, his fingers biting deep into her tender flesh. 'You promised me a child and you'll do your duty, madam, or I'll beat you until you are black and blue.' As yet he'd done little more than pinch Madeline and shake her or throw bitter words at her, but something told her that he meant this new threat and next time he punished her it would be severe.

'I have not repulsed you,' Madeline said, raising her head. 'If you want more than I can give, I am sorry. I cannot give what I do not have—and I do not love you.'

'Who is he?' Count Lethbridge's eyes narrowed in fury. He was a man of five and forty, not ill favoured though harsh of expression and tongue and of a violent temper. He shook her until she went limp like a rag doll and, when he let her go, she sank in a faint to the floor. 'Your fainting will not save you, madam. I've paid for your services and even a whore would smile at me when I took her.'

Coming to herself, Madeline looked up at

him. 'I have not betrayed my vows despite your unkindness to me. I do not see what more I can do to please you, sir.'

'The reckoning is coming, madam. I shall have you even if I force you. Your coldness will not deny me next time.'

Madeline had not answered him. Sometimes she wished that he might take what he needed from her, by force if necessary. In truth, a child might have helped to fill the emptiness inside her, but though he might bluster and threaten, she knew that when he came to her again it would be useless. She would lie unresisting, her eyes closed, but after some fumbling he would curse, angry at his failure, and then start to pinch and abuse her.

If only she could bear him a son and be allowed to retire to the country, leaving him to his mistresses and the life he enjoyed in London, but until that happened he would keep her here and she must bear his unkindness.

Her only defence was to face him proudly. He had done little more than bruise her, but she knew that he no longer felt tenderness towards her and had regretted his bargain. He feared being ridiculed and would not divorce her or let her live alone, which meant there was only one way he could be free of her.

Only her death would set them both free.

Lethbridge was a brute, but she did not think him a murderer. Perhaps he hoped that she would become so unhappy that she would save him the bother and take her own life? Perhaps it *would* be the best way for both of them.

Madeline held back her tears. She would make herself think of something else…of the look in Hal's eyes when he'd seen her. Just for a moment she'd thought he smiled before turning away…

'You look so beautiful, my lady,' Sally said, recalling her thoughts to the present. Then, touching Madeline's arm gently, 'Why do you not run away? Leave him and return to your family?'

'My father would send me back,' Madeline said sadly. 'I am his wife and in law he could force me to return. My father would suffer if he defied him for my sake.'

Nothing had changed since their marriage. The count had not returned her father's notes as he'd promised when she married him, but simply kept them as a threat to use against

her. Her father could not offer her a refuge
because if he did Lethbridge would ruin him.

Tears caught in Madeline's throat as she allowed her maid to place the confection of lace
and ribbons on her head. A glance in the mirror showed her perfectly arranged red-gold
hair that hung in one long ringlet over her
shoulder. Magnificent pearls hung from her
lobes and she had one string of large creamy
pearls about her white throat, which were
fastened with a diamond clasp. On her right
hand she had a ring of diamonds and emeralds and a large splendid teardrop diamond
adorned the third finger of her left hand, together with the thin band of gold that marked
her servitude as a wife.

For a moment she was tempted to tear off
all her jewels, refuse to accompany Lethbridge to the wedding and run away. If only
there were some way that she could simply
disappear and never be forced to return to
her unkind husband.

Giving her head a little shake, she dismissed the idea. She must honour her bargain or her father would be punished in her
stead. She painted a look of cool pride on her
face, for she would never allow her husband
to see that she was distressed.

She was going to a wedding and she must be gay and bright so that everyone would tell Lethbridge how fortunate he was to have such a beautiful wife and then perhaps he might forget his threat to punish her.

If only she'd run away with Hal the day he'd asked her…but her loyalty to her father had prevented her from seeking happiness then, just as it did now.

Yet only her memories of Hal sustained her when her life seemed too terrible to bear.

Standing up with Adam in church, as his best man, was a pleasure and helped to dispel the dark clouds that had hung over Hal since the murder of his cousin Mark. He, Mark, Paul and Adam had come through the war with Napoleon's France together, only for his eldest cousin Mark to be shot down in cold blood by a rogue at his own home. Between them, Adam, Paul and Hallam had caught and punished Mark's murderer, but it had left a shadow on their lives.

Adam's wedding was the time for them to put the sadness of the recent past behind them. Lord Ravenscar had wanted it to happen, because he said it was what Mark would have wanted.

'My son would not wish us to mourn him for month after month, even if we do so in our hearts,' he'd told Adam when he offered to postpone the wedding until a year had passed. 'You must marry, Adam. Miss Jenny Hastings is a beautiful young lady and I shall be glad if you will bring her to stay with me sometimes.'

Adam had promised he would when they returned from their honeymoon. After a stay in Scotland, they were to return to Ravenscar for a time before taking a long journey to France and then on to Italy, where Paul had gone in an effort to forget the pain and grief his brother's death had caused him. Hallam suspected that there was more to Paul's extreme distress...a little matter of being in love with Lucy Dawlish, the girl who had been expected to marry Mark Ravenscar.

Women could be the very devil, Hallam thought, his thoughts drifting away from the ceremony after he'd done his part and supplied the rings. He watched his cousin and Jenny approach the high altar for the private blessing they would share with the vicar before going off to sign their names. His mouth hardened, as he thought of the woman that he'd been so much in love with some four years previously. Maddie had married her count, and he'd seen how well she'd settled into her new life at Devenish's ball. How beautiful she'd looked that evening, pale and lovely like a marble statue. The young vibrant girl he had known was nowhere to be seen.

The thought caught at his throat, restricting his breathing and causing him pain somewhere in the region of his heart. What a fool he was to care what Maddie might or might not be doing! Hallam had done his best to forget her in the arms of a mistress, but after the first flush of anger had passed, he had parted company from the very obliging married lady. He believed she was now enjoying a similar arrangement with another officer. Her husband had his heirs and was apparently content to allow his wife her pleasures providing she did not interfere with his; he'd married her for the fortune she brought him.

Hallam's mouth curled at the notion of such an arrangement, though he knew that several of his friends had married either for money or land and were seemingly content in similar marriages. It would not do for Hallam. He would not have taken up with the obliging Lady Meadows had she not made it clear she was interested in an arrangement.

In truth, it had brought him only physical relief, for his heart belonged to one woman—a woman he could never have.

What had Madeline done to him that he could not be interested in any other woman? Bitterness swept through him, because he wanted neither a marriage of convenience nor the caresses of a mistress. Even in the lady's bed, he'd known a sick longing for the woman he could never have.

His frown increased as he watched Adam and Jenny walk arm in arm from the church, the happy smiles on their faces telling of their pleasure in each other. Why could he not find a woman to love so completely that she swept the memory of Madeline from his mind? Miss Carstairs would make someone a delightful wife, but not him. He was a man haunted by the past, unable to forget the torment that had begun when Madeline broke his heart.

Could a man ever put the past behind him so completely that his heart was no longer shadowed by an old love? For him it seemed impossible. He gave himself a mental shake.

He must forget his own problems. Hallam had duties as Adam's groomsman and he pushed the worrying thoughts away, smiling as he looked about him at the guests. He must make certain that everyone had a carriage to convey them to the house, where the reception was being held.

As they left church, Adam and Jenny were showered with rose petals and rice, the guests laughing and cheering as the happy couple ran for their carriage. Hallam stood outside the church, greeting people and overseeing the carriages as they lined up to collect their passengers. Suddenly, his breath caught as he saw a woman in a pale-blue silk gown. She wore a lace fichu at her throat and carried a fine, lacy wool stole over her arms, a long ringlet of fair hair resting on one shoulder.

Obviously the wife of a rich man, her clothes and jewels of the finest money could buy, Maddie looked beautiful but cold. A proud beauty, heartless and carved of ice. Hallam's heart felt as if someone had thrust a dagger into it.

She had noticed him. He saw her green eyes gleam suddenly and for one moment she seemed to come to life, the colour washing into her cheeks, but in the next she had turned to the man next to her and they moved away to their carriage. He watched as she was assisted inside the splendid equipage, but she did not turn her head to glance at him, though he knew that she had seen him.

She had deliberately drawn her husband away so that she did not need to acknowledge him. Hallam felt the knife twist inside him. Had she become indifferent to him? He'd thought not when they met at the ball, but now he was unsure. She had deliberately avoided speaking to him at the supper party. He was the fool for carrying a torch—a memory that was sacred to him was less than nothing to her. She probably found it amusing.

Recalling himself to the task of making sure the guests were all on their way to the house, Hallam finally settled into the last carriage with some of the other ushers. He had by this time steeled himself for the inevitable meeting with Madeline. She would be at the reception and he would find a way of speaking to her. He wanted to know that she was well and happy and then he would forget her.

Yes, he truly would, he vowed. If Madeline told him that she was content in her life, he would make up his mind to find a good-humoured lady who would be happy with a home and children—perhaps a widow who had memories of her own and would not expect love. If he could put the past behind him, then he would be content with a comfortable arrangement—perhaps even the lady he'd enjoyed a relationship with in Spain, though he believed her to have another lover now.

Hallam was here! Madeline had felt such a rush of emotion as she saw him that she had known she could not—dare not—meet him in her husband's company. Lethbridge had demanded to know the name of the lover he imagined she had—and if she betrayed a sign of her feelings for Hallam Ravenscar, he would immediately believe that it was he.

Oh, how she wished that it were true. Madeline would give much to be in Hallam's arms, to be kissed and caressed with tenderness. She recalled the sweet meetings beneath the apple tree that summer when she'd first fallen in love with the handsome young man. He had been home on a visit to his uncle and swept her up in a whirlwind of romance, vowing that he would return as soon as he could to ask her father for her hand in marriage. She'd believed that everything would be wonderful when he had leave from his regiment and that she would spend her life travelling with him wherever he was sent—but then his father had lost so much money gambling, as had her own. By the time he'd been given leave again, everything had changed.

No, she must not think of all she had lost. She must control her feelings and be careful to show nothing if they were forced to speak with Hallam at the reception.

By the time they arrived at the house and joined the line waiting to greet the bride and groom, Madeline was much calmer. She was able to bestow a warm smile on the bride and groom and wish them happiness and was in turn thanked for the beautiful gifts they had received. As Lethbridge had neglected to tell her what he'd considered fitting for the daughter of his old friend, she had no idea what those gifts were, but murmured something appropriate.

Moving away from the happy couple, Madeline was offered a glass of champagne, which she accepted and sipped delicately. It was very good and she could see that a wonderful buffet was awaiting the guests, with all kinds of delicious foods. She had little appetite, but would make an effort to eat something later.

The guests were mingling as the queue

gradually wound to an end, and Madeline's smile felt frozen on her lips as she saw Hallam enter the hall. Now people were beginning to approach the buffet and select their preferences.

'Go ahead and join your friends, Madeline,' Lethbridge said. 'I wish to speak with someone on a matter of business.'

He always had another reason for attending any social event. Madeline moved away; she was relieved to be dismissed from her duty. There were a few people she knew well socially, but no one she would call a particular friend. However, she had met Lucy Dawlish once or twice during a stay at Bath and went to stand beside her, glancing at the loaded table.

'How nice to see you,' Lucy said and smiled at her. 'Jenny looks beautiful, does she not?'

'Yes, lovely,' Madeline said. 'I believe you are particular friends?'

'Yes, we are,' Lucy said. 'Jenny has been exceptionally good to me and I shall miss her, though Mama says we shall travel abroad next month.'

'How pleasant to spend the winter away in warmer climes,' Madeline said, a little sigh leaving her. 'Such an array of wonderful food—how does one choose?'

'I think the crab tartlets look delicious,' Lucy said, 'and I always love a syllabub, do you not, Lady Lethbridge?'

'Oh please, call me Madeline. Yes, I am partial to a syllabub but I suppose one ought to eat something savoury first. Perhaps I will try a tartlet, though the prawn, not the crab, I think…'

'May I help you to choose, Lady Lethbridge?' A man's voice made Madeline's heart jerk and she turned her head sharply to look at Hallam, as Lucy Dawlish moved further down the table.

'Thank you, but I think I prefer to help myself.' She moved away from Hallam, but he followed her, looking puzzled. Madeline felt compelled to explain. 'Please…my husband watches everything I do. You must not pay me any attention.'

'How ridiculous,' Hallam said, frowning. 'What harm can there be in a few words exchanged at a wedding?'

'Please, leave me,' Madeline said. 'I beg you, do not continue with this…'

She moved away, putting tasty morsels on her plate without seeing what she was choosing. Hallam did not follow her and she found a place at a table with several other ladies, who were laughing and eating, clearly enjoying themselves. Madeline bit into a tart, but found it difficult to swallow the soft flaky pastry, which at any other time would have been delightful. What little appetite she'd had had quite vanished.

She sat silently, listening to the conversation flow around her, and sipping her wine now and then when the toasts were made, but her throat was tight with misery and her smile felt frozen. When Hallam called everyone to attention and began his speech as the groom's best man, she could no longer bear it and excused herself, saying that she needed a little air, then got up and walked from the room.

She was aware that her progress was remarked and knew it was rude of her to leave during Hallam's speech, but could not bear to stay another moment, for if she did not escape she would weep. She left the house through a side door and went out into the garden. She needed to be alone for a time, because she was so desperately unhappy. Seeing Hallam, speaking to him, had brought home her misery and she had rebuffed him more out of fear of giving into her tears than for fear of her husband. After all, what more could he do to her?

Walking swiftly, Madeline sought out a secret arbour amongst the roses and sat down, staring unseeingly at the beauty all around her. Her eyes filled with tears, which began to spill over as she realised how very much she had lost. She ought to have been braver, to have stood up to her father's blandishments, and refused to marry the count. Yet if she had chosen happiness for herself, her family must have faced ruin. It was all too late. Regrets would not help her now.

She bowed her head, covering her face with her hands. How Hallam must hate her now—and she loved him still.

Hallam was feeling angry. He had meant to offer Madeline the courtesy any gentleman would offer a lady and she had rebuffed him in the coldest manner—and then she had left the room while he was making his speech. Had she meant to be deliberately rude? Yet she'd seemed agitated, even frightened. What had she said about her husband watching her every move?

Did Lethbridge mistreat his wife? Anger

curled inside Hallam at the thought and he balled his fists at his sides. There was little he could do for the moment, because he did not wish to cause a scandal at his cousin's wedding, but if he knew Maddie was being bullied or actually harmed he would kill Lethbridge with his bare hands!

Hearing the count laugh at something a rather grand lady was saying to him, Hallam knew that he could not bear to be in the same room with him. He must go out for a breath of air or he might explode. His hands itched to land a facer on the vile fellow and he turned away, walking swiftly from the room and out into the gardens.

He had been wandering for some minutes, his mind seething with anger and bitterness as he tried to come to terms with the tormented feelings inside him, when he heard the sound of a woman crying. Following the sound, he saw her sitting alone in a secluded rose arbour and his heart caught with pain.

'Maddie,' he said and walked swiftly to her side. 'Please, you must tell me what is wrong. Does that devil hurt you? I swear I'll kill him if he has harmed you.'

Madeline had risen to her feet at his approach. She looked about her anxiously, as if fearing that someone might see them. Her gloved hands held before her, she moved them restlessly, clearly in distress.

'Hal, you should not have come,' she said on a sob. 'I know you mean to help me, but if he should see you he will think the worst. I…I cannot explain, but he imagines I have a lover and has demanded the man's name. If he thought…' Hallam reached out for her restless hands, catching them in his. 'Oh, you must not…' Her voice broke and a tear slid down her pale cheek.

'Tell me, does he beat you?'

'No, of course not,' she said quickly, but in her agitation her stole had slipped and he saw the dark bruises on her upper arms. He exclaimed wrathfully and touched one gently with his finger, his mouth hardening as she flinched. 'He did not beat me. He…pinches me when he is…frustrated.'

'The evil brute!' Hallam bent his head to kiss the bruise. 'My sweet Maddie. I shall call him out and kill him.'

'You must not,' she said, her eyes wide with fear. 'They would arrest you—and you might be tried for murder, even if he did not kill you first.'

'Then I will force him to call me out,'

Hallam said. 'Or you may run away with me, Maddie. You cannot wish to stay with such a brute?'

'I never wanted to wed him,' she confessed. 'He holds my father's notes and if I tried to leave him he would ruin my family. I cannot bring shame on my mother and sister. My father would bear it, but my family… where would they live? How would my sister ever find a suitor?'

'It is unfair that you should sacrifice everything for them,' Hallam said, staring at her in despair. 'So you had no choice—you sent me away for their sakes? You do love me, Maddie. I know you do.'

'No, you must not think it. You must forget me,' she whispered, throat catching with emotion. 'I am desperately unhappy, Hal, but I am caught fast in a trap and I cannot escape.'

He moved closer, looking down at her for a moment before he bent his head to kiss her lips. They parted beneath his and for a moment she allowed his kiss, but then, as his hand slid into the hair at her nape, she froze and moved away, turning her back to him as her shoulders shook.

'I cannot…please, do not waste your life

loving me. I can never be the wife you deserve.' A sob broke from her then, 'I never wanted to hurt you. Please believe me, Hal. I was forced to wed him and I cannot leave him no matter how I feel…'

'I shall find a way to set you free of him somehow,' Hallam said. He was reaching out to touch her cheek, but she flinched away when they heard someone call her name and the colour left her face.

'I must go,' she said and tears stood in her eyes. 'Please forget me, forget what I just said. You cannot help me. Lethbridge would ruin my family and kill you. Honour demands that I keep the vows I made when I married. I beg you, forget me.'

Hallam tried to hold her, but she slipped away and walked from the rose arbour into the open garden. He heard the sound of voices and knew that she was speaking to her husband. The count's voice was harsh and it took all Hallam's will-power to stop himself from rushing out to confront him, but Maddie had begged him not to and he could not make a scene here.

He must seek Lethbridge out another day and see what could be done to help Maddie. If she would go with him, he would take her away to France or Italy. He had little fortune and she had none, but he would find a way of supporting them both somehow. His estate might be sold and perhaps he could become a soldier of fortune, offering his sword to any that would pay.

Yet she'd spoken of honour and her family's ruin. It was foolish of her to think of honour when her husband was so cruel to her, but her family's ruin was another matter. He could do little for them and he knew that she would never walk away from her unhappy marriage if it meant their downfall.

The only way was to force a quarrel on Lethbridge. If the count would call him out it would be an affair of honour, and though he might be brought before the magistrate and even imprisoned for a time, he would not hang for it. He thought that he would bear even that if necessary to free Maddie from what must be a living hell for her.

If the count would not call him out, he must be the one to do it and would probably have to flee to France until the storm blew over. His mind busy with his thoughts of revenge on the evil count, Hallam waited until he was sure he would not be seen leaving the rose arbour before returning to the re-

ception. He did not wish Maddie to be punished for meeting him, for if her husband had
seen them together he must have thought the
worst.

Taking great care not to follow too close on
the count and Madeline, he did not notice the
servant lingering in the shrubbery, watching.

His mind with Madeline, Hallam could
only pray that Lethbridge would not harm
her again. Somehow, he must find a way to
set her free. He would not think of his own
future or the happiness he hoped to gain one
day, but only of Maddie.

As a widow she would be safe and perhaps one day she would allow him to take
care of her.

'Who were you talking to?' Lethbridge
demanded, as he took his wife by the arm,
pushing her in the direction of the courtyard
where his coach was awaiting them. 'I told
you what I would do to you if you saw your
lover again—and I shall thrash him.'

'There is no one else,' Maddie said, lifting her head defiantly. 'You are foolish to be
jealous, sir. I do not have a lover.'

'Lying bitch,' he muttered as he thrust her

towards the coach. 'Get inside. I'll teach you to behave when I get you home.'

'May I not say farewell to my friends?'

'You chose to leave the reception and I am ready to leave,' he said looking at her coldly. 'I have made your goodbyes. I was forced to say you were feeling unwell.'

'You did not lie, sir. It was because I had a terrible headache that I left the reception. I swear to you on my mama's life that I did not go to meet anyone.'

Lethbridge glared at her. 'You swear that you did not meet a lover, madam?'

'I swear it,' she said, but could not look at him.

He grabbed her arm, swinging her back to face him. 'Swear it on your mother's life or I shall thrash you when we get home.'

Madeline felt a surge of anger. Lifting her head, she looked him in the eyes. 'I swear in on my own life, my mother's—and anyone else's you care to name. I did not meet my lover for I have no lover.'

Lethbridge stared at her for a moment, then inclined his head. 'Very well, I shall accept your word—but if I discover you have lied to me you will be very sorry, madam.'

Madeline turned her face from him, the

tears stinging her eyes, but she refused to weep or beg. He was a brute and she hated him. He had made her life intolerable and she would almost rather be dead than married to him. Yet if she took her own life, he would seek revenge from her family.

Her throat was tight with tears, for she could discover no way of escape. All she could do was to try to block out her unhappiness…and perhaps to allow her thoughts to drift back to the time when Hallam had made love to her so sweetly beneath the apple tree.

Yet even that memory was ruined for when Hallam kissed her, she'd known that something inside her had flinched away. How could it be that she could not welcome Hallam's kisses when they had always been so sweet to her? Had her husband's cruelty made it impossible for her to accept even the touch of the man she loved?

If that were the case, there was no help for her.

Chapter Three

Hallam looked at the invitation tucked into the gilt-framed mirror in the front parlour of his lodgings. He'd taken a small house in town for a time, though he was not certain what had made him decide to come up— but a chance remark from one of his friends had told him that Lethbridge and Madeline were in London for a few weeks. The invitation was to a prestigious ball and he was almost certain that Madeline and her husband would be there. Somehow, he must find a way to talk to her. Since speaking to her in the garden of Lord Ravenscar's home, he had not been able to rest for thinking of her unhappiness.

Try as he might, Hallam had been unable

to discover a solution to their problem. If it were not for her father's debts to Lethbridge, he would have carried Maddie off with him, but he knew that she would not snatch at happiness for herself while condemning her family to ruin. Had Hallam the money, he would have paid her father's debts, but he could not pay those his own father had left, without disposing of most of his estate. It seemed that the count had them in a cleft stick and there was no escape—but there must be! Lethbridge must have a chink in his armour. Hallam would just have to discover what it was and plan his strategy accordingly. If there were no other way, he must kill him. Yet he would prefer to get his hands on the notes Sir Matthew Morris had lost to the count and then force him to let Maddie go.

Hallam had never taken life in cold blood, and it would be his last resort, but if it was the only way...

Lethbridge was a gambler. It was possible that Hallam might contrive to win the notes from him. But would he part with them? Perhaps only if he were entirely ruined.

Somehow Hallam did not think it likely the count would gamble away his whole fortune just to please him. Yet gambling was the way to get close to him, he was sure. If Lethbridge should be at the ball, he would most likely spend much of his time in the card room. Hallam decided that he would attend. If he were fortunate, he would be able to speak to Maddie or perhaps, make an arrangement to meet in private…and if he could find the count at the tables he would find a way of making his acquaintance.

Yes, he would go to the ball that evening and discover what he could of the man who was causing Maddie so much unhappiness.

'You look lovely, my lady,' Sally said as she finished pinning Madeline's fair hair into a knot of curls high on her head. One ringlet fell on to her shoulder and she wore a collar of magnificent diamonds about her throat, together with huge teardrop earbobs. Her gown was white, the bodice encrusted with tiny sparkling *diamanté*, which sprayed out like a stem of flowers over the skirt. Her shoes were white satin and the heels were also studded with crystals that caught the light whenever her skirt moved to reveal them.

'You have done well,' Madeline said and smiled at her. Sally had applied the merest touch of rouge to her cheeks after powdering her face and neck. Her bruises had faded since the wedding, because for some reason known better to himself, her husband had not come near her for the past ten days. 'Thank you, Sally. I do not know what I should do without you.'

'You know I would do anything for you, my lady.' Sally would have said more, but at that moment the door from the count's dressing room was thrown open and he entered his wife's bedchamber. Madeline stood up and turned to face him. Inside, she was trembling, but she gave no outward sign of the fear and revulsion he aroused.

'You look beautiful, madam,' Lethbridge said. 'That gown was worth its price. I am pleased you have made an effort, for I wish you to do something for me this evening.'

'You may go, Sally.' Madeline dismissed her maid and then looked at her husband. 'How may I be of service, sir?'

'I wish you to charm someone—a gentleman, a marquis. He is necessary to a scheme I have in mind. It will be of some considerable financial benefit to me if you can twist him around your little finger. I intend to ask him to dine here, but he has been evasive. If you smile on him, he will be eager to visit us.'

'Are you asking me to encourage this gentleman to pay me compliments, to dangle after me?' She was incredulous, for he had always been angry if she spoke more than a few words to another man.

'To put it crudely, madam, I want you to make him mad with lust for you—if you can manage it? I find you too cold, but some men love a challenge and I've been told Rochdale cannot resist a woman who is not easily won.'

'And if he should ask me to dance, or to walk outside in the air?' She was trembling with indignation that he should ask such a thing of her but managed to hold her disgust inside.

'Anything within reason. You will not allow him to bed you, Madeline, but if he imagines you might so much the better.'

'I find your suggestion insulting, sir.'

'Indeed?' Lethbridge moved closer, a nerve flicking at his temple. 'You know how to smile and charm, Madeline. You deceived me into believing you warm and loving before we were wed. Now I ask you to do the same to the marquis.'

Anger raged inside her as she said impulsively, 'And if I do—what will you give me?'

His mouth tightened. 'Do I not already give you sufficient, madam?'

'I want nothing for myself, but I would have my father's notes. You promised them when we married, but you reneged on your bargain. I ask for no more than my rights. My father lives in fear of you. Give me the notes and I shall do as you ask.'

He glared at her, reached for her wrist as if he would subdue her, then changed his mind. 'Very well. Charm Rochdale into accepting an invitation to dine at our house and I will give you the notes.'

'I do not trust you. Give them to me now and I swear I will do as you ask.'

'You deserve that I should teach you a lesson,' he threatened. 'However, I need you to look at your best this evening. I will give you some of the notes now and the rest when you have finished your work.'

Madeline held out her hand. 'Give me my father's notes and I shall make every effort to charm this man for you.'

Lethbridge swore under his breath and went into the dressing room and through to his own chamber. Madeline could hardly believe that she had won and held her breath until he returned. He was carrying a bundle of notes, which he thrust at her.

Madeline glanced through them. Her father's signature was scrawled on a dozen notes of sums from five hundred guineas to two thousand. Her fingers closed over them and she felt a thrill of triumph.

'Is this all of them?'

'Most,' he said, clearly furious, but with a look in his eyes that told her he was lying. He held many more notes, she was certain, but she had recovered at least a part of her father's debt. 'You will get the rest when you've done as I wish.'

'Thank you. You will not be angry if you see me dancing this evening, sir? I must make this gentleman a little jealous if you wish him to fall in love with me.'

'Do whatever you need to bring him into my house and I shall do the rest.'

'Very well,' Madeline said, raising her head proudly. She had no idea why her husband was so eager to have the marquis dine with them, but she would find it a small price to pay if she could free her father from the shadow that had hung over him for so long. 'Just one moment…' She walked to the fireplace and cast the notes into the fire, watching with a smile as the flames consumed them. Had she left them in her drawer her husband might recover them by force or stealth. 'I am ready now.'

Walking from the bedchamber with her husband close behind her, Madeline's thoughts were racing. If she could but obtain the remainder of her father's notes, she would be free. Money and jewels meant little to her. If her family were safe, she would leave her husband and go away somewhere quiet. She was not sure how she would live, but perhaps she could earn her living with her sewing needle.

Hallam saw Madeline almost as soon as he entered the ballroom. She was the centre of a small group of gentlemen, laughing as if she had not a care in the world. A picture of loveliness in white silk and lace embroidered with beads that sparkled like diamonds, she was magnificent, so far removed from the pale shadow of the girl he loved that he'd seen at Adam's wedding that he could scarce believe his eyes. She'd wept and told him that she feared her husband's jealousy if he saw her speaking to Hallam and yet now she was flirting with the men that clustered about her.

Had she deceived him to the true nature of her life?

Just what kind of a woman was she—and could he trust anything she said?

He stood for several minutes just watching her laughing and teasing one of the men in particular—by his elaborate clothes and exquisite laces, he was a wealthy nobleman. Hallam had never met the gentleman, but his jewels flashed in the light of the candelabra and his clothes were fashioned by the best tailors, though in Hallam's eyes his cravat was too high, his collars too wide for taste. He was one of the dandy set. Hallam's lips curled in disgust as he saw the man carried a fan and, still worse, wore rouge on his cheeks—a fashion that had long since been discarded by most men in England. He was a man of middle years, thin with a cruel mouth, and he wore a powdered wig. Another fashion Hallam scorned as being foppish.

He preferred the clean, plain look that Mr Brummell had brought into fashion before he'd fallen so deep into debt and been forced to flee abroad, leaving an unpaid gambling debt—something no gentleman would ever do unless forced. Society had turned against Brummell, though Alvanly and some others were known to speak of him kindly and to send him money in his exile in France.

Why was Madeline looking up at that fop in such a coquettish manner? He had never seen her flirt with anyone so outrageously. As a girl she'd had shy pretty manners that had touched his heart, but now…he hardly knew her. If her husband were truly the brute she'd described to him, how dare she behave so recklessly?

A glance around the ballroom told Hallam that Lethbridge was not in the room to witness his wife flirting with the fop. Frowning, Hallam watched as she gave her hand to one of the other gentlemen and was whisked off to the dance floor. Her ardent suitor seemed annoyed—or perhaps frustrated. He had the look of a hunter intent on cornering his prey.

'How are you, Ravenscar?' The voice at his elbow distracted Hallam. He turned to look at the gentleman, a fellow officer who had seen service in France with him. 'She is a beauty, isn't she? But off limits unless you wish Lethbridge to call you out. I've heard he is like a dog with a bone over his wife as a rule.'

'Good to see you, Mainwaring. Who is the wealthy fop?' Hallam nodded in the direction of the frustrated suitor. 'He looks dangerous.'

'Yes, I dare say he might be. I've heard he is a crack shot and even more deadly with the sword. He was in France with us, though a line regiment, has some French relations, I understand. Rich, they say…some whisper he absconded with jewels, *objets d'art* and pictures that belonged to Napoleon in the last days of his reign. They also say his relations worked for the secret police in the time of the Terror and became rich by robbing the wretches condemned to be guillotined. Marquis of Rochdale…the third of his line, I believe.'

'A pretty fellow, by all accounts, and old enough to be the countess's father.'

'Perhaps she likes them that way. Lethbridge must be twelve years her senior.'

'She married to save her family from ruin,' Hallam replied, stung to defend Madeline, even though he felt annoyed with her for flirting so openly—and for spinning him that tale at the wedding.

Yet she had been crying when he discovered her in the rose arbour. Something was wrong, but he could not decide what to believe.

Moving on, Hallam greeted friends and danced with a couple of ladies—wives of his particular friends—and his hostess, but most of the first part of the evening he spent watching Maddie. She danced several times, twice with the Marquis of Rochdale. He began to notice that she behaved far more demurely with her other partners, actually seeming a little reserved, but let down her guard whenever she was speaking with the marquis.

What on earth did she think she was doing? Did she not realise that to flirt so dashingly with a man like that was to play with fire? Unless, of course, she wished him to think her available. The girl he remembered would not be so fast or so foolish.

It came to Hallam in a blinding flash. She was deliberately leading Rochdale on! What on earth had got into her? Did she not know that Rochdale was dangerous? The marquis was not a man to be trifled with—surely she must sense that she was in danger of being seduced by the man?

At the supper interval he saw her seated at a table with two other ladies and a little cluster of gentlemen. He'd hoped that perhaps he might have an opportunity of speaking with her, but the men vied with each other to fetch her drinks and delicate trifles and she was never alone.

Annoyed and frustrated, he decided to take a walk in the gardens and smoke a cheroot. He'd come to the ball to speak to Madeline before deciding on a course of action, but now it seemed that perhaps she did not need rescuing from her husband. Perhaps her tears had been the result of a quarrel and meant little.

He was wasting his time here, he decided. Having finished his small cigar, he threw the butt into the flowerbeds. Walking towards the house, he had made up his mind to take his leave of his hostess when he heard a cry from behind one of the shrubs.

'No, sir! I did not give you leave to molest me—'

'You have been leading me on all evening, *madame*. Am I to understand that you did so without the intention of responding to my ardour?'

'You go too fast, sir,' the voice Hallam knew as Maddie's replied. 'A little flirtation does not mean—' There was a little cry of alarm and the sound of a struggle. 'No, no!'

Striding towards the scene, Hallam saw the marquis trying to force Maddie to lie back on a bench in a small summerhouse at the far edge of the lawns. His intention was all too obvious; he was bent on having his way with her. She might have brought it on herself by flirting so outrageously, but Hallam could see that she was trying to throw the fellow off and he strode towards them, grabbing the marquis by his coat collar and hauling him off her.

'How dare you?' the marquis spluttered as he was bodily flung away and landed on his knees. As he rose, the grass stain on his satin knee breeches was evident. 'You will meet me for this, sir.'

'Willingly, sir, but then all London will know that you are a damned rogue. No gentleman would try to force a lady when she says no.'

'She was willing enough earlier,' the marquis snapped. 'She has been inviting me to seduce her all evening.'

'Flirting is one thing—forceful seduction is another,' Hallam said. 'Will you choose swords or pistols?'

'Neither,' the marquis said, dusting himself off. 'I have decided that the whore is not worth the effort. I bid you goodnight, sir.'

'You will not so insult a lady—' Hallam
bristled, but Maddie tugged at his sleeve.

'Let him go, Hallam. It would only cause
a scandal—and it *was* my fault. I flirted
with him and allowed him to bring me out
for some air. I should have known what he
would expect.'

'Why did you do it?' he demanded, his
own anger coming to the fore now the marquis was dismissed.

'Lethbridge promised to give me my
father's notes if I intrigued the marquis
sufficiently to get him to accept a dinner invitation.'

'Your husband told you to flirt with him?'
Hallam looked at her in disbelief. 'Does he
not know of the man's reputation? He is a
dangerous rake, Maddie.'

'Yes, someone warned me earlier, but what
could I do?' Madeline's hand trembled she
put it to her mouth. 'Lethbridge will not be
pleased with me. I made him give me some
of the notes and then I burned them—now I
have failed him. Rochdale will never accept
that invitation now.'

'If you fear your husband, come away with
me now,' Hallam said. 'I will hide you from

him and find a way to make him release you from the promise you were forced to give.'

'If only I could,' she said and her eyelashes were wet with tears. 'I feel so ashamed. That horrible man has been pawing me all night and now…it was all for nothing. But you must not risk your life for me. I am not worth it. I am soiled…not worth your notice.'

'It is not your fault if the man is a rogue,' Hallam said. 'Do not tell Lethbridge what happened out here. He need only know that you did as he asked. It is not your fault if the marquis refuses your husband's invitation.'

Hallam took his clean white kerchief and wiped her cheeks with it. He smiled down at her, then gave her his hand and helped her to rise.

'Thank you. You are so kind to me and I do not deserve it.'

'You deserve far more, but I am not sure how much I can do—other than to call Lethbridge out.'

'If I had succeeded in getting all my father's notes, I should have left him,' she said. 'He will be so angry when he realises I have not done what he asked.'

'I will do what I can. If I could win the notes back in a card game, would you leave him?'

'He would never stake them. Besides, he is very lucky. He wins far more than he loses.'

'Does he, indeed? Do you think he wanted the marquis to dine at your house so that they might play cards?'

'Lethbridge often has his friends to dine. I am his hostess at dinner—but when they play cards I retire for I am not allowed to gamble more than a few shillings at the loo table.'

'Do you wish to?'

'No, not at all, but neither do I wish to watch others gamble. I believe Lethbridge and his friends play deep at times.'

Hallam nodded. He had heard that the marquis was wealthy and perhaps that was why Lethbridge hoped to lure him into one of his card games. Perhaps it would be better to watch the count and his friends at play before taking a hand himself.

'May I take you home, Madeline?'

'Thank you, I shall go alone—if you would send for my carriage for me, please?'

'Yes, of course. Go up and put on your cloak. I will make your excuses to your husband…tell him that you felt a little faint and decided to leave.'

'Thank you. He will be angry, but perhaps he will wait until tomorrow before venting his anger on me. And I truly have the headache.'

Hallam smiled at her, then bent his head to kiss her hand. They parted, he to order her carriage brought round and she to put on her cloak.

When she came downstairs, Hallam escorted her out to her carriage and assisted her inside. He held her hand a moment longer.

'I should like to meet somewhere—do you walk or ride?'

'Sometimes I walk with my maid in Hyde Park on fine afternoons.'

'Can you trust her?'

'Yes, with my life.'

'Then meet me one day this week—perhaps tomorrow.'

'I am not sure. Perhaps the following day?'

'I will visit the park every day between two and three,' he said. 'Do not despair, Madeline. I will find a way to free you from Lethbridge.'

She smiled, but said nothing, sitting back in her carriage. Hallam told the man to drive on and then went back into the house.

It was time to seek out Lethbridge and discover what kind of a man he was—and why he was so fortunate at the card tables.

Hal had rescued her from the marquis. She trembled as she recalled the way he'd looked at her. At first he'd blamed her for her shocking behaviour, but he'd understood once she'd told him that her husband had forced her to flirt with the marquis. He'd asked her to run away with him...he must still care for her a little, if only sufficiently to protect her from her husband's spite.

If only she dared to run away. And yet could she ever find happiness after the pain Lethbridge had inflicted on her? There were times when she thought she had been scarred too deeply. He had done such things to her... things that shamed her and made her feel unworthy of a good man's love.

Madeline lay in bed for some time, wondering whether her husband would come to her in a rage, and, when in the early hours of the morning, she heard him enter the house, she tensed to receive the onslaught. However, he did not enter her room and after half an hour or so she fell into a deep sleep.

* * *

It was morning when her maid drew back the curtains and presented her with a tray of hot chocolate and sweet rolls.

'Did you sleep well, my lady?' Sally asked.

'Yes, I did eventually.' Madeline sat up and smiled at her. 'Has my husband asked for me?'

'No, I do not think so, ma'am.'

'Very well. I shall get up when I've eaten my breakfast. Is it a nice day?'

'A little wet this morning,' Sally replied, 'but Cook says it will clear this afternoon.'

'We might go walking this afternoon,' Madeline said. 'I shall decide later.'

Sally nodded and left her to the enjoyment of her hot chocolate. She was just finishing her rolls and honey when the door to the dressing room opened and Lethbridge entered her room. Madeline put her tray to one side and waited, expecting the tirade to begin. She was surprised when her husband looked at her with a wry smile.

'It seems that you have charmed Rochdale, madam,' he said. 'I invited him to a card evening next week and he accepted. He does not yet know that he is to be my only guest. You must have intrigued him for he told me to give you his best wishes and tell you that he looked forward to seeing you soon.'

'Oh…' Madeline was surprised for she had quite expected the marquis to refuse after the scene in the garden. 'May I have the rest of Papa's notes now?'

'Later,' he said and glared at her. 'I do not see why you want them. I shall not ruin my wife's father. Unless…' His eyes narrowed. 'Do you think to get them and then leave me?'

'No, of course not,' she said, but her cheeks were warm.

'You are ungrateful, Madeline. Why I bother with you I do not know. I could find a dozen willing women to fill your place— and I'll warrant they would give me a child in return for what you have.'

She raised her head. 'Yes, I dare say they might. Yet I have never refused you, sir.'

'I've paid for you and I intend to get my money's worth out of you yet. If I can't get a son from you, I'll bring the boy my mistress bore me here. She's a whore, but worth two of a sourpuss like you. If she were a lady, I would marry her. I dare say her son would make me a better heir than any you could give me. At least he would have some spirit in him.'

Madeline felt the colour drain from her cheeks in shock. How could he say such cruel things to her?

'Why do you not divorce me?' she asked, her throat tight with misery. 'You could marry again and get yourself a legitimate heir.'

'Maybe I shall,' Lethbridge said. 'God knows, I am sick of your pale face and your complaints. Yet I may need you again to persuade Rochdale to my way of thinking. Behave yourself and do as I tell you and I may give you your father's notes *and* your freedom.'

Madeline watched as he walked from the bedchamber. What did he want of her now? She had cheapened herself by flirting with the marquis and she knew that Rochdale would not be denied a second time. She'd imagined he would be angry and refuse her husband's invitation to dine, but he had accepted and sent her a message. Was it some kind of a veiled threat?

Was he imagining that he could seduce her under her husband's nose—perhaps with Lethbridge's permission?

What did her husband want from the marquis? He had always been possessive and jealous, but now it was almost as if he were prepared to give her to Rochdale—but in exchange for what?

Madeline shuddered. She had felt sick and ashamed after that encounter in the garden. He had meant to force himself on her, she was certain, and might have succeeded if Hallam had not arrived in time.

She would not allow it to happen. Madeline knew that her husband still held the biggest part of her father's debt to him and nothing would make him part with it. He'd promised to give it to her if the marquis accepted his invitation, but now he wanted more from her. It was always the same; he would never keep his promises whatever she did.

She would not give him what he asked of her. The very idea of allowing the marquis to paw at and kiss her made her feel ill. Was Lethbridge trying to humiliate her, because she had been cold to him—or was there a deeper reason for his hints?

Lethbridge was a cheat. Hallam was as certain as he could be without proof that the count had been systematically robbing his friends at the card table, perhaps for months or even years. He was not certain whether Lethbridge marked the pack or kept important cards tucked into the frills at the ends of his sleeves. He was almost certain that he'd seen a card disappear into the count's sleeve, but he'd also noticed him stroking the corner of a card as if feeling for a mark, though he could not have sworn to either at this stage.

What was certain was that the count was very careful if he was cheating. He usually lost the first couple of hands and then began to win steadily throughout the evening. He was said to have the devil's own luck, but it seemed no one suspected him of cheating—though Hallam had seen someone else watching him closely at the table.

He decided to seek Captain Mainwaring out and ask him his opinion. After searching various coffeehouses and clubs, Hallam ran his friend to earth at Cribbs's Parlour, where he had been watching a bout between one of the professionals hired to help the gentlemen learn the science of the game.

'I had begun to think you had gone out of town,' he said. 'Lunch with me at my club, Mainwaring? I want to ask your opinion of something.'

'Delighted. I've been wanting to see you. I heard a rumour I think may interest you, Hal.'

Hallam waited as his friend watched the bout conclude, paid a small gambling debt, and then they left together, strolling through the chilly streets towards White's, where they could be sure of a decent meal.

'You're interested in Lethbridge, aren't you?' Captain Mainwaring said as they began to walk. 'Mind telling me why? I have my own reasons for being interested.'

'He is a bully and a brute and mistreats his wife,' Hallam replied. 'If you will keep this to yourself—I intend to do my utmost to set her free of him.'

'That will not be easy. Lethbridge is a jealous man, which was why I was surprised to see her flirting with Rochdale the other evening—until I heard a whisper concerning a certain evening at the card table…'

'What happened?' Hallam raised one eyebrow. 'I do not follow you?'

'Lethbridge lost a great deal of money to the marquis—several thousand pounds, I understand.'

'But he can stand the nonsense.' Hallam frowned. 'He is very wealthy, I imagine?'

'He was certainly wealthy even a year or

so back, but I've heard whispers that he has lost money in other ways…investments that turned bad. And he had a long run of bad luck at the tables, until it miraculously turned.'

'Miraculously? You think there is a reason for his change of luck?'

'Lethbridge is a cheat.'

'Yes, perhaps but can you be certain? On the face of things, he appears to be a gentlemen of unblemished character.'

'Hardly that, Hal. He is known to haunt certain vice dens of the worst kind, besides being a cheat and perhaps more.'

'What do you mean more?' Hallam asked. 'I knew he was a bully and I suspected him of being a cheat—do you know how he does it?'

'I think he must mark the cards very lightly, because he never wins at the first or second hand, which means he must need time to mark a few cards.'

'Yes, I thought it might be that—a pinprick or something no one would notice unless they looked for it.'

'Yes, I dare say.' Captain Mainwaring frowned. 'I believe him to be responsible for the death of my young cousin Roger some years back. The lad came into his fortune at eighteen and his only guardian was his mother, who could deny him nothing. Imagine the result when he found himself let loose on the town with money to burn. I was fighting in Spain at the time, but his mother tells me Roger played too deep and was found with a pistol to his head in his lodgings.'

'My God! You suspect Lethbridge of fleecing him at the tables?'

'He and a few others, I dare say—but I do not believe Roger killed himself. He was badly dipped, but the estate was intact. He could have recovered with some careful management—and a magnificent diamond parure was missing, which he'd taken from the bank. As far we know it did not form part of any wager he made, though he may have sold it to pay his debt.'

'You think he was murdered?'

'Yes, I do.' Captain Mainwaring frowned. 'I do not think it was merely robbery—there must have been another reason, perhaps a fear of blackmail. Something that Lethbridge feared to have known.'

'What leads you to believe so?'

'Because of something I discovered in my cousin's things.' Captain Mainwaring frowned. 'I discovered it only a few weeks ago. Roger's mother asked me to sort out her son's personal possessions, because she could not bring herself to do it. Everything had lain untouched for four years…and I found a letter addressed to Lethbridge. It was the letter of a young man with more passion than sense—and it threatened to reveal a secret. But it had never been sent.'

'A secret?'

'The secret was that Lethbridge was a cheat. It was written just before Lethbridge married, and spoke of "the means you used to force that sweet lady to wed you"—which suggested some sort of coercion on the count's part. When you told me she had been forced to wed him I knew that I must be correct in my assumptions.'

Hallam stared at him in horror. 'So he cheated Sir Matthew at the card tables and then blackmailed him into allowing Maddie to marry him. He is a worse rogue than I imagined.'

'A cheat, a blackmailer and a murderer,' Captain Mainwaring agreed, looking grim. 'We need say nothing of his other vices, for he is not the only one to have such secrets— but cheating at cards and blackmail are surpassed only by murder.'

Hallam nodded, his expression grave. 'Where does the marquis come into it?'

'I believe he's won rather too much money from Lethbridge of late—but there may be more.'

'I am not sure I understand you?'

'Supposing Rochdale knows that he is a cheat and has threatened to expose him?'

'He would want to lure the marquis into some kind of a situation where he could be rid of him?'

'If Rochdale has some hold over him, Lethbridge must murder him or face exposure… unless he can buy the marquis off in some way.'

'My God!' Hal shuddered with disgust. 'Maddie told me that her husband had ordered her to entice the marquis. He would sacrifice her to keep his secret? His own wife! Could any man be that vile?'

'A man such as Lethbridge would do anything to save his own skin.'

'Yes, I dare say,' Hallam said, his mouth curling in distaste. Captain Mainwaring's revelations were so disgusting that it made it imperative to free Maddie from her marriage—and urgent.

'I must get her away from that devil!'

'And how do you intend to do that?'

'I can see only one way—and that's to accuse him of being a cheat in public. If I did so in private and asked for her release, he would simply deny it and find a way to murder me. No, I must contrive to play cards with him and accuse him in front of reliable witnesses.'

'He will call you out if you do, for he has no choice.' Mainwaring frowned. 'He is a crack shot, Hal, and good with the foils.'

'I am also thought an excellent marksman and sufficiently skilled with the foils.' Hallam's jaw hardened. 'It is the only way to put an end to her misery, Jack. And if what you believe is true, he deserves to die. I cannot allow him to use her…to sell her to Rochdale in return for his silence.'

'I should have liked to see him hang, but as yet I have no proof that his hand was on the pistol that took Roger's life. Though I would swear I've seen him cheat.'

'We must have proof of it,' Hallam said. 'I want you to sit down with him at the table while I watch. As soon as I know how he does it, I will accuse him.'

'And I'll stand by you as your second. He plays tonight at Lord Hartingdon's house. Do you have an invite?'

'Yes,' Hallam said. 'And you?'

'Tonight it is,' Jack Mainwaring said. 'If you can spot him cheating, we'll break him one way or the other.'

Chapter Four

Madeline's heart thudded wildly as she saw Hallam coming towards her. Hyde Park was filled with people, walking or riding, some in open-topped carriages. Once wild and teeming with game and the favourite hunting ground of a king, the park was now a popular place of pleasure and amusement for people of all classes and ages. It was a favourite haunt for ladies, because they could be sure of meeting friends as they drove or walked in the beautiful surroundings.

Lethbridge's coachman had dropped Madeline and her maid at the park gates and would return in two hours, which should be sufficient for them to walk around the park and greet friends. She had not been sure that

Hallam would be there that afternoon and she felt a surge of pleasure as he came up to her.

'Maddie, I hoped you would come,' he said, taking her hand to bow over it. 'How are you? I have been thinking of you. He did not punish you for your behaviour at the ball?'

'No, for it seems it had the desired effect, even though I thought the marquis angry with me when he left us. Yet he has accepted an invitation to dine next week.'

Hallam nodded. 'I believe Lethbridge has a plan to save himself from ruin and it involves using you.'

'Save himself? Is he in some trouble?' Madeline said and frowned. 'He was pleased because I had done what he asked, so the marquis could not have told him what happened in the garden. He sent me a message to say he was looking forward to meeting me again.'

'You must be careful not to be alone with Rochdale,' Hallam warned. 'I believe him to be both depraved and ruthless. Your husband is a fool to court his company for he may discover that the marquis is more deadly than he knows.'

A little shiver went through her. 'I fear that Lethbridge hates me now. He blames me for not giving him a child, but indeed, it is not my fault. Now he speaks of a bringing an illegitimate child to his house and making him his heir.'

'He could not so insult you?'

'He could and would do anything that pleased him. While he holds Papa's notes he knows I cannot defy him.'

Hallam glanced back at Sally, who was following them a short distance behind. 'She is to be trusted?'

'Yes, of course, always.'

'Have you tried searching for your father's notes?'

'No…' Madeline bit her bottom lip. 'I believe he keeps them in his bedchamber. I had thought to honour my promise, but he does not honour his.' She lifted her gaze to meet his as a thought occurred to her. 'Would it be very wicked of me to steal and destroy them?'

'I think your husband does not deserve loyalty, Maddie. After the way he has behaved to you, you are entirely justified in stealing the notes. They belong to you for you were promised them when you wed him.' His eyes held hers with a burning look that made her tremble inside. 'You know that I would be happy to take you away. We could go to Italy or

Spain or perhaps further away—somewhere that your husband would never find you.'

His words aroused new hope in her. Perhaps there was a chance of escape if she could recover her father's debt?

Yet might Hal demand more than she could give? Madeline knew that she felt tender love for Hal, but was she too deeply scarred to love him in a physical way?

'I think once I had gone he would not bother to search for me, at least if I were no longer in England,' she said, her throat catching. 'He spoke of giving me my freedom if I do what he wants.'

'I thought you had already done so.' Hallam frowned. 'He has no right to demand more of you, Maddie. Do you know what he wants of you?'

'No...' She hesitated, then, 'I fear it may be something to do with the marquis. I think... but no, he could not want me to allow Rochdale to my bed, could he?' She shivered at the thought.

'Damn the man,' Hallam growled low in his throat. 'If he asks you to allow Rochdale to seduce you, refuse him, leave the house and come to me at once. I will promise to give your family a home at my estate if he turns them from their home.'

Madeline's eyes were misty with tears as she attempted to smile at him. 'Lethbridge is a gentleman. I cannot think he would do something so vile as to give his own wife to a man like the marquis.' Her words were meant to reassure him, but in truth she knew that her husband might stoop even that low to gain what he wanted.

'If you think that, you do not know him,' Hallam said. 'I cannot tell you just what kind of a man your husband is, because what I know was told me in confidence—but do not trust him, Maddie. I believe him to be in desperate trouble and he might be capable of anything to protect himself.'

Madeline inclined her head to a passing lady and gentleman, then turned to look at Hallam once more. 'You should leave me now, Hal. People I know are walking here and if you stay with me longer my husband may come to hear of our meeting.'

'Very well. I would not have harm come to you,' Hallam took her hand in his for a moment, looking at her tenderly. 'Do not despair, Maddie. I have not been idle. Perhaps your release may come sooner than you think.'

'What do you mean?' she asked, but he inclined his head and walked on past her. Sally joined her and she resumed her walk about the park, stopping to talk to various friends for a few moments here and there, before making for the park gates where the carriage was waiting to take her home.

What had Hallam meant when he spoke of her release? She prayed that he would not do anything foolish, for unhappy as she was she would rather continue in the same way than have him risk his life for her sake.

Returning home an hour or so later, Madeline discovered that her husband had left word that he would not be home until late that evening. She was free to spend the time as she wished, for he had an appointment that did not include her.

Glancing through the invitation cards she'd received for that evening, Madeline thought that there was nothing she really wished to attend. Instead, she would spend a quiet night at home, perhaps reading or playing the spinet for her own amusement.

She went up to change for the evening, but then decided it was not necessary. She would take off her walking clothes and wear a loose sacque gown because she had no need to go downstairs for dinner.

'You may bring me a tray up, Sally,' she had told the girl and when she did so, 'I shall spend the evening in my rooms reading. I will not need you again tonight. You may retire early or go out for an hour or two with a friend.'

'I should like to visit a friend for an hour or so, but I shall be back by ten should you need me, my lady.'

'Thank you, but I do not think I shall require help,' Madeline said.

She had ordered a light supper and ate a few of the tasty morsels her cook had prepared, then picked up a book of Lord Byron's poetry and begun to read. However, her mind was not at ease and after some minutes she put it down, rose and went through the dressing room. She paused and knocked, but there was no answer from her husband's chamber so she turned the handle and went in.

Her heart began to race because she was very conscious of being where she had no right to be. Lethbridge did not encourage her to enter his rooms and she knew that he would be angry if he returned and found her here. She had come to search for her father's notes. Hallam's words had lingered at the back of her mind since leaving him and now she had gathered sufficient courage.

Her eyes moved round the room, lingering on the opulent bed with its four mahogany posts with the heavy silk curtains, the matching chests that stood each side, and the magnificent armoire, also a large mahogany desk with an elbow chair. It had not taken her husband many minutes to fetch the notes he'd given her the other evening so he had not locked them away in a secret compartment. No doubt he believed that she would not dare to touch them if she found them— and indeed, until this moment that had been the case. She would not even have considered searching for them, but something had changed in her and she no longer felt that it would be wrong of her to touch her husband's things.

Breathing deeply, she began to search the chests, opening each drawer in turn and being very careful to return everything exactly as it had been. She glanced in the armoire, looking in the drawers that contained silk stockings and cravats, also several handkerchiefs, with embroidered initials in the corners. There were no papers of any interest other than a few receipts for items of clothing.

She walked softly over to the desk and pulled out the top drawer and discovered a leather folder. Opening it, she saw the sheaf of notes immediately: one that signed over her father's estate and another for ten thousand pounds.

No wonder he had been unable to pay. What could her father have been thinking of to play so deep? He had gambled away more than his estate was worth and must have been ruined and shamed had Lethbridge demanded payment.

Madeline held her breath, her hand reaching towards the papers when she heard a sound outside the door. Snatching up the notes, she closed the drawer and fled into the dressing room just as the door into the hall opened. From behind the open door of the dressing table, she saw her husband's valet enter carrying a pile of clean linen. He began to place the things in the drawers of the armoire. Madeline fled through the dressing room into her own bedchamber.

She was trembling, though whether from excitement or the fear of being caught she was not sure. For a moment she could not move, because she felt too weak, then she walked towards the fire and stood before it gazing down into the flames.

She had her father's notes. She could destroy them by casting them into the flames and then... Her heart was racing so fast that she could scarcely breathe. It was what she wanted to do so very much, but did she have the right? Lethbridge had promised to return them to her father when she married him, but he had reneged on his promise. According to the bargain they had made, the notes were truly her father's property. Madeline had every right to destroy them. Tearing them across three times, she tossed the pieces onto the fire and watched them burn. A feeling of elation rushed through her. Her father was free of the threat of shame. Madeline would send him a letter in the morning, telling him that the notes were destroyed.

Her elation lasted only a few moments. She had made certain of her father's freedom— but was she herself truly free?

Hallam had told her that he would take her away with him and care for her. She could leave her husband this very night. Yet she knew him to be a vengeful man. Would he not seek to take revenge on both her and Hal? Would she in fact endanger the life of the man she loved?

Madeline was tempted to run, but fear held her. If she took the chance for freedom, Lethbridge would find some way of seeking his revenge—either upon her and Hal or her family...

Tears slipped slowly down her cheeks. She brushed them away, feeling empty and drained of hope. For years she'd thought of the notes as being the tie that kept her chained to a husband she did not love, but now she was frightened to leave him.

What ought she to do? If her husband discovered the loss of the notes he would be so angry and sure to punish her—but if she ran he might kill both her and Hal.

Did she have the right to endanger Hal's life? Perhaps she should simply slip away somewhere by herself....and it would be best not to see Hallam again. Her life meant nothing to her, but she could not bear it if Hal died for her sake.

She would write to him, tell him that she could not see him—and then she would slip away, go down to the country and hope that her husband did not force her to return.

* * *

Hallam read the note that had come to him that morning. He knew Madeline's hand immediately and his heart quickened with excitement. Was she ready to come away with him?

Scanning the brief lines, he stared in disbelief for some minutes before screwing the notepaper into a ball and tossing it into the fire. She did not wish to see him again. She had considered his offer and decided that she could not leave her husband. She begged his pardon and asked him to forget her.

'Damn the rogue!' Hallam exclaimed aloud. What had her wretched husband done to her now that she felt forced to write this letter to him? Had he not known better he would have thought her indifferent to him, but the look in her eyes when they met in the park told him that she still felt something for him.

Why did she feel constrained to stay with a brute who hurt and humiliated her?

Hallam found it impossible to understand. Of course there were the notes, but something could be done—and her family could live on his estate if the worst happened.

He must see her again despite this foolish

letter, but first he had business with her husband. Mainwaring had played with him the previous evening and lost a thousand guineas and Hallam had watched, positioning himself so that he could see in a mirror on the wall at Lethbridge's back. The count had made one fatal mistake. Hallam had seen him prick the corner of a card and them push the pin into the cuff of his velvet coat. Because of his frills and the heavy embroidery on the sleeve of the evening coat, it would be almost impossible for anyone to see the pin, but Hallam had seen him use it twice and was now certain of his facts.

It only remained for him to call the count a cheat and arrange the duel that would free Madeline of her husband once and for all. However, he had been unable to establish when the next opportunity might arise for the count had spoken of perhaps going to the country shortly. If he did so that would mean postponing the confrontation, for he could hardly force his way into the count's home to call him a cheat—nor could he follow him to the country. He could only hope that Madeline would be safe until the opportunity arose to force a quarrel on her husband.

* * *

Madeline saw Hallam as she entered the ballroom that night and her heart caught. She longed to go to him, but knew she must keep a distance between them. It would be foolish to arouse her husband's suspicions for nothing. Lethbridge was in a better frame of mind than of late. Nothing more had been said of the marquis, nor had her husband mentioned anything he wished her to do for him, and she began to think she had imagined that he had some idea of giving her to the marquis.

'I shall go to the card room,' Lethbridge said. 'Sit with your friends, Madeline. If you are asked to dance this evening, you may do so.'

'Thank you, sir,' she replied, glancing at his profile. A little nerve flicked at his temple, but he gave no other sign of emotion. Yet she guessed that there was conflict at work within him, though she could not think what it might be.

Seeing Lady Jersey sitting with some other ladies that she knew well, Madeline went towards them and sat on an available chair. She was soon drawn into a discussion about a young lady who was said to be the latest rage and watched Miss Catherine Anderson being courted by her admirers with amusement.

'Will you dance with me, Lady Lethbridge?'

Madeline glanced up as Hallam spoke. She knew that she should refuse him, but seeing Lord Rochdale approaching her at that moment, she stood up with Hallam before he could reach her.

'You ought not to have asked me,' she said as he placed a hand at her back and drew her into a waltz. 'It is useless, Hal. I cannot leave him…'

'But he lies to you, he cheated you of your father's notes.'

'No, I have them back. My family is safe now.'

'Then come away with me now—I beg you to leave him now, tonight.'

'I am afraid of what he might do. Forget me, Hal. I am not worthy of you. I beg you to forget you ever knew me.'

'Madeline…' Hal stared at her in dismay. 'Have you taken leave of your wits? Or is it that you care for him?'

Madeline met his eyes, tears hovering on her lashes as she said, 'You must believe what you will of me.' Breaking from him, she walked swiftly away from him and left the ballroom.

She went up to the bedroom given over for the use of female guests that evening and shut herself away in the closet provided for relieving oneself. There, she allowed her tears to fall until she could recover her composure. Returning to the bedroom, she washed her face in cool water from a porcelain jug and tidied herself before going downstairs. No trace of the tears remained, though she looked pale.

It was as she reached the bottom of the stairs that she saw the Marquis of Rochdale. He was about to enter the ballroom, but stopped and waited for her.

'May I escort you back to the dancing, Madeline?'

'I did not give you permission to use my first name, sir.'

'Did you not?' His lips curled in an unpleasant sneer. 'You think to flirt with me and then spurn me, madam, but you will learn to know better. It will give me great pleasure to teach you a lesson.'

'Sir, I think you forget yourself. I shall speak to my husband of your discourtesy.'

He laughed low in his throat. 'Say what

you will, Lethbridge may not be listening,' he said. 'A reckoning is coming, Madeline. Next week I dine with you—and then you will discover I am a man of my word.'

Madeline lifted her head proudly and walked past him into the ballroom. Her heart was thumping madly, but she gave no sign of it as she looked about her.

She was afraid of the marquis, afraid of what her husband had done—but she'd sent Hallam away. Oh, how she longed for a shoulder to weep on and a strong arm to hold her!

But it was best this way. She could not bear that Hal should know the depths to which she had fallen. It was best that she never saw him again, for she was soiled and shamed, no fit companion for any decent man.

Lethbridge rose from the card table after the Marquis of Rochdale had departed, taking his winnings with him. He had lost ten thousand pounds in one sitting to that detestable man and was now ruined. He could not pay without selling his country estate, and if he did that he would lose everything he cared for. His estate had been in his family for four hundred years and it was the source of his income—and his pride. Once it had gone, he would be dunned by all those he owed money to—and then...there would be nothing left.

There was only one thing that stood between him and complete ruin—his wife. Unless he forced Madeline's father to sell his estate and pay his debts, in as far as he could...but even that would not suffice for he'd given Madeline more than twenty thousand and she'd destroyed them.

But there was one way that he could buy time. The marquis had made it plain to him what he wanted. If he gave him Madeline, he would return the notes and Lethbridge could carry on as before. He would take good care not to sit down with Rochdale again and somehow he would come about. He'd done it before and he could do it again—though never had he been as deep in debt as now.

He'd attempted to cheat this evening, but somehow Rochdale had known which cards he'd marked and turned them against him. He'd actually played into the devil's hands. How could he have known which cards to look for? But of course, he must have learned to feel the corners for that slight unevenness caused by a pinprick. Most men never knew it was there—but Rochdale did.

Rochdale had made it clear that he would

demand payment of Lethbridge's debts, and he would use the cards to expose the count as a cheat—unless he gave him Madeline.

He must reply by noon the next day or he would lose all he had. He was caught fast in a trap—unless....

A plan had begun to form in Lethbridge's head, a plan so wicked and devious that it made him shake with excitement. He would agree to the marquis's demands—he should have his time in bed with Madeline when he came to dine, but then...

No court in the land would convict him of murder for shooting a man he discovered raping his wife.

He smiled unpleasantly. He would allow Rochdale to come to the house and to have Madeline once the notes were returned to him, but then he would burst in on them and shoot him as he lay in her bed.

Once, he could not have borne another man to touch her, but she was cruel and proud. Why should he care what happened to her? He could use her to destroy his enemy and then he could divorce her because she was spoiled goods and had shamed him.

It was such a neat plan that his good humour was restored. And since he was deter-

mined to be rid of his wife, why not foreclose
on her father and make him pay with the sale
of his estate?

Hallam left the ball feeling angry with
Madeline. How could she stay with her husband when she knew what a worthless wretch
he was?

Hallam had no idea of the turn events had
taken that evening, but what Mainwaring had
told him was enough to convince him that the
count was close to desperate. His mind was
made up—he must engage him in a game
of cards as soon as possible for Lethbridge
would certainly try to cheat and then he could
expose him.

Hallam was torn by his doubts. He hardly
knew Maddie these days. As a young girl he'd
found her sweet and innocent, incapable of
hurting anyone, but then she'd sent him away
and married Count Lethbridge. He'd seen her
flirting with the marquis and though she'd
claimed Lethbridge might ruin her family if
she left him, once she had destroyed her father's notes, she said it was best if Hal forgot her. He was baffled. Was she the girl he
loved or someone very different?

Walking home, he turned the thoughts over

and over in his mind, trying to discover the truth, but he could not puzzle her out. How could he know whether Madeline truly cared for him or not?

Madeline rose the next morning feeling heavy-eyed. She'd hardly slept, her thoughts going round and round in circles. She'd regretted dismissing Hal so coldly and wished the words unsaid. Her husband was an unkind man and she feared him more now that he had become a harsh stranger, barely speaking to her unless absolute necessary, than she had when he had visited her bed and abused her both physically and verbally.

When he looked at her now she saw calculation in his eyes and wondered what he was planning.

Feeling close to desperation, she sat down at her desk and wrote a short note to Hal, begging him to meet her again in the park. She wanted to apologise, to make her peace with him and try to explain why she could never be the wife for him even if she were free. How could she when she feared that her husband had destroyed her ability to respond to physical love?

Lethbridge had abused her both physically and mentally; the physical scars were slight and soon mended, but she feared that he had made it impossible for her to welcome a man's kisses…his loving…even if that man were the only one she'd ever loved.

When Hal had kissed her in the gardens on the day of Jenny and Adam's wedding, she'd wanted to melt into his arms but then, suddenly, a feeling of fear and revulsion had made her draw back. How could she bear anyone to touch her intimately after…? Even the thought turned her cold and caused an acid sickness in her throat.

Her mind told her that it would be different with Hal, because he was a gentleman and he loved her, but her body had learned to fear the intimate side of marriage.

Somehow, she must explain to Hal. Tell him that she loved him, but could never accept him as a lover. She could never bear anyone to touch her again for she was soiled… shamed beyond bearing.

Her eyes filled with tears as she sealed her letter and summoned Sally. Even though she knew the future held nothing for her, she longed to see Hal just once more…

Chapter Five

Madeline encountered her husband as she went downstairs just after noon the following day. She had been hoping to escape to the park, where, if he'd received her letter, she hoped Hal would come to meet her. Her heart raced with fear for she saw her husband's icy eyes and knew he would question her about her intentions.

'You know that the Marquis of Rochdale is dining with us this evening, Madeline. You should wear the green gown I had made for you in Paris—and do not wear a fichu in the neck. Instead, wear your diamonds.'

'I do not like that gown, it is too low and reveals too much. It makes me look like a whore,' Madeline said, her cheeks flushed.

Did he intend to humiliate her? 'The marquis…he is not what you think him, Lethbridge. He may think…he may believe I wear the gown for his benefit.'

'That is exactly what I wish him to believe,' Lethbridge said. 'If he wants to touch or kiss you, you should allow it. I want something from him and if he wants you, then he may have you. You have given me nothing and I may as well get some benefit from all you have cost me.'

Madeline stared at him in horror, her worst fears confirmed. 'Am I to understand that you would condone…a liaison between us?'

'Why not?' her husband sneered, his thick lips curving unpleasantly. 'You are of no use to me. I might as well lie with a block of wood. Rochdale has something I desire more than I ever desired you, madam. If he will take you in exchange, then good luck to him.'

'How dare you suggest such a thing to me?' Madeline cried in utter disgust. 'You have gone too far, Lethbridge. I shall not do what you ask and I shall leave you. By insulting me so you set me free of any debt of honour I felt towards you. Our marriage is at an end. I no longer owe you any duty.'

'Damn you,' he muttered and moved towards her. One hand grabbed her wrist and she saw that he was considering whether to strike her. 'No, I shall not punish you yet. I would not have you ill before he takes what he wants. But after he has done with you, I shall teach you to obey me. You will not defy me again, madam.'

'No, I shall not allow it. No matter what you threaten. I shall run away—'

'Then I'll lock you in your room until he arrives.' Lethbridge grabbed her by the hand and started to drag her with him, out into the hall and up the stairs.

Madeline struggled against him, crying out as his fingers dug into her soft skin, but although the servants saw her struggling none attempted to help her. They dared not. He would have them thrashed and they would be dismissed without a reference, cast out without hope of finding another employer. It was useless to ask for help and she did not, though she fought him all the way, but to no avail. He was much too strong for her. She was thrust into her bedchamber, her husband standing in the doorway, glaring at her.

'Make yourself ready to receive the marquis this evening,' Lethbridge growled before the door closed. 'Please him or I shall beat you until you weep for mercy—and I'll ruin your father.'

'You may do what you wish to me,' Madeline said defiantly. 'I shall run away as soon as I can and you may do your worst.'

'If you think to run to your lover, think again,' Lethbridge muttered. 'I know who he is and I shall kill him.'

'I have no lover.'

'I saw you with him in the gardens at Miss Hasting's wedding—and you've been seen with him in the park and other places. Do not try to deny it, madam. I had not decided what to do to him, but it would be better to have him dead. Then you will not have foolish ideas of escaping me by running to Ravenscar.'

Madeline gasped, feeling the colour drain from her face. He knew of Hal! His words were not merely bluff or vain threats this time—she'd been seen in the park with Hal.

'Yes, I see your guilt and by it you seal his fate,' Lethbridge said. 'Tonight you will play the whore for my guest. If you do not, you know what will happen.'

Hearing the door slam and the key turn, Madeline sagged with despair. Hal was in danger. It hardly mattered what her husband did to her now for if Hal were lost to her for ever she did not care if she died.

Sinking down on the edge of the bed, she bent her head and wept. She should have gone with Hal when she had the chance.

Lethbridge would give her to the marquis in return for something he craved. Clearly, he no longer valued her and, perhaps, wished to be rid of her. Was he planning to bring his bastard here—and his mistress? Or did he simply wish to be free of a wife whom he thought of as useless? If she were forced to lie with the marquis, her husband could claim that she had betrayed her vows and divorce her. She would be utterly ruined and ostracised from society.

It was a fiendishly clever plan for he gained something he craved and rid himself of an unwanted wife in one swoop.

'My lady, you must come now,' Sally's voice called to her. Madeline looked towards the dressing-room door and saw her maid beckoning to her. 'Your husband has gone out and we have a carriage waiting for you—but you must come quickly before he returns.'

'Sally, you know what he would do to you if he catches us?'

'I would give my life for you,' Sally said

and smiled bravely. 'I have packed a bag for you, my lady. Come quickly, I beg you.'

'But how have you done this? My husband has the keys.'

'There are other keys,' Sally replied. 'I overheard what he was planning to do to you—and Thomas was willing to risk everything for you, as I am.'

'But where can I go? My father would send me back to my husband.'

'Not if he knew the truth,' Sally said. 'Thomas knows of a place that you can hide, my lady. It will be safe for a few days, but then you must decide where you will go next.'

'I must send word to Major Ravenscar. My husband means to kill him.'

'Thomas will take your letter later, but first we must go, before anyone realises what we mean to do.'

'Yes.' Madeline stood up. She caught up her cloak, which was lying on a chair where she'd abandoned it earlier, then went to her dressing chest and took out a small box containing the jewels she wore every day. Lethbridge kept the valuable things in his strongbox and gave her what he wished her to wear when he dictated, but she would take the jewels that she had brought with her to the marriage and the few gold coins she had in her reticule. She looked about her chamber, praying that she need never see it again. 'Let us go now, before my husband returns.'

'Where is she?' Lethbridge thundered at the luckless servant that brought him the news. Arriving home late in the afternoon, he'd gone to his room to change for the evening and then sent a servant to tell Madeline to make ready. 'By God, if you've allowed her to leave, I'll have you beaten to an inch of your life!'

'I don't know where she is,' the servant said, cringing as his master struck him a blow on the shoulder with his ivory cane. 'Sally and Thomas must have spirited her away by the back stairs for no one has seen them for hours either.'

'Damnation!' Lethbridge glared at him, a vein bulging in his neck. 'If I discover any of you turned a blind eye, I'll make you sorr—' He broke off as the door to the salon opened and his butler announced the arrival of the Marquis of Rochdale. 'Get out, dog,' he hissed at the servant, then turned and smiled at his guest, as the footman shot from the room like a scared rabbit. 'Ah, Rochdale, my dear fellow. I am glad you could come this evening. I'm sorry to have to tell you that Lady Lethbridge is indisposed. I fear she will not be joining us this evening.'

'Indeed? How very disappointing,' the marquis said and his lips curled in a sneer. 'Since the lady is ill I shall not waste your time or mine. I shall be plain with you—unless you give me what you promised, I shall call in my notes. You know what I want, Lethbridge. You implied it would be mine this evening. If you renege on your bargain, I shall ruin you for good in society.'

'No, no, you shall have her another time,' Lethbridge said. 'You know how much I want what you have.'

'You have three days to bring her to heel,' the marquis said. 'I shall not stay. Perhaps another time?'

Lethbridge cursed as the marquis walked out, leaving him staring after him. Damn the woman! He would make her father pay. That would bring her to her senses. He strode up the stairs and into his bedchamber, pulling out the drawer where her father's notes were kept. Taking out the leather folder, he stared to see it empty and then, realising what must have happened, swore furiously.

She had stolen them! Madeline had outwitted him by taking the notes and then running off with her lover. He had not thought she had the courage to do it or he would have stored them more securely. His own carelessness was to blame, but he did not consider that—only her perfidy in taking them behind his back.

If he could not find her and get her back, he was ruined.

Fury whipped through him. He would find her and kill them both—but before she died, she should suffer agony. His plans for the evening were in ruins and the chance to recoup his notes was lost to him, for if the marquis knew she'd gone to a lover he would waste no more time in claiming his dues. Slamming out of his room, he went down the stairs and out of the house. He must find entertainment elsewhere that night. He would go to his club and see if he could find a plump pigeon to fleece.

Madeline would not be allowed to escape him. She had few jewels and little money for he kept her on a tight string. She could not go far. He would find her—and when he did, he would give her to Rochdale to do with as he pleased, if he would still take her.

The man was depraved, far worse than Lethbridge knew how to be—but if he humbled
the proud beauty it would serve her right, and
he would recover his losses at the card table.

He must find his wife, he would find her!
He would fetch her back—and this time she
would do what she was told.

Hallam was seated with a party of gentlemen when Lethbridge walked into the card
room at Lord Sawford's London house. He
had been finding it hard to keep his mind on
his cards for most of the evening, because all
he could think of was Madeline. She'd sent
him such a strange note, begging him to meet
her in the park. He'd gone to their meeting
place and waited, but she had not come. Why
had she not kept the appointment she'd made?
Ought he to have gone to her house and asked
for her? Yet she had begged him not to do so
and he'd feared she might suffer if he had.

Seeing the count entering the room, Hallam was instantly alerted. Something was
wrong.

Why was Lethbridge here when he was
supposed to be dining with the Marquis of
Rochdale that night? Frowning, he watched
as Lethbridge wove his way through the

room, stopping to talk to various gentlemen before arriving at Hallam's table.

'Thought you were entertaining at home this evening?' one of the gentlemen seated at Hallam's table offered.

'My guest had another appointment he was forced to keep,' Lethbridge said, but the look in his eyes was furious, as if he could barely keep his anger inside. 'May I join you, gentlemen?'

Hallam glanced at Mainwaring. He sat up, suddenly all attention as there was a polite murmur of acceptance and Lethbridge drew out a chair and sat down. He would have preferred to leave the table and take his place behind the count so that he might see what was going on while his friend played, but Lethbridge's request left him no choice but to play on.

He actually had winning cards that hand and took the pot of five hundred guineas. Since he'd won it was his turn to deal, which he did with a new pack. It was brought to the table and broken open by the waiter, as was the custom when a new game began.

Hallam realised that he must be alert at all times. The cards were clean now but, if Lethbridge played as usual, by the third hand after he joined the table they would be marked.

Lethbridge ordered a bottle of wine and glasses were filled, but Hallam noticed that the count merely sipped his. He did the same, watching as the first hand played out. Mainwaring won easily, and another gentleman won the second, but Lethbridge took the third and the fourth.

'What do you say to raising the stakes?' he asked pleasantly.

Hallam hesitated. He would not normally play so deep, but he had won a large pot and could afford to lose a hand or two even at the higher stake of fifty guineas a hand—and it was the best way to discover what Lethbridge was doing.

He went down heavily the next two games and then, having discovered which cards were marked, watched Lethbridge's hand reach beneath the table. When the count began to deal again, he stood up.

'I do not play with cheats,' he said. His announcement sent shockwaves through the company and all eyes turned on him. 'I am speaking of Lethbridge. I know that you have marked the cards, sir.'

'How dare you!' Lethbridge was on his

feet, a vein bulging at his temple. 'You will answer to me for that.'

'Here is your answer, sir.' Hallam handed three of his cards to the other gentlemen to examine. 'The ace is pricked twice, the king once and the queen three times.'

'And why have you decided that I am the culprit?' Lethbridge demanded, glaring across the table at him. 'It might as well have been you, sir.'

'This is not the first time I've watched you cheat,' Hallam said. 'Mainwaring—would you mind looking at the edge of his coat cuff, just below the brocade? I believe you will discover that there is a pin stuck into the material.'

'Certainly,' Jack Mainwaring agreed and reached for Lethbridge's arm. His hand was struck away angrily, but the movement caused a card to fall from beneath his ruffle. One of the other gentlemen reached over to pick up the jack of clubs, which, his fingers soon told him, was still unmarked. 'I think that proves your guilt, Lethbridge. For myself I have lost to you too often of late to doubt Ravenscar's word. I had wondered why you won so consistently.'

'Nonsense. I lost heavily to Rochdale the

other night—anyone will tell you so. Anyone could have marked those cards. Why should it be me?'

'Why did you have the jack hidden in your cuff?'

'Damn you and him!' Lethbridge said, his neck and face brick red. He'd been exposed as a cheat in public and knew that his days of winning large pots at the tables of his society friends was over, because the news would spread like wildfire, but was determined to bluster it out. 'I know not where that card came from. It was probably planted on me—'

'For shame, sir,' came a new voice. 'I wondered why you were so damned lucky at the tables and now I know.' Lord Sawston stood up. 'I, too, refuse to play with a cheat.' The other gentlemen followed his suit, saying that they would never play with Lethbridge again.

'You will meet me for this, Ravenscar!' the count cried. 'Name your weapon, sir.'

'I choose pistols,' Hallam said. 'Mainwaring, Sawston—you will stand up with me?'

'Aye, I will,' Lord Sawston said. 'Though the fellow is finished and does not deserve that you should honour him in duel.'

'Name your seconds, sir,' Hallam said. 'Perhaps they would wait on me at my lodgings later.' He looked at the gathering, a faint smile on his lips. 'Will you bear me company, Jack? I think I shall go down to supper. And then perhaps we might make up another table?' He nodded to the gentlemen with whom he'd been playing earlier.

'You'd best go home and get some sleep,' one of the gentlemen advised.

'You think so?' Hallam said and sent a deliberate and insulting look at the count. 'I hardly think I need bother. I believe I shall make a night of it and go to the meeting place from here. You may inform your seconds they will find me at the tables rather than my lodgings, sir.'

Lethbridge cursed and turned on his heel, walking from the rooms. Men who had hailed him when he entered turned their backs on him. Their message could not be clearer. Hallam was believed for the thought that Lethbridge might have cheated had crossed a few minds before that night, though none had been sure enough to accuse him.

'He's a damned good shot,' Sawston said when he accompanied Hallam and Jack down to the supper room. 'Are you certain you wish to continue playing cards? He's killed his man before now.'

'So have I on the field of battle,' Hallam said. 'We didn't get much rest then and if he is a good shot I'm better. Never missed my man in battle.'

'I can vouch for that,' Jack Mainwaring said and laughed, clearly delighted with the night's outcome. 'Well, he's ruined now, Hal—it's what I hoped for. And if you kill him, I'll bear witness that he called you out.'

'We all will,' Lord Sawston said. 'Lord, I'm hungry. I hope they have a decent supper tonight.'

Hallam laughed. He could hardly believe that Lethbridge had been so easily brought to a duel. If Hal's aim were true, Maddie would soon be free of her cruel husband.

'Did you take the letter?' Madeline asked, as the footman Thomas entered the small private parlour of the riverside inn to which he had taken them. The inn belonged to his brother and he had assured her that she would be safe there until she decided where to go next. 'Was he there?'

'No, my lady. His landlady said that he was out, but promised to give the letter to him as soon as he returned.'

'Thank you,' she said. 'I think I shall go up

to my room now, for I am very tired. Sally, you may stay and talk to Thomas if you wish. I can manage my gown if I try.'

'I shall come and assist you as always, my lady,' Sally said. 'Thomas has things to do and I shall sleep with you on a truckle bed, for there is but the one room.'

'Very well.' Madeline left the parlour and walked swiftly past the taproom, from which came the sound of hearty laughter. It was a busy inn and not truly a good place to hide, for she was almost certain to be seen before many days had passed. However, she was grateful to be away from her husband's house and the hateful attentions of the marquis.

'It is not fitting for you, my lady,' Sally said, glancing around the bedchamber they had been given. It was furnished with the essentials, but not pretty or comfortable enough for a lady of quality. 'We did not have much time to plan, but we must find somewhere more suitable as soon as we can.'

'I do not object to the room for it is clean and adequate,' Madeline replied with a little smile. 'If the bed is comfortable, I shall sleep well enough. Yet I fear that I shall be seen sooner or later and my husband will discover where I am. I must find somewhere else to stay—somewhere quiet where I can remain hidden.'

'You will not return to your father's house?'

'I shall send word that I have left my husband,' Madeline said.

She would tell her father that his notes were burned and that he was free of the debts that had shamed him, but he was in general an honourable man and she feared that he might feel it his duty to tell Lethbridge where she was staying. She might be forced to return to him under the law. She was, after all, still his wife and some might say as much his property as his horse or dog—and therefore in his gift if he chose. It was barbaric that a woman should be obedient to a husband who treated her ill, but the law was too often on his side. Madeline could not prove that he had been planning to sell her to another man. Society would be shocked if they believed her, but he would deny it and the scandal would be unbearable either way. No, she must simply hide until she could find somewhere she might live in safety—perhaps abroad?

'I have a little jewellery. Perhaps Thomas could sell some of it for me? It might pay our way until I can find work of some kind.'

'You cannot work, my lady. Who would

employ you?' Sally frowned. 'We must take a rented cottage somewhere and Thomas and I will work to keep us all.'

'I could not ask so much of you,' Madeline said. 'If Major Ravenscar gets my message, it may not be necessary. He promised to help me if I left my husband.'

'Then I am sure he will come as soon as he has your letter,' Sally said. 'Now let me unlace you, my lady, for I think you must be tired. You will not mind my sleeping in your room? I do not snore—at least, I do not think so...'

'Of course I do not mind,' Madeline said and laughed softly. 'I am no longer a grand lady, Sally. I must learn to live by my own means somehow.'

She stood patiently while Sally helped her to disrobe and put on the nightgown her thoughtful maid had packed for her. Sally had smuggled her things downstairs to Thomas, who had carried them away from the house, to the carriage, which had brought them to his brother's inn. Madeline had observed that the young footman was devoted to her maid and knew that she was his reason for risking so much for her sake. He'd given up a good position and would not find it easy to find another in society without a reference, but Sally had asked and he'd agreed because he loved her.

'You know that I will give you a reference, Thomas, but my word will not carry against that of my husband.' Madeline had told him when he helped her from the carriage on their arrival at the inn. 'I can never tell you how grateful I am.'

'It's time I stood on my own feet, milady,' the young footman said and grinned. 'I've been saving my money and I'll be buying an inn myself soon enough. The truth is, I should have left your husband's employ long ago if Sally would've come with me—but she refuses to leave you.'

'She is very loyal, but I would not wish to stand in the way of her happiness if she loves you, Thomas.'

'She'll come round when she sees you happily settled, milady. And I can wait.'

Madeline had thanked them both again. Now, as she lay in the bed, which had proved both clean and comfortable, she allowed herself a few tears. Everything had happened so swiftly and she hardly knew where she was or what to do. If Hal came for her she would go with him, but they would need to go abroad for, if they remained in England, she feared that her husband would find a way of disposing of her lover and killing her.

She wished with all her heart that she'd run away with Hallam when he'd asked years ago, but of course she had married to save her father from ruin. At least she had freed her father from his debt. She could no longer feel remorse in having stolen the notes after the way her husband had behaved.

At last she settled and drifted into a gentle sleep, a little smile on her lips because her dream was sweeter than of late.

Hallam buttoned up his coat against the cold night air. Dawn was just breaking and the scene in the park was bleak, just a small group of men waiting for the arrival of Lethbridge and his seconds. As the church clock struck the hour, three men came walking towards them. Hallam had begun to think the count would not show, but now he was here and he must keep his nerve. If Madeline was to be set free, Lethbridge could not be allowed to leave here alive. Yet Hallam must hold his fire until the other man shot, because otherwise it would be murder.

The count's seconds had brought pistols

with them, which Lord Sawston insisted on examining. He suspected foul play, but declared the pistols beautifully balanced, though, as Lethbridge had used them before they gave him the advantage.

'You could insist on using the pistols I provided,' he suggested, but Hallam shook his head.

'One pistol is as good as another to me. Let it take place immediately.'

Hallam glanced at the doctor, who had been summoned to attend whichever man was shot. He had an unpleasant feeling in the pit of his stomach: it was one thing to kill the enemy in battle, another to kill an English gentleman in cold blood. However, it must be done for Madeline's sake.

'Does either of you wish to withdraw?' Lord Sawston asked.

'No,' Lethbridge growled. 'He insulted me—I want satisfaction.'

'I have no intention of withdrawing,' Hallam said.

'Then take your places. I shall count to fifteen and you will take one pace on each count. On the count of fifteen, you will turn and fire.'

Hallam nodded and stood back to back

with Lethbridge. He took a step forwards on each count, but on the count of fourteen something alerted him and he half-turned as Lethbridge fired. Because he turned the ball struck him in his left arm rather than his back. He recoiled, steadied himself and then took aim, but he could not quite bring himself to press the trigger and before he could fire, a shot came from out of the trees at Lethbridge's back. It struck him in the centre and his body jerked. He looked stunned as he sank to his knees, blood trickling from the side of his mouth. His mouth opened as if he wished to speak, but only a gurgle issued from his lips before he fell forwards flat on his face.

'Good grief, that's murder!' Sawston cried. 'Did anyone see who fired the shot?'

'I was watching Ravenscar. He did not fire,' Sir Andrew Meechin said. He had accompanied Lethbridge as his second. 'The shot came from behind us and I saw nothing of the rogue—did you?'

'I was also watching Ravenscar. I believe he meant to fire in the air,' Lord Sawston replied. He walked towards Hallam, who was clutching at his arm, swaying a little as the blood oozed through his fingers. The doctor was already with him, binding a tourniquet below the wound to stop the bleeding.

'I'll do,' Hallam said through gritted teeth. 'Take a look at Lethbridge if you will, sir.'

'He's dead,' Mr Phillips, the second of Lethbridge's friends, confirmed. 'It was a foul shot and I caught sight of the rogue in the shadows as he fled—looked like a hired assassin to me, dressed in dark clothes and masked, hat low over his brow.'

'Are you saying one of us arranged this?' Jack Mainwaring demanded.

'No, not at all, but someone did,' Meechin said. 'Let us not forget that there were others the count cheated at the tables. Last night he was exposed for the rogue he was. The man had enemies and someone saw an opportunity to kill him while we were all looking the other way.'

'We must report this to the magistrates,' Lord Sawston said. 'You did not fire, Ravenscar. You are in the clear—but murder was done here this night. Lethbridge is no great loss to the world, but the law must be enforced. Whoever did this thing must be brought to justice.'

'I very much fear I may be—' Hallam got no further as he fainted into Jack's arms.

'We must get him to his lodgings,' Jack said. 'He doesn't need to spend the day kicking his heels in prison in this condition. We can all swear to his innocence.'

'I'll speak to the magistrate and sort this mess out,' Lord Sawston said. 'You may accompany me, Meechin. Jack, you and Phillips should help Hal into a carriage and see him home.'

'It would be better if you brought him to my house,' Dr Phelps said. 'I shall tend him more easily in my surgery. That ball needs to come out and he is going to feel a little the worse for weather for a while. I shall care for him until he feels able to return home. My wife is an excellent nurse and I believe he lives alone.'

It was agreed that this was the best strategy since one could not expect his landlady to nurse him. Grooms were called to assist Hallam into a carriage and others to help transport the lifeless body of Count Lethbridge to his home.

Hallam came round a little in the carriage, but was given a drink of brandy by his friends and soon fell into a swoon again.

'Damn it, I hope his wound isn't fatal,' Jack said. 'He fought the French and came through it—and that devil shot on the count of fourteen. If he were still alive, I would see him hang.'

'It is as well justice was served then,' Meechin remarked. 'I had no wish to act for the fellow in the first place and if I'd known what he meant to do I should have refused. He's a damned scoundrel—or was.'

'Someone had to do it,' Jack said. 'Waste no tears on Lethbridge, sir. He was a cheat, a liar and a murderer and I for one believe that he got what he deserved. I just hope that Hal does not pay too harsh a price.'

Chapter Six

'I think I shall go into the country,' Madeline said on the morning of the third day after she'd fled from her husband's house. 'Last night, when I glanced down into the hall, I saw a gentleman I know—a friend of my husband's. He glanced up, but whether he glimpsed me in the shadows I do not know. I think we should leave London before Lethbridge comes looking for me.'

'We always knew we could not stay here for long,' Sally agreed with an anxious look. 'But where will you go, my lady?'

'I pray you, do not call me my lady. It is best that you call me ma'am or by my name. We are friends after all.'

'I shall call you ma'am,' Sally said. 'You

will always be my lady in my heart. Where in the country shall we go?'

'Are you sure that both of you wish to come with me?'

'I shall not desert you, ma'am,' Sally said, 'and Thomas vows he will go wherever I lead.'

'I have a friend in Cambridgeshire who will take me in for a while,' Madeline said. 'Hattie was my governess, but she left us to marry a gentleman farmer. She will allow me to stay until I can find a cottage of my own. Thomas must take a necklace and sell it for me to cover the costs of the journey.'

'You will not sell your trinkets yet,' Sally said. 'Master Hobbis told Thomas that he would loan us a chaise and pair for the journey. Once we are safe, Thomas can leave us and return them and make his own way back. He has a horse stabled here and will need it in the country.'

'I feel much obliged to you both. Thomas must thank his brother for me, but he has already done so much.'

Madeline's throat caught. She wished that she had found a way to bring more of her jewels with her, for she would like to reward her good friends and did not like to ask so much of them. However, she could not refuse their kindness and must seek a way to repay them in the future—surely there must be a way for her to be independent?

She was determined not to be a burden to anyone for long. Hallam had promised to help her, but he had not answered her letter and she could not help being anxious. He'd spoken of calling her husband out— had he been injured himself? A terrible fear gripped her that he might be in pain or even dying.

She could not make enquiries herself for fear of betraying her whereabouts, but Thomas must go again to Hallam's lodgings and enquire after him. Madeline would not beg for his help and so would not send a second letter, but she needed to know that he was well and not in trouble.

Accordingly, the former footman was dispatched with a pearl necklet she insisted on selling and instructed to make enquiries concerning Hallam's health. While he was gone, Sally packed their few possessions and Mr Hobbis had them loaded on to the chaise ready for his return.

Madeline spent the time at the window looking down into the yard, standing just behind the curtains to avoid being seen whilst on the look out for Thomas's return or Hallam himself.

Two hours passed before she saw Thomas crossing the yard. He came upstairs to them immediately. He had sold the necklet for fifty guineas, which Madeline was pleased to have, but his news was not good. Hallam's landlady had not seen him in three days and she had heard nothing of him since he went out the last evening.

Madeline felt a surge of despair sweep through her, for she could only think that Hal had met her husband in a duel as he'd promised and been killed. Fighting the urge to scream and weep, she sank down into a chair, her hands to her face.

'If he is dead, what have I to live for?' she said, the tears she could not control trickling through her fingers. 'I knew in my heart something was wrong, for he would have come to me when he had my letter.' Unless he was angry with her, for sending him away with harsh words that night at the ball?

If only that were so.

She would rather he hated her than that he should be dead.

Thomas frowned. 'I heard a rumour of a duel, my lady…they say a man was killed by foul play, but I do not know the details. Would you have me ask my brother to make what enquiries he may? He has friends who will discover the truth, and when I return the chaise to him he may have more news for us.'

'Thank you,' Madeline said. 'How good you and Sally and Mr Hobbis have been to me. Will you take some of these guineas for your brother?'

'He would not accept your money, my lady. Jake has a big heart and he told me he would willingly do more for you.' What he'd actually said was that he would like to break the count's neck for treating a lady so ill, and since he was a big strong man with huge hands, given the chance he could do it.

'Then I can only thank you all for your kindness. I do not know what I should have done without my friends.'

Had she been forced to submit to the marquis, she thought she might very well have taken her own life. Her heart was aching, but she was determined to be brave and carry on, because her friends had done so much for her that she could not give in to her private misery.

'We should leave, ma'am,' Sally said. 'Thomas, pray ask your brother to have the chaise made ready. We shall be more than two days on the road and we must seek out small quiet inns, otherwise the count will find it easy to follow us.'

'Yes, we must be careful for all our sakes. It is not just I who would suffer if we were caught,' Madeline said. Her friends had risked much for her sake and if Lethbridge caught up with them he would punish both Sally and Thomas, as well as forcing Madeline to return with him.

'We'll be on our way in a few minutes,' Thomas promised. He patted his coat pocket. 'Do not worry, ma'am, I am armed and I would die before I let that devil take either you or Sally.'

'You should stay in bed another day, sir,' Dr Phelps said as he saw Hallam up and dressed. 'We were lucky that the fever soon passed and your wound is healing well, but I would have preferred to see you rest a little longer.'

'I thank you for my good health. Your wife has been an excellent nurse,' Hallam said and offered his hand, which was firmly clasped.

'Please render your bill to me at my lodgings as soon as possible. I am very much in your debt.'

'Captain Mainwaring, who has called every day to see how you went on, has paid the bill. He would not disturb you for you were sleeping when he called, but says he has news for you and will come to your lodgings soon.'

'Have the magistrates asked you for an account of that shameful affair?'

'I have given a statement in writing. You may receive a rap over the knuckles for having taken part in a duel, but I think there will be no further charges, Major Ravenscar. There are plenty to speak against the late count and you have more friends than you may realise.'

'I thank you, sir, and will take my leave of you.'

Once he was out in the cool air of early morning, Hallam felt the pain in his arm. It had taken him four days to recover from the wound and the bout of fever that had kept him restless and tossing for the first two days. The wound itself was not serious and healing well, but the fever had pulled him down more than he liked and he was anxious.

What had happened to Madeline during the last few days? Her husband could no longer bother her, but he could not rest easily in his mind. Lethbridge had been ready to give her to the marquis.

But surely she was safe at home, preparing to wear black for her husband and instruct her advisers to arrange a fitting funeral? All she need to do now was to wait a short time and she would be free to live her life as she chose. Her husband must have left her some sort of jointure and so she would not be penniless. If she could be persuaded to marry Hallam, he would have no use for her husband's money—but would she be satisfied to live quietly in the country as his wife? He had so little to offer her.

He could not quite forget that she had chosen to marry the count after Hallam's father had lost his fortune. Madeline had explained that her father would have been ruined had she refused—but now that she was free, might she prefer to find herself a wealthy husband, a man she could respect and love?

There was only one way to find out. He would call on her at her London home and ask to see her. If she received him kindly, he would ask her to marry him. Out of respect for her late husband's family, she could not marry again for at least six months, but if they had an understanding it would not matter. Hallam would spend the months between preparing his home and doing what he could to pay off his father's debts.

He saw a cab drawn up at the side of the road and spoke to the driver, giving him the address of the countess's home.

'I am sorry, sir. We are a house in mourning,' the butler said in answer to Hallam's request. 'My late master was foully murdered and my mistress is out of town.'

'Out of town?' Hallam frowned. 'When did she leave? Do you know where she has gone?'

'I fear I am unable to answer those questions, sir. My late master's lawyer, Mr Symonds, is arranging the funeral since there is no one else. He is not here at the moment, but should call in later this afternoon. If you wish to know more, you might like to return and speak with him.'

'Thank you… Answer me this, if you will—did the countess leave before or after her husband was killed? I am her friend and very anxious to find her.'

The butler hesitated, then glanced over his

shoulder. 'I understand it was the previous evening, sir, but I can tell you no more. None of us know anything, but the count was angry and—' He shook his head. 'It is not my place to say, but things were not right here.'

'I see.' Hallam nodded and thanked him, giving him a guinea before taking his leave. He was thoughtful as he walked back to his lodgings. If Maddie had left the previous night and her husband was angry, had she run away—or, more worryingly, had she been abducted by Rochdale?

His pace increased, for if she'd left on her own account, surely she would have contrived to send him word somehow? He was on fire with impatience, cursing the ill luck that had caused him to lie in a weak state for so long. Doctor Phelps was correct in saying that he needed to rest, for he was not yet himself and began to feel a little light-headed as he hurried home.

When he let himself into the house, Mrs James, his landlady, came hurrying out into the hall. She gave a little shriek as she saw him, her face stripped of colour.

'Lawks a' mercy, Major,' she cried. 'I'd given you up as dead, so I had. Not a word in four days and people asking after you—I was sure something wicked had happened.'

'Someone was asking for me? Was it a lady?'

'No, sir. A footman by the looks of him, handsome he was and had a nice smile. He brought a letter first and then came asking after you three days later—seemed anxious to find you.'

'You have the letter?'

'Why, yes, sir. I kept it in my parlour for you, just in case.' She went back into her parlour and then returned with two small sealed notes. 'This came that day as well, sir. I meant to give it to you, but you left and I couldn't catch you.'

Hallam took the letters and broke the seal of the first in haste. Madeline had asked him to meet her that afternoon. Opening the second letter, he scanned the few lines and frowned. Maddie had fled from her husband because he had threatened to kill Hallam and to force her to lie with the marquis.

'You say this came three days ago?'

'It would be four now, sir, for it was the day after you went missing.'

Hallam cursed softly. Maddie would think he had deserted her!

'Thank you. I am sorry to have worried you. I shall be back later.'

'You're not going out again, sir? It's a raw day and you look as if you could do with a warming drink and a good meal inside you.'

'I shall hold that thought, Mrs James,' Hallam said and smiled at her. 'A lady needs my help, but I shall return as soon as I can.'

Madeline stared out of the window at the countryside. It was a cold bleak day and there was a light coating of frost on the trees and bushes. The hot brick a thoughtful landlady had placed at her feet had gone cold now, but her hands were warm inside the fur-lined muff that Sally had brought for her. She was fortunate in having all the comforts that two small portmanteaux could provide. Thomas had not had time to bring more, but she must be grateful that she had so much. Had she tried to flee without their help she would have had nothing.

She would not need expensive silk gowns in the country, but had she been able to bring more, she might of course have sold them. Try as she might, Madeline could not think how she was to live without money. Lethbridge had paid her bills, but never gave her more than a few guineas to play at loo. She supposed he had wanted to make her dependent on him, which she had been. Had she planned to leave him in advance, she might have kept a valuable necklace or bracelet, which might have paid her lodgings for months. Surely there must be some way she could earn her living without being a burden to her friends?

Yet what did any of this matter if Hal were dead? Emotion caught at her throat, but she would not allow herself to weep. She must remain calm. Somehow she must make a home for herself and her friends, for they could not live on charity for ever. Hattie would take them in for a time, but after that?

It was too difficult to think about. Madeline's thoughts returned to Hallam. He'd been so passionate, so determined to save her from her cruel husband and she feared that he had suffered for her sake.

'Oh, Hal, my dearest,' she whispered. 'I pray that we shall meet again, if not in this life then the next.'

Hallam stared at the innkeeper. He was looking back at him with suspicion in his eyes and a slightly hostile manner.

'And who might you be, sir, if I may make so bold?'

'I am Major Ravenscar and a friend of the countess. She wrote to me, telling me that I might find her here, sir. Will you please ask her if she will see me?'

'Ah…would you mind a showin' me the letter, sir?'

'Here, read it for yourself,' Hallam said and thrust it at him. 'It bears her seal. For God's sake, tell me she is here and safe!'

Hobbis stared at the seal, which had been broken, but could still be seen for what it was, then shook his head. 'You must be the cove what my brother asked me to enquire after. The lady ain't here, sir. She left yesterday afternoon, my brother and her maid with her.'

'Where did she go?' Hallam asked. 'Was it to her father's home?'

'I wouldn't rightly know about that, sir. My brother told me they was goin' into the country, but he'd bring the chaise back and take his horse what he keeps here. He'll know where they're at when he returns, but it will be a few days yet, I reckon.'

Hallam cursed beneath his breath. 'Are you certain you know nothing more? I assure you I only wish to help her.'

'That's what the other cove said what came askin' after her. I told him she'd gone and no more—I've told you more, but I can't tell you what I don't know. My brother spoke of going to East Anglia, but that's all I can tell you.'

'The other person who came enquiring— what sort of a man was he?'

'I don't rightly know, sir. Spoke with a bit of an accent, he did. Might have been from the north, but he weren't no gentleman, nor were he from London. Looked as if he were a servant to a gentleman, if you ask me.'

'Thank you.'

Hallam frowned. Lethbridge was dead and his servants believed their mistress to be out of town. Who else might look for her? He could think of only one man who might try to trace her—the Marquis of Rochdale. If he'd been prepared to forgive a large debt at the card tables for a night with Lethbridge's wife, he must want her almost to the point of obsession. Now that Lethbridge was dead, he could gain nothing by taking his wife.

It was unnatural for a man to be so obsessed and Hal wondered what could be behind his desire to pursue a woman who did not want him—or was that it? Was it simply that he believed she had snubbed him and was determined to make her suffer for her pride?

The man must be deranged, surely?

Or was there some other reason? If there were, Hal could not fathom it. Yet he believed that Rochdale must be the man who was making enquiries about Madeline's whereabouts.

Yes, he would try to find her now that the count was dead, for he would think her vulnerable and alone. Hallam guessed that the marquis had sent one of his servants to look for Madeline—but how could he have known she was here? Had he had someone watching the house? Or agents searching for her?

If Rochdale was searching for her, it meant she was not as safe as Hallam had supposed. Somehow he had to find her before the evil marquis did.

'If you hear anything, will you let me know, please?' Hallam said and gave Hobbis a gold coin. 'If your brother returns, please tell him that Major Ravenscar is searching for the countess—and warn him that a very unpleasant gentleman may also be looking for her. He is dangerous and not to be trusted if he comes here.'

'Right you are, sir. I'll send word to your lodgings as soon as I hear.'

Hallam thanked him and left the inn. He walked home deep in thought, unaware that he was being shadowed. Hobbis had seemed genuine, but was he hiding something? East Anglia was a large place with many isolated dwellings and he could search for months and not find Maddie.

Where could she have gone? For the moment he was lost, unable to think of anyone she knew in that part of the country.

His arm was hurting quite a bit and he needed food. He would return to his lodgings and enjoy the meal his landlady had promised. After that he would make a plan of campaign. He was too impatient to sit around waiting for Hobbis's brother to return.

Perhaps if he wrote to her father and told him she might be in danger, he would provide a clue as to where she might have sought a refuge…yet that would take time and he was on fire to see her.

'That is the house just ahead,' Thomas said and steadied his horses. 'Your friend will be expecting you, ma'am, for I took the liberty of sending a groom to warn her when we reached the inn last night.'

'You sent a groom?' Madeline said. His

thoughtfulness overwhelmed her and she said, 'You must keep an account of what you spend on my behalf, Thomas. I shall find the means to repay you.'

'It cost me nought but a bit of time, for I cleaned the stables in his place and he was glad to do it.'

Madeline accepted his word, but she still felt indebted to him for he must have been tired after driving them for the past two days, and was not used to such a manual job. However, he wanted no thanks and, once again, she could only smile and think how fortunate she was to have such friends.

She was a little apprehensive as to what her former governess would think at having three guests thrust upon her, but as the chaise drew up in the yard, the front door of the large, rambling farmhouse flew open and a woman came running out.

'Miss Maddie, is it truly you?' she cried. 'Oh, lord above, how good it is to see you. Come in, come in to the warm, my dove— and your friends with you. My Bert is at work, but he will be as pleased as can be for me to have you stay, for he says I never stop talking of you.'

'Hattie,' Madeline said and her eyes stung

with tears. 'I am so glad to be here. May I truly stay for a while—just until I can find some employment?'

'Employment—what's this?' asked the good woman, who was a deal plumper than she had used to be. 'You'll do no such thing while I have breath in my body. You have a home with me—and your friends too, though they might prefer their own cottage?'

'They are not yet married, though I believe it is what they both wish for,' Madeline said and laughed. 'We shall stay with you for a time, but then we must find a place we can manage ourselves—and perhaps I shall find some kind of work. I might take in sewing.'

'We'll talk of that another time,' Hattie Jenkins said. 'Come to the fire and warm yourselves for it is cold enough to freeze and I dare say we'll have snow before long.'

Maddie laughed. She'd always been fond of her former governess and missed her company when she had left to marry. Their letters had been infrequent after she married for the count did not approve of her having a friend he considered below his wife in the social scale.

'It is so good to see you,' Madeline said

and smiled. 'I missed our conversations. Reading poetry together...'

'I've had little time for poetry of late,' Hattie said and laughed. 'A farm kitchen is always busy and always dirty from muddy boots, my love, but I shall enjoy talking of it with you.'

Madeline followed her into the large kitchen. Furnished with a huge dresser, the shelves of which were crammed with china, glass and pans, also a long pine table and chairs, a black cooking range, several painted cupboards and chests of drawers, it was as clean as a new pin, the red tiles on the floor polished and gleaming.

'Your kitchen is spotless,' Madeline said. 'You must work hard to keep it so clean.'

'I have some help, but Bess is away at the moment. Her mother took sick and she asked me to let her go until the good lady recovers.'

'I should be glad to stand in for her,' Sally said at once. 'I can scrub floors and wash dishes, Mrs Jenkins. I'll be glad to earn my keep—and Thomas will help your husband in the yard, if he would be of use.'

'Well, bless you, my love,' the kind woman said. 'I won't say no to a bit of a hand now and then, Sally. I shan't take advantage, but an offer of help now and then won't be refused.'

'I can help, too,' Madeline said, but Hattie shook her head.

'Now that you won't, my dove—leastwise, not with the rough work. We don't want to spoil your pretty hands. I might find you a bit of sewing, if you need employment. I never find the time for it and you always did set a neat stitch.'

'That is why I thought I might earn my living with my needle,' Madeline said. 'I must do something after all.'

'But why?' Hattie asked, looking puzzled. 'You've run away from your husband, I know, for the message your groom sent me told me so—but surely you have a little money of your own? Did neither the count nor your father settle anything on you when you married?'

'You do not know what happened after you left us,' Madeline said. 'I did not tell you when I wrote for there was nothing anyone could do—Papa lost everything to Lethbridge at the card tables and I was forced to accept him. My father made no settlement himself, for he could not, and the money Grandfather left me went to Lethbridge. It was meant to be my pin money, but my husband gave me only a few guineas when he felt like it. I do not know what happened to the capital, though I think it was put in a trust in my name.'

'Cry shame on him,' Hattie said in high disgust. 'How could he treat you so ill? It is no wonder that you left him.'

'You do not know the half of it,' Madeline said. 'I shall tell you later when we have a little time to talk.'

'I'll take you up to your rooms,' Hattie said. She looked at Sally. 'You'll be next to your mistress—and your man can sleep over the stables for the moment. If you would care for it, you'll find the things for making tea on the dresser. We'll be down again by the time you've boiled the kettle.'

She took Madeline by the arm and steered her from the welcoming kitchen up a wide staircase to the landing above and then led the way to the end of the right-hand passage. Opening the door, she ushered Madeline inside a neat, pretty room furnished in cool colours of blues and greens with a dash of white.

'It isn't quite what you're used to, Maddie, but it will do until we can sort you out,' she said. 'So tell me why you decided to leave him. Something must have happened.'

'Yes, it did,' Madeline said and described the last scene with her husband.

Hattie listened in silence, saying nothing, but shaking her head sorrowfully from time to time. 'I never heard such wickedness in my life,' she said when Madeline had finished. 'The man deserves to be flayed alive, so he does. Any decent man would take a horsewhip to him for his treatment of you. Well, if he comes looking for you, my Bert will see him off.'

'I do not think he will know where to look. I never told him where you lived, but of course my father might do so, for he may guess where I have gone.'

'Surely he would not? Knowing what that man did to you he could not wish you to return to him.'

'I hope that he would not, but I would rather he did not know where I am, at least until I am ready to move on.'

'Is there no one to help you, Maddie?'

She hesitated, then sighed. 'I believed there was, but I wrote to him and he did not come. I fear he may have been wounded or killed…'

A tear ran down her cheek. 'Otherwise…he would have come for me, I am sure.'

'Well, perhaps he was prevented by some circumstance you know naught of,' Hattie said in a practical tone. 'Does he know where to find you?'

'No, for we thought it best to tell no one. Thomas is to return his brother's chaise in a few days and he will try once more to contact Major Ravenscar.'

Hattie stared at her for a moment, looking surprised. 'Would that be the Honourable Mr William Ravenscar's son by any chance? My Bertie speaks of Major Ravenscar highly. He says that if he'd been in England at the time, his father would never have got in with a bad crowd and lost his money at the tables.'

'Oh!' Madeline stared at her. 'Does the family own an estate near here? I had not realised.'

'It is not the family estate—for that is nearer Hampshire, so Bertie tells me—but the house and land in Fenstanton came to the major through his mother. It is not a large place, but a pleasant family house and some acres of land.'

'I did not know.' She bit her lip. 'Does Hal come down often?'

'He was here a few weeks back, just before his cousin Captain Miller was married. He was talking to my Bertie about the possibility of selling the place. His father's estate is mortgaged to the hilt and he thought selling Highgroves Hall might help pay the debts.'

'Oh, I see. Has it been sold yet?'

'No, for my Bertie advised him against letting it go. He thinks the major would be better off selling his father's property and settling here. It's good fertile land and the house is sound. Only needs a spring clean to make it a lovely family home… It's about the same size as this house and Bertie said he would buy it if he had a son, but we've no children yet and it looks as if we shall not.'

'I am sorry to hear that,' Madeline said. 'I know what a sadness that is. I felt I could have borne my marriage more easily had I had a child.'

'You are still young,' Hattie said. 'We married late, but Bertie has a nephew who will inherit this place. He is still considering buying Highgroves, but isn't sure whether it would be of use to him, because it is a bit too far from us to make it viable. Besides, the major said he would consider taking Bertie's advice and keeping it rather than his late father's estate.'

'Then perhaps he will come again soon,' Madeline said, praying that he was still alive. If he came down to visit his mother's estate, he might learn where she was staying and then surely he would call on her? Even if he no longer wished to marry her, he might know someone who would give her a position as a companion or a seamstress. She desperately wanted to see him again to know that he was alive and unharmed.

'I'll leave you to tidy yourself,' Hattie said. 'The kettle will be boiling so come down when you're ready.'

'Yes, of course.'

Left to tidy herself, Madeline sat on the edge of the bed, feeling the softness of a feather mattress. She could be quite content here for the rest of her life, she thought, if only she had enough money to pay her way. Perhaps she could find some work that would be sufficient to pay for her board and lodgings.

She went to the dressing mirror and patted her hair. She did not intend to waste her time moping. She was safe and free of both her husband and the marquis for the moment.

Until she could make contact with Hal she must make the most of her circumstances… if only he were still alive.

It came to Hallam as he was on his way to the club to speak with Jack Mainwaring. The innkeeper had mentioned East Anglia. Madeline had told him something once about her former governess. A Mrs Hattie…what was the woman's married name? He could not recall it or be certain that Madeline had ever used it in his hearing, but he did know that her husband had a farm somewhere in Cambridgeshire.

He knew most of the farmers in the area reasonably well. Since his mother's death he had employed a manager to look after the land and the house. He'd been down only a few weeks before Adam's wedding, wanting to see the house again before deciding whether to sell and pay off his father's debts, or at least some of them—or to sell what remained of his father's estate.

Hal's mother had come from a wealthy country family, and as Hal's roots were set firmly in a country way of life, he thought he would be satisfied to settle for the life of a well-to-do farmer. His Uncle Philip lived in

Norfolk and had a large and fine estate, but while Hallam was in France, he'd learned that his uncle had lost both his wife and daughter to a virulent fever. He had other nephews on his wife's side, but no surviving children of his own. Hal had written to him concerning his sad loss, but his uncle had not replied, and he'd felt some reluctance to intrude on his grief.

He would go down to Cambridgeshire, Hal decided. If Thomas Hobbis came looking for him, he would leave his direction, and in the meantime he would employ an agent to help him search for Madeline.

She must be somewhere and in her position she would most likely seek refuge with someone she trusted. Mrs Hattie… If only she'd told him her former governess's married name!

Hal's determination hardened. He would not sit in London twiddling his thumbs, but go down to Cambridgeshire and ask a few people he was acquainted with if they had heard of the lady. At least he knew that her name had been Miss Hester Goodjohn before she was wed. Someone would surely know of her.

On his way to his mother's estate, he would

take a detour and speak to Madeline's father. It was time that he was made aware of what an evil man his former son-in-law had been.

'I should return the chaise,' Thomas said when they had been living at the farm for three days. 'My brother may have need of it—and he may have news for us by now.'

'You will go again to Major Ravenscar's lodgings?'

'Yes, of course, my lady,' Thomas said. 'I shall discover what I can and return as soon as is humanly possible.'

'We shall miss you,' Sally said. 'You will not be too long, Thomas?'

'Never fear, I shall not desert you,' he said. 'When I return I shall look for an inn I may purchase, where we may all live in comfort, if my lady will deign to come with us.'

'I cannot leave her while she needs me,' Sally said, though a look of longing was in her eyes.

Thomas reached for her hand and held it. 'Her ladyship does well enough here, but I pray that when I return I shall have news that will bring her much happiness—and then she will not need you so much.'

Sally watched as he mounted his horse

and rode away, then went back to the large kitchen. She noticed the muddy footprints on the floor she'd scrubbed that morning and sighed, thinking that life in a farmhouse would not suit her for long. Despite Hattie's kindness, Sally would feel happier in a nice little inn with the man she loved—but she could not and would not desert her mistress.

Chapter Seven

'Had I known what kind of a man Lethbridge was I should not have allowed the marriage,' Sir Matthew said. 'I would rather have faced ruin than had my poor daughter suffer such cruelty.'

'You could not have known to what depths he would sink,' Hallam said as he prepared to take his leave. 'You say that you believe Maddie's former governess to live in Cambridgeshire on a farm, but you do not know her married name?'

'Forgive me, I would tell you if I could. I should have paid more attention, but I had much on my mind at the time,' Sir Matthew said. 'We must find Madeline, for now that Lethbridge is dead she is entitled to her endowment and the money her grandfather left her—and certainly her jewels and clothes belong to her. Alone and with no money, I dread to think what may become of her.'

'She is not entirely alone for she has friends,' Hallam said. His expression did not alter, but he detected a degree of enthusiasm in Sir Matthew at the thought of the money his daughter might inherit, and fought to keep any sign of censure from his tone as he said, 'It is my intention to find her, sir. I shall not cease to look until I find her.'

'And you will let me know when you do?'

Hallam inclined his head, but made no promises for he must consult Maddie's wishes before giving her father that information. She'd been married once against her will and he did not quite trust her father. He was a selfish man, who had used his daughter ill once and might seek to use her to build up his own fortune given the chance.

After taking his farewell, Hallam set off for his mother's estate in Cambridgeshire. At least he had some idea of where Maddie might have gone, though he was still in ignorance of her exact location. However, there were one or two farmers he knew well enough to exchange words with, as he rode about the countryside, and surely one of them could tell him something.

'What have you learned?' the marquis demanded from his henchman. He'd had the inn by the river watched since he'd first discovered where that interfering footman had taken Madeline and her maid, also Hallam Ravenscar's lodgings, and now it had paid off. 'Tell me, sirrah! Damnation! Am I served by imbeciles? Have you lost your tongue?'

'I kept watch on the inn as you told me, my lord,' the man said, watching his master warily. The marquis's temper was violent when he was thwarted. 'I saw the footman you wished to speak with and followed him to the lodgings of Major Ravenscar...'

'Where is he now?'

'He returned to the inn where he lodged for the night.' Seeing the fury in the marquis's eyes, he said quickly, 'He left word for the major, sir—the lady is fled to Cambridgeshire, to a farm.'

'You know the name of the farm—or the people she fled to?'

'Yes, sir,' the man said with a gleam of triumph in his face. 'I stood beneath the open

window and heard the footman give the landlady an address—the farm belongs to a Mr
Jenkins and it is called Buttercup Farm. It is
situated some ten miles beyond the small village of Fenstanton in Cambridgeshire.'

'My God! I shall have her yet,' the marquis
cried, a gloating look in his eyes. 'You have
done well. Go to the kitchen and eat something. We leave within the hour.'

No woman could be permitted to slight
him. He had desired her from the first moment of seeing her, but her behaviour in first
refusing his help in the rain and then flirting with him, only to repulse him when he
attempted to make love to her, had aroused
his fury. And that interfering fellow Hallam
Ravenscar had dared to threaten him!

Rochdale suspected an intrigue between
them. If he could take his revenge on the
wench, the annoying major would be well
served—it would kill two birds with one
stone, for once he had his hands on Madeline he would make sure she would never
welcome the touch of another man.

He would marry her whether she wished
it or no and secure what remained of Lethbridge's fortune to himself, for a run of ill
luck at the tables had made his own finances

temporarily difficult. Then, when he was finished with her, he would decide whether or not to let her live.

Madeline stood at the bottom of the stairs, listening to the sound of voices and laughter in the kitchen. She was pleased that Sally was settling in so well, though she knew that the girl had been restless since Thomas left seven days earlier. His journey was obviously taking longer than he'd envisaged and both Madeline and Sally were awaiting his return eagerly.

Perhaps he would have news of Hallam, Madeline thought. She glanced out of the window. The wintry sun was bright and it had been dry for two days. She was too restless to sit in the parlour with her sewing and knew that Hattie would not allow her to do anything in the kitchen. She envied Sally, because she was busy and could fill the empty hours with little jobs that she enjoyed.

She would take a little walk in the fresh air. It might help to clear her mind. Slipping her cloak about her shoulders, Madeline called out that she was going for a walk, but was unsure whether her friends had heard her. Leaving by a side door, she walked across an expanse of lawn and into the orchard. Birds were singing in the branches above her head and, as she left the orchard and passed into a narrow lane bounded by high hedges, she saw Hattie's husband and waved her hand to him in greeting.

He lifted his hand to acknowledge her, but was talking to two of his men and in truth could hardly have realised who she was for there was a distance between them and she had a hood over her head.

The sun was warm enough, but the ground was still hard, because there had been a heavy frost overnight. It had not yet snowed, but the promise of it was in the air and the sky was dark grey. On the way here they had passed a small village with a pretty church. Madeline thought it would be pleasant to visit and perhaps make the acquaintance of the vicar and his wife. If she were to settle in the area, and she thought it was as good as any, she would need an interest and the vicar or his wife might know of some work she could do.

Her spirits lifted a little as she walked. It was unlikely that her husband would find her here and she would like to live near her friends. Thomas had spoken of finding a cottage or an inn where they could all live. If he purchased an inn she could pay something for her lodgings—or perhaps she could find a position where she would be required to live in as a companion or a lady's maid.

Her thoughts went round and round in her head because as the days passed she had begun to fear that something must have happened to Hallam. Her father would know where Hattie lived, because she'd told him, but would Hallam have gone to him? And would her father think it Madeline's duty to return to her husband?

She could never do so! Her whole being recoiled from the thought of living with Lethbridge again. No, she would make a new life for herself somehow.

She reached the village and went inside the church to admire the beautiful stained-glass windows, the altar with its gleaming brass and the displays of greenery and deep-crimson chrysanthemums. Decorating the church with flowers was something new and Madeline thought it a pretty change from the green boughs that had always been used at certain times of the year.

The vicar entered as she was about to leave and Madeline exchanged greetings with him, promising that she would attend a service at the church very soon and venturing to ask if he knew of any work as a gentlewoman's companion. She did not give her true name, but on the spur of the moment, used her mother's maiden name, for she thought it would serve her better than her father's. She would be Miss Madeline Heath, a spinster of good character recently forced to find work by a change in her circumstances and introduced herself as that lady.

The vicar nodded, listening kindly to her request and then replied, saying that he would welcome her to his committee meetings and promised to make enquiries about a position as a companion, for he knew everyone in the district.

Feeling more hopeful of the future, Madeline began to walk home. She decided to stroll back past the river and stopped to admire some majestic swans as they made their graceful way down the smooth surface of the softly flowing water. It was then that she heard something behind her—the snapping of a twig underfoot—and turned just as a man tried to grab her. Screaming, Madeline dodged past him and started running. From the corner of her eye, she saw another man coming at her from the side and gave a cry of despair. Her husband must somehow have discovered where she was staying and his henchmen had followed her. She should never have come out alone!

They were gaining on her. She tried to run even harder and caught her foot in a rabbit hole, stumbling and almost falling. Before she could recover her balance the men were on her, one each side, holding her arms as she struggled and screamed.

She could see a closed carriage waiting a short distance away and, as they began to drag her towards it, she screamed once more, knowing that once she was inside it she would be his prisoner.

'You'd better come quietly, lady,' one of the ruffians said. 'Or we'll have to knock you on the head. If we don't take you, he'll have us flayed.'

'No, never! I shall never return to him! I would rather die!'

Madeline kicked at his skins and fought harder, straining with all her might to break free, but they held on to her relentlessly. Then, suddenly, out of nowhere, she heard a shout and then a shot went over their heads. The men were startled and stopped trying to drag her towards the coach, looking about them to see where the shot had had come from. A man had pulled his horse to a standstill just a few yards from where she stood, placing himself between them and the coach. A little cry escaped her lips. It could not be… yet it was!

'Stand away from her or I'll shoot you like the dogs you are.'

Madeline stared at the man on horseback and her throat tightened with emotion. Hal was here! He had found her…he was not dead, but very much alive and here. She could not wonder why or how he'd known where to look, but only be grateful that suddenly he was here when she needed him. Tears pricked her eyes and she felt relief rush through her. Hallam was here!

'Let her go—he means it,' one of the men holding her arm said, his grip slackening. 'I'm off. You do as you please.'

He then broke away and ran for his life. The second man looked at Madeline speculatively, before growling deep in his throat, 'You've got away this time, but he'll have you yet. My master always gets what he wants in the end.'

Her throat was too tight to answer him. She could not move, but stood where she was shaking, as the second man ran towards the coach. He scrambled inside and was driven away at speed. Hallam had dismounted and came towards her, a pistol still in his hand. He thrust it into his coat pocket and held his hands out to her.

'Thank God I came this way,' he said as he caught her to him. 'I've been searching for you for days, Maddie. Your father knew the farm was in the area somewhere, but not its name or the name of your friend.'

'She is Mrs Hattie Jenkins of Buttercup Farm,' Madeline said and he nodded, as if he were aware of the fact. 'You've been there?'

'I went to ask a friend if he knew of your former governess and was taken into the house to meet her. Sally was there helping with the baking. She looked for you, but could not find you, then Mr Jenkins recalled seeing a woman walking towards the village. I came at once to find you and thank God I did. Another few minutes and I might have been too late. What made you venture out alone without telling anyone?'

'I called to tell them, but perhaps they did not hear me. It is too difficult to explain, but I felt…so useless and thought a walk would do me good. I did not think anyone would know I was here.' Madeline felt the shudder that ran through him at the thought of what might have happened. She gazed up at him, her eyes wet with tears. 'Oh, Hal, I thought you might have been killed. I wrote to you, but you did not come...'

'I was wounded and laid low of a fever for a few days.' He gazed down at her, an expression of hurt mixed with bewilderment in his eyes. 'Why did you not tell me where you meant to go? I could have been here so much sooner.'

'I was not sure...' Madeline looked away from his searching gaze. How could she explain the doubts and fears that assailed her whenever he was not by? 'We were afraid my husband might discover where I had gone—and it seems he has.'

'No,' Hallam said and frowned. 'Those men did not come from Lethbridge.'

'How can you be sure?'

'Because he is dead.' She gasped in shock and he held her hands tighter. 'We fought a duel, Maddie, but it was not I who killed him. He fired on the count of fourteen, but I turned as he did so and his shot struck my arm. Had I not turned, he would surely have killed me—just as he was murdered by an assassin's ball that struck him in the back.'

'He fired too soon in the hope of killing you? How could he be so vile?' Madeline was stunned and amazed. 'My husband was murdered, you say…but by whom, do you know? Have they caught him?'

'No one saw who did it. He was just a shadow in the trees. I was injured and my friends thought first of me—Lethbridge's seconds of him. The rogue had the advantage of surprise and disappeared before anyone thought of going after him.'

'But who could want him dead?' It did not seem possible that such a thing could have happened.

'Lethbridge may have had many enemies. He was a cheat, a liar and a murderer himself, Maddie. Do not waste your pity on him.'

'No, I shall not,' she said and shivered, her hand trembling in his. Whoever had killed Lethbridge had released her from a marriage she had never wanted and her stunned mind could not quite take it in. 'It is a horrible thing to say, but I can only feel relieved that he can no longer command me.'

'You will never be at his mercy again,' Hallam said. 'I would have killed him had I the chance, for your sake—but the assassin struck first.'

'For that I am glad. I should not want his blood on your hands, Hal.'

'I admit that it would not have been pleasant, but I would have done it to set you free.'

'Thank you…' She gazed up at him, looking puzzled as she began to think more clearly. 'But if those men who tried to kidnap me just now were not sent by my husband, who sent them? I cannot think who would want to kidnap me.'

'I am not certain, for there might be several men who would wed you for your fortune,' Hallam said.

'My fortune?' she asked in a bewildered tone. 'I have nothing but a few clothes and trinkets Sally packed for me.'

'I do not know exactly how your fortune stands after your husband's death, but I believe he has no other family—unless there may be a distant cousin. I imagine that much of what he owned will come to you once any debts have been paid, though of course the title will lapse since there was no son, unless a relative is found.'

'I think he had none…that I've heard of.'

'A distant cousin could inherit the title and

the estate if it is entailed—but your settlement, jewels and carriages would belong to you and you might have a claim on at least one of the houses.'

'I want only my jewels and sufficient to live on,' she said, instantly repulsed by the idea of a fortune from her late husband. 'The settlement that should have been mine on marriage is all I require.'

'I think your father may have other ideas about what is your due. After I told him of the way you were treated, he said that you were welcome to return home and he would claim your rights on your behalf.'

'I am glad Papa accepts that I was not treated fairly but…' She looked up at him. 'I do not wish to live with my family. I fear that Papa might try to marry me to another rich man when my period of official mourning is done. If I place myself under his jurisdiction he can command me to obey him once more.'

'Yes, he might,' Hallam agreed. 'You alone should decide what you wish to do about your husband's fortune, but I imagine your father has already claimed it in your name. I know he intended to contact the count's lawyers immediately.'

'Please, do not ask me to go home,' Madeline said, her throat catching with emotion. 'I would prefer a house of my own if I can afford it.' She could not beg him to take her to his home unless he asked her to be his wife. Yet had she the right to ask so much of him? Would he want her if he knew what the count had made her suffer—and its terrible toll on her?

'No, I shall not take you to your father's house,' he said, thinking that he would not truly trust Sir Matthew to take proper care of his daughter. 'I want to make you safe, Maddie. I want to protect you and care for you—if you will let me?'

'Oh, yes, please, Hal,' she said on a sob. 'Take me somewhere safe. I cannot stay here after what happened this morning. Who do you think sent those men to kidnap me?'

'I cannot be certain, but I suspect the Marquis of Rochdale.'

'Lord Rochdale…' Madeline's throat tightened and she swayed towards him. 'No, oh, no. I could not bear to be his prisoner, Hal. I fear that man more than my husband…he will not forgive me for leading him on and then repulsing him in the garden that night. It is surely his reason for trying to have me kidnapped. He wants to punish me.'

'That may be part of his reason for wanting you in his power,' Hal said thoughtfully. 'But there may be others.'

'You think he wants Lethbridge's fortune?'

'Perhaps. I think your husband may have owed him a large sum of money from a gambling debt.'

'He shall be paid somehow. If the estate passes to me, I shall pay all his debts.'

'You are owed something after the way he treated you, Maddie. You must keep enough for yourself.'

'I wish that I need take nothing from Lethbridge. I hated him at the end. My settlement is mine by right and it would surely be sufficient—if my husband has not already spent the capital. He was deeply in debt to Rochdale, I believe…'

'I have little fortune, but I should be honoured to offer what I have.'

'Oh, please, do not speak of the future yet. I feel…abused, unclean,' Madeline said and shuddered. 'If only my father had not been so foolish with his money and I need never have wed him.'

'As to that, I have been told that Lethbridge cheated your father at the card tables, just as he cheated others. I exposed Lethbridge for a cheat at the tables and he challenged me to a duel…but a friend of mine believes that he once killed a young man to protect his secret.'

'He was an evil man and I shall not mourn him,' Madeline said and now the shine of tears in her eyes had been replaced by anger at the way that both she and her father had been tricked. 'I refuse to wear black for him. Why should I?'

'I do not require it of you,' Hallam said, 'however, I fear we must observe a period of mourning. If you were to marry before six months were out, people might suspect that I tried to murder your husband to get you. And I *would* have killed him if I'd had to, Maddie.'

'Hush,' she said and pressed her fingers to his lips. 'Speak of him no more, Hal. I would prefer to forget him.'

'We shall do our best,' he said and smiled at her. 'You asked me to take you away. My cousin, Adam Miller, has just returned from his honeymoon in Scotland. He is to stay at Ravenscar for a few weeks before travelling abroad and my uncle has asked me to join them for a time. Adam and I have business to discuss. I shall take you there for you will be safe with my family.'

'What if the marquis finds me again?'

'Adam will have the keepers patrol the grounds, Maddie. Ravenscar is well staffed and protected and you will be safe there.'

She was hesitant. 'I hardly know them. And Lethbridge was a friend of Mrs Miller's father...'

'Jenny is a lovely person and I know she will welcome you, as will Adam,' Hallam said. 'I would take you to my home, but it needs refurbishment and is too close to your friend's farm to be safe for you until we have settled with whoever is trying to abduct you. I intend to sell out my army commission, but I may be called back to the regiment in the meantime. If that happens, I would wish to know that you were safe with my cousins. If I left you alone, I should not know a moment's peace.'

'Yes, perhaps that would be best,' Madeline said, giving in because she had nowhere else to go, though she could not like the idea of imposing on people she hardly knew. 'You, Hal, shall guide me, for the time being. I have nothing until Lethbridge's affairs are settled and must rely on the generosity of others...'

'You know that all I have is at your disposal, Maddie,' he said. 'There is little enough, God knows, but I hope to settle things soon and then I shall at least be able to provide a comfortable home for you should you wish it.'

Madeline hesitated. He was gallant and generous and she wanted to accept his offer, but he'd made no mention of his feelings. She could only accept if he were to offer her his heart. And even then, could she be the wife he deserved?

Lethbridge had soiled and despoiled her. Now that she was free of him she should be thinking of the future, and she wanted nothing more than to be Hal's wife, but she was not certain she could ever allow a man to touch her again—even the man she loved.

Would Hal still love her if he understood what her husband had done to her?

'I am sorry you must leave us,' Hattie said and kissed Madeline on both cheeks. 'Yet I know that it would not be safe for you to stay here if this wicked person is bent on kidnapping you. We would care for you as best we could, but we could not protect you if he is determined to take you captive. You will be safer with the major's family.'

'I would not wish to bring harm to you,' Madeline said. 'I've been content here and thought I might like to live nearby, but for the moment it may be best if I live with Hal's family. They have a big estate and if I stay within its bounds I should be safe enough. Once again this man—whoever he may be—must find me before he can harm me.'

'It beats me how he came to find you here,' Hattie said, looking distressed. 'He must have had you followed.'

'Yes, or someone followed Thomas perhaps, which makes me anxious for him, though I would not say so to Sally,' Madeline said. 'I believe Hal scared the rogues off this time and it will be a while before *he* sends someone else to hunt me down. Perhaps he will not bother now that he knows I have such good friends.'

She could only hope that the marquis would decide she was not worth the bother and forget her. There were many women richer and more beautiful than she—even if her husband's money came to her. Why should he waste his time pursuing her?

'We must pray he will not.' Hattie nodded and patted her hand. 'You will write to me and let me know how you are?'

'Yes, of course.' Madeline embraced her. 'Perhaps I can visit again soon in happier times. If God wills it I may even come to live near you one day.'

'He's a good man,' Hattie whispered in her ear. 'I think you could not do better than wed him when he asks.'

Madeline felt the heat rush into her cheeks and glanced at Hal, but he was speaking to Sally and noticed nothing. He'd hired a chaise for her and Sally and would himself ride beside them with a groom he'd found somewhere. The man was ex-army by his look and no doubt handy with his pistol. Thomas had not yet returned from London, but Hattie had promised to tell him where to find them, though she swore that she would not say a word to anyone else.

'Wild horses would not drag it from me,' she said, 'but I'll send your young man to you, Sally, when he returns.'

Sally blushed, but she was feeling too anxious over Thomas's late return to do more than thank their kind hostess. She gathered up a few of their belongings and went out to the chaise.

Madeline followed, glancing back to watch as Hal took his farewell of the farmer. They seemed to have much to discuss and she wondered what could be keeping him, but then they shook hands and Hal came out just in time to hand her into the chaise.

'Jenkins was telling me of some land that has come up for sale,' he said. 'I've asked him to buy it for me if it goes for a price I can afford.'

'You are thinking of settling here, then?'

'Yes, I believe it will suit me,' Hal said and smiled in a way that made her heart beat faster. 'I have good friends here and with some improvement and perhaps in time an enlargement, the house will make a comfortable home. To settle my father's debts I must sell his estate. What little remains may be invested here. I do not have a fortune to offer any lady, Maddie, but I hope it may be enough for the woman I care for—if she loves me.'

'I am certain it would be,' she said and her heart fluttered.

'I am not yet in a position to ask anyone to wed me,' Hal went on, 'but we shall speak more of this another time.'

She murmured something appropriate for although she longed to declare her love for him, she did not wish to make him feel he *must* wed her. Hal had loved her to distraction once, but she'd hurt him, sending him away with harsh words. He'd fought a duel with her husband for her sake, and he would protect her from the marquis, if it was he that was bent on abducting her. But did he still love her? He had spoken vaguely of caring for her and keeping her safe, but Hal was a man of honour. By his code he could do no less. Madeline was not certain that he loved her as he once had, for she knew he would do his utmost to protect any lady he discovered in trouble.

When he looked at her sometimes her heart raced and she believed that he did love her, but at other times she was uncertain. He would wed her rather than see her at the mercy of unscrupulous rogues who wanted her for her beauty and perhaps the fortune they imagined Lethbridge had left her—but Madeline wanted him to love her as he had before she married.

Perhaps if she was certain of his love she would be able to give herself to him…to welcome his touch in their bed. It was what she wanted, longed for—to be loved and to be able to love in return. Yet even the thought of intimate relations brought a rush of unwelcome memories, making her stomach twist. If she shuddered when Hal touched her intimately, he would be hurt. In time he would turn from her as her husband had and then he might hate her.

What was she to do if this feeling of being soiled never left her? Must she remain unwed and alone for the rest of her life? Tears caught at her throat, but she could not let them fall. She could not tell Hal of her fears—because she could not bear to see the gentle kindness in his eyes turn to scorn. How could she expect him to understand her fears…the revulsion for the intimate side of marriage that Lethbridge had instilled in her?

No man would continue to love a woman who could not bear his touch: it was not to be expected.

What would become of her if she sent Hal away?

She was a widow now and Hal would not be the only gentleman to admire her. If she chose to re-enter society once her period of official mourning was over, she might find a man who loved her for herself and took no account of her fortune or lack of it. In her heart, she knew there was only one man for her—but she was already in his debt and could not allow him to offer for her out of sympathy or a misguided sense of duty.

Oh, how she longed to be as she'd been when she was a young girl and first in love, when she had not known what it was like to be abused and scorned, to think of herself as worthless. Lethbridge had told her she was frigid, and could not give a man what he needed.

What if he was right? What if she could not make Hal happy, even though her heart ached with love for him?

Glancing sideways at his handsome profile, Madeline felt her love for him warming her, melting the ice she'd built inside as a barrier against pain. She hoped that they would have time to get to know each other again before Hal was forced to report to his regiment. Perhaps they might fall in love all over again… perhaps she would be able to make herself smile when he touched her.

She must conquer her fears. She was determined to put the past behind her. She would forget the things her husband had done. She would find happiness again…

Oh, please God, let her find a way to overcome this fear inside her.

Chapter Eight

'Hal told us that he intended to bring you here,' Jenny Miller said. She was a pretty, spirited girl and looked very happy. Madeline took to her instantly. 'You are very welcome to stay for as long as you wish, Lady Lethbridge.'

'Please, do not call me by that name—it is distasteful to me. I am Madeline or Maddie to my friends.'

'Then I shall call you Maddie, if I may,' Jenny said and took her arm. 'I am sure you are weary from the journey and would like to go to your room and make yourself comfortable?'

'Yes, I should,' Madeline said gratefully. 'You have a beautiful home, Jenny.'

'Ravenscar Court is not truly our home,' Jenny confided as they walked up the magnificent staircase arm in arm. 'Adam is having some work done at his estate, and, besides, we are staying here to keep Lord Ravenscar company while his son Paul is in Italy. He has been in terrible affliction over the death of his eldest son, as have we all. Mark was to have married my best friend, Lucy Dawlish, and it was to be with her and attend the wedding that I came down. The tragic events of that time drew Adam and me together—and we feel we would wish to keep Lord Ravenscar from feeling lonely until Paul returns. We hope for his return by spring and then we shall take a trip to France or Italy.'

'I heard something about Lord Ravenscar's son Mark being foully murdered, but do not know the details,' Madeline said. 'Please tell me only enough so that I may not trample on his father's feelings unaware.'

'Mark was murdered here at his home,' Jenny said. 'Adam, Hal and Paul discovered the murderer's identity and he has paid for his foul deed. But do not let us speak of it, for you have problems of your own.'

'You must not pity me,' Madeline said. 'My marriage was not a happy one and I am relieved to be free of it, though shocked, of course, by the circumstances of his death. This other business remains a mystery for we do not truly know who tried to have me abducted, though we suspect it to be the Marquis of Rochdale.'

'Adam told me that he knew the marquis to be a wicked man who might stoop to an act of this nature. You must be very careful not to give him an opportunity to harm you.'

'Yes, I know. It is the reason I am so grateful to you for giving me a home until things are settled. I am not certain of my situation, though I hope to have a home of my own in the future.'

'You do not wish to return to your family?'

'No, I think not—if I have a choice.'

'Is Hal to act on your behalf in the matter of your settlement?' Jenny asked. 'I know that Adam or Lord Ravenscar would be glad to help if you needed advice.'

'I think my father intends to claim the estate in my name, but I need very little,' Madeline said. 'I dare say there may be papers from the lawyers to sign—and I should be glad of advice if Hal were not here when they came.'

'He has promised to stay with us for a few

weeks while his estate is being refurbished,' Jenny said, smiling. 'He and Adam are good friends and I think they intend to go into business together—and of course they both wish to be of help to their uncle until Paul returns.'

'Yes, I believe Hal mentioned something of the sort,' Madeline agreed. They had reached the upper landing and Jenny stopped outside one of the guest bedchambers. She opened the door and invited Madeline to enter. 'This is one of my favourite rooms in the house. It is normally given to a couple, but it is large and I thought you would find it comfortable. If you stay with us some weeks, as I hope, you may spread your own things about and make it home.'

Madeline thanked her and after some more conversation, Jenny left her to make herself comfortable. Sally had already unpacked her small trunk but she was aware of how few clothes she had at her disposal. It had been well enough to wear the same simple dress for three days at the farm and then let Sally wash it, but it would not do here. Somehow she must acquire more clothes, even if it meant parting with some of her precious trinkets.

Madeline allowed herself a sigh. She did not wish herself in possession of a great fortune, but she could wish for some of the clothes and personal possessions she'd been forced to leave behind.

Her life was still precarious for she did not truly know how she was to go on in the future. She must discover how she stood with regard to the settlement that ought to have been hers from the start of her marriage and at least to recover some of her own things. If nothing more, she must be entitled to recover her clothes.

She would speak to Hal about it later, she decided. She ought to write to her father, but she did not wish him to demand her return to his house, which he had the right to do since she was not yet five and twenty and no longer a wife.

Glancing at herself in the beautiful dressing mirror, she tidied her hair and her gown before going down to join her hostess in the parlour for tea.

'I can see why you were devastated when she married Lethbridge,' Adam said when he and Hallam were alone in Lord Ravenscar's library. 'She is very lovely—and will be quite wealthy, I imagine, once his estate is settled.'

'From what Sir Matthew told me, the count had no family whatsoever. I suppose that was why he was desperate to get himself an heir. One can understand it in the circumstances, but he was a devil to Madeline. I cannot be sorry he is dead, Adam—though to shoot a man in the back is cowardly work.'

'Yes, most disagreeable. It leaves one with a bad taste in the mouth. But Madeline must be relieved to be free at last.'

'He treated her abominably.'

'Yes, most unfortunate for her. Still, I confess I am glad you were not the one that killed him, Hal. I know you would have killed him for her sake, but it would have been a shadow over your life.'

'Yes, perhaps,' Hallam agreed. 'Murder is a foul crime, Adam, and it did feel a little like that to shoot in cold blood. But he shot first and would've killed me if he could. I feel no regret for his death.'

'Nor should you—though someone undoubtedly took advantage of the situation to murder him. You have no idea who it was?'

'No…unless…' Hallam shook his head. 'It occurs to me that it may have been the same person who tried to abduct Madeline. Rochdale wants her and I believe Lethbridge owed him a large sum of money.'

'Would any man do murder for such a thing?'

'A man like that would do worse. I fear for her, Adam. If I should fail her, she would be at his mercy.'

'You should not doubt your abilities, Hal.'

'I would back myself against any man in a fair fight, but a damned rogue who could murder a man and then attempt to abduct his wife does not fight fair.'

'Indeed, you are right. I've spoken to my uncle. We shall double the guards patrolling the grounds while she is here,' Adam said and frowned. 'If you fear for her, you must expose this man for the devil he is, Hal. It would not be possible for you to protect your own estate as we may Ravenscar.'

'I know—but it will not be easy. Rochdale covers his tracks well. I made a few enquiries in London and, apart from a few whispers of depravity was unable to discover anything that could have him arrested.'

'I trust you do not plan to challenge the marquis to a duel?'

'No, for it would not serve. I have never

met the man to my knowledge, other than to glimpse him at a large gathering, and I doubt he would oblige me.'

'Have you considered going abroad to live?'

'It would not be my first choice,' Hal told him. 'I shall try to discover what Rochdale wants of Maddie. If he is willing to settle for money, she would be better paying him off.'

'It seems to me that her family has served her ill. Her father should never have let her marry Lethbridge.'

'He had little choice for the count could have ruined him.'

'Yet to give one's daughter to such a man…' Adam shook his head, then his gaze narrowed. 'Do you intend to ask her to marry you?'

'Yes, of course, in time. I must settle my affairs first and she must observe a period of mourning. I would marry her at once, but I must have thought for the future. I should not wish her to be censured by society.'

'No, most certainly not,' Adam agreed instantly. 'She will be safe enough here, Hal. But I should not permit her to return to her father if I were you. He might see a way to use her to his own advantage.'

'Yes, I did see a gleam in his eyes when he learned she was a widow.'

'He sold his daughter to a man not fit to kiss her feet,' Adam said. 'A man like that might do anything.'

'Well, Maddie thinks much the same and has expressed a wish not to return to her former home. I intend to enquire into the particulars of the count's estate. While I am uninterested in his fortune, she is entitled to the settlement left her by her grandfather, which ought to have been protected in law. I should wish her to have that for her own use. You know my circumstances. I cannot give her as much as I would wish, Adam. Indeed, had she not been in danger, I dare say I should not have thought of approaching her again.'

'Because she broke your heart?'

'That…and the fact that she could do so much better. She has been used to moving in the highest circles. I can offer only a medium-sized house in the country and a comfortable living. If she had something of her own, it might serve and she could spend a few weeks in town if we had what is due to her. I do not wish to make her a prisoner of poverty after the life she has led.'

'You are worthy of any woman,' Adam said. 'Pray do not undervalue yourself, Hal. Besides, your fortunes will come about in time. We shall make a reasonable living from importing wines together. I believe you have more to offer than you know.'

Hal smiled and agreed, but he could not help wondering how Maddie would take to living in a small country house. He would naturally give her all the comforts he could, but he was unable to offer a smart London house or to give her all the jewels and clothes she deserved. It was his intention to see what could be recovered of her personal possessions, but as to the huge fortune that might come her way...it was his opinion that they would do better without it, even if it was on offer to them.

'You look lovely this evening,' Hal said when she came down to the drawing room before dinner that night. 'That colour becomes you, Maddie.'

'The gown belongs to Jenny,' she replied, a faint flush in her cheeks. 'Sally had time to put up only a few gowns for me and she chose the simplest she could find, for she knew we must go into hiding. They were very well for the farm, but not right for dinner here. Jenny saw my lack and loaned me this gown. It fits well enough for we are much the same size, though I prefer my gowns to be a trifle more modest. Jenny bought this in Paris and it was all the rage there—but I am glad to have a stole to cover my shoulders.'

He smiled and reached for her hand, carrying it to his lips to place a kiss within the palm. 'You are too modest, Maddie. You look charming—and this style is all the rage even in London now.'

'Yes, perhaps.' A flush of heat touched her cheeks. 'I fear to wear such gowns for they draw the eye of gentlemen I prefer not to notice me. Lethbridge liked even more immodest gowns—I believe it was the gown he forced me to wear that night that brought the marquis to attempt seduction.'

'Rochdale is not here, Maddie,' Hal said gently. 'Adam is a perfect gentleman and I would never do anything to hurt or distress you.'

'I know.' She lifted her eyes to his with a look of appeal. 'You do not know what my husband did to me sometimes. The different ways he hurt me, Hal. I have not told you, but after the first few weeks of our marriage he was unable…he could not play his part in my bed…and he blamed me.'

'Was he violent to you?' Hal asked, a little nerve flicking at his temple.

'Yes, sometimes. He often pinched me, but his rages took all forms. He would shout and throw things, smash things I liked and tear my pretty gowns. He accused me of pride and coldness and withheld anything he knew might please me'

'I wish that I had known—that I could have taken you away.'

'Until I had discovered and burned my father's notes I dared not leave him. He gave me jewels, but only allowed me to wear them when it pleased him, and he never released my settlement. When I fled I had only a few trinkets of my late grandmother's.'

'I shall recover what I can for you,' Hal promised. He reached out and touched her cheek. Madeline did not draw away, but he saw a flicker of something in her eyes and knew that he would have to be careful with his lovemaking. She had been ill treated and would need to overcome her nervousness of physical affection.

'I know…I do not trust my father to handle my affairs, Hal. He is a gambler and even though he no longer has the threat of his debt to Lethbridge, he might seek to keep as much of my late husband's fortune as he can. And he might withhold what is rightly mine to force me to return home.'

'I shall look after everything—if you give me your permission?'

'I wish you would do so,' Madeline said fervently. 'I want only my clothes, my personal possessions and the settlement that was mine on marriage, but withheld.'

'You may be entitled to more,' Hal said. 'If you refuse it, Lethbridge's fortune might revert to the Crown with his title.'

'Please do what you think right,' Madeline said, looking at him with such appeal that it took all his strength of will not to gather her into his arms and tell her of his love. 'I know only that I want to forget that I was ever married to that man.'

'You shall forget it,' Hal promised. He leaned towards her, brushing his lips lightly over hers, keeping his hands away from her so that she should not fear what he might do next. 'I want you to be happy, Maddie. You have told me how he hurt you. Please believe that I would never hurt you in such a way. I care for and respect you too much—and it is my hope that we may marry one day.'

'Oh, Hal,' she said, her voice catching. 'I think I should like that so much, but…'

'You know it cannot be yet,' he said and ran a gentle finger down her cheek. 'We need time to get to know one another again. You were badly hurt…'

'Yes.' She did not deny it, her voice faltering as she added, 'I would wish to be the wife you want, Hal, but…I do need time to know you, time to forget what happened.'

'Of course,' he said. 'We are fortunate to have such good friends. Here we shall have all the privacy we wish for and the time to become accustomed to one another.'

Hal stood back, controlling his raging emotions. Once he would have swept her into his arms and kissed her passionately, but he was afraid of frightening her, of giving her a disgust of him. He'd seen her reaction to the marquis's lovemaking and would not have her recoil from him in that way.

Hal must show her that there was another side to loving, a sweetness and satisfaction that came from tenderness and concern one for the other. He knew that if he could ease away the painful memories she would respond with all the sweetness and trust that she'd once had towards him. He would need to be patient, but she was worth waiting for... if only that devil Lethbridge had not made it impossible for her to love and trust again.

Afterwards, when she went up to her bed-chamber, accompanied by her smiling host-ess, Madeline thought it one of the most pleasant evenings she'd ever spent. For the first time in years she could retire to a com-fortable room and bed without the fear that her husband would arrive to pinch and taunt her. Even at the farm she had not been able to sleep because she feared her husband would discover her.

Lethbridge was dead. She was no longer bound to him by her father's debt and could follow her own inclinations. The feeling of freedom was wonderful and she was smiling as she sat down and allowed Sally to brush her long hair free of its pins and curls.

'Are you feeling happier now, my lady?' Sally asked as she smoothed the brush over her thick hair.

'Yes, and more relaxed.' She looked at Sally's reflection in the mirror and noticed that she was tight with anxiety. 'You must not worry too much. Thomas was delayed for some reason and when he gets to the farm he will have yet another journey here.'

'Yes, I know, but I cannot help thinking if someone took him prisoner to make him tell where you had gone...'

'Oh, but you must not fear him dead. Thomas is too clever to be taken in by their threats. I am sure he will come to us soon, Sally—and if he does not, I will ask Major Ravenscar to make enquiries.'

'I pray you are right, my lady,' Sally said. 'Thomas spoke of buying a small inn for us. You would not wish to live with us now, but if I knew you were safe here I might agree to wed him.'

'I know you love him,' Madeline said and smiled at her. 'I may have some money of my own soon, Sally. I could then pay your wages and employ Thomas as my secretary for he is too clever to be a footman all his life—but if you prefer, I will give you something and you may marry him with my good wishes.'

'I should like to remain with you, at least until I had a child,' Sally told her, 'but I must ask Thomas what he wishes to do for I love him. I would not like it if he took another girl in my place.'

'I am sure he would not. He adores you,' Madeline said. 'You are fortunate to have such devotion, but I know you love him in return.'

'Yes, I do,' Sally agreed and smiled.

The following morning Jenny took Madeline visiting with her in the carriage. They were accompanied by two grooms and driven by Lord Ravenscar's own coachman, ensuring their safety.

'Adam insisted we use the carriage. I should have driven us in my phaeton, for he has been teaching me to drive a pair and I enjoy driving a team about the estate, but he thought it best we take the carriage and grooms to accompany us in the circumstances.'

'How you must curse me,' Madeline said. 'To have your freedom curtailed because of me must irk you, Jenny.'

'No, of course not, think nothing if it.' Jenny smiled and shook her head. 'Adam fusses over me too much—but he loves me and I do not wish him to be anxious.'

'Certainly not,' Madeline agreed. She said no more about it, but Jenny's careless remark had made her realise that her presence at the house might place Hal's friends in some danger and was certainly inconvenient.

She enjoyed the morning spent visiting Jenny's friends and envied her, her uncomplicated life and the happiness her marriage had brought her. How wonderful to be that confident, to love and know you are loved—to have no fear of love. Having seen the way Jenny went to her husband's arms so willingly, lifting her face for his kiss with such a look of joy, made Madeline realise that there must be pleasure to be found in marriage—if only she could forget the hurt inflicted on her.

Madeline would wish to live quietly in the country with the man she loved, but for the moment she was obliged to live beneath the shadow of fear—fear of another attempt to abduct her. And even if that fear were somehow removed, could she be sure that she was worthy of Hal's love?

Madeline was able to accept the shadow that hung over her for herself, but she had not realised until Jenny mentioned it that she was bringing a deal of trouble to the kind people that had taken her in. Hal had spoken lightly of the arrangements Adam would make, but Madeline must be aware that she had disrupted their lives.

She comforted herself that it would not be for ever, but she felt under an obligation and that made her uncomfortable. For the moment there was little else she could do, but once her affairs were settled, she would find somewhere else to live.

On their return to the house, she went upstairs to her room to discover Sally unpacking several trunks. An array of elegant silk gowns were spread over the bed, gowns she recognised as being her own. Spinning round, she saw the silver brushes, perfume bottles and other glass trinkets on the dressing table and gave a cry of pleasure for she'd been forced to leave many trinkets behind, things that had been given her by her mother and grandmother when she was a girl.

'These are mine,' she said, turning to look at Sally with a surge of delight. 'Where did they come from?'

'Thomas brought your things, my lady,' Sally said and her eyes were bright with excitement. 'He discovered in London that the count was dead and went to the house. He told them that you were staying with friends until your husband's affairs were settled and said you'd ordered him to fetch your clothes.'

'And they packed them—just like that?'

'Thomas said they could not do enough for him. Apparently, they believe the house and its contents belong to you and asked him if they should close it down or continue in their duties. He pretended to have your authority and ordered them to keep all in readiness for your return and to wait for your further orders.'

'They took their orders from Thomas?'

'Yes, for they believed he had your authority.'

'How clever he was. I am grateful to him.'

Madeline stared at her, hardly believing that it had been so simple for Thomas to bring her all these clothes. Seeing a small trunk standing on an oak hutch, she went to investigate further and discovered it was the strongbox in which her husband had kept her jewels and a quantity of gold.

'The key is in the top drawer of the dressing table,' Sally told her. 'I put it away when Thomas gave it to me, but did not open the chest for I thought you would wish to do that, my lady.'

'How could he have brought this? My husband never allowed me to touch it.' Madeline fetched the key from the drawer and approached the trunk with some trepidation. She would never have dared to ask for something of such value and felt almost guilty as she inserted the key. Opening the lid, she saw row after row of jewel cases and a metal box. She lifted out the box and opened the lid, catching her breath as she saw the gold coins inside. 'There must be five hundred... perhaps a thousand sovereigns here.'

Sally came to look over her shoulder. 'I should think more,' she said. 'Thomas said the trunk was heavy.'

'I'm not sure he ought to have brought this.'

'It belongs to you, my lady,' Sally said. 'You were denied your rights—now you have them.'

'Yes, I think I do,' Madeline breathed as she began to open the jewel cases one by one. All the trinkets and sets of diamonds, pearls, rubies, sapphires and emeralds that her husband had given her to wear when she was going out were there. 'Yet are they mine? Are some of them not heirlooms that should go to the next heir?'

'Who should have them if not you?' Sally asked. 'Most of the jewels were given to you, though your husband kept them under lock and key—besides, the entail is broken for there is no male heir.'

'None that carry the Lethbridge name, I know,' Madeline said. 'But I believe there may be some distant cousin on his mother's side, who might have a claim to the estate, though not the title.'

'And why should some distant cousin have what belongs to you?'

Madeline shook her head. 'I do not know… I am not sure.' She took out a string of pearls and placed it on the dressing table, then removed a diamond pendant that had been her mother's as a girl. 'These pearls were a gift for my wedding and the pendant is my own— and I shall take the gold, for I am entitled to my settlement, but the other things must be kept safe in case they are not mine.'

'But who else should they belong to?' Sally said. 'No one knows Thomas brought the box for he was given access to your rooms—and he hid it with your clothes. He thought you were entitled to it, my lady.'

'It was good and loyal of him,' Madeline said, but felt doubtful. She was not yet certain if she was her husband's heir and would not feel justified in disposing of heirlooms if there was another—though there was enough here to keep her in modest comfort for the rest of her life.

'You should keep the box,' Sally said. 'Your husband was a rich man and even if there is a distant cousin to inherit his estate, you are entitled to this much.'

'Perhaps,' Madeline agreed. 'Thomas has been thoughtful and loyal—and I wish to give you both a present to thank you. He has done nothing wrong, Sally, for he thought only to serve me.' She would give them a hundred sovereigns each for it would secure their future when they left her and she owed them more than she could ever repay.

'The contents of that trunk make you independent, my lady,' Sally said. 'You should keep it safe and tell no one—it is owed to you for all you suffered.'

Chapter Nine

'I understand that Thomas was able to bring you some of your clothes,' Hal said when Madeline went down to tea a little later that afternoon. 'You will be more comfortable now, I think.'

'Yes, it is more comfortable,' Madeline said. 'Jenny was kind to lend me her gowns, but it is better to have my own—though there are some I do not care for. They were very costly, Hal. I should like to sell a few of them for I shall never wear them again. They were my husband's choice and I hate them.'

'Then I dare say it could be arranged,' he said and nodded. 'Some of them are unsuitable for life in the country, I imagine—and you might wish to use the money to purchase something simpler.'

Madeline's reason for not wanting to wear some of the gowns her husband had forced on her was very different, but she merely smiled and agreed.

'Perhaps they could be taken to a merchant in town?'

'Adam was speaking of sending in a wagon for supplies the day after tomorrow. Your maid and Thomas could take them in and dispose of them—if you are sure you no longer require them?'

'I am quite sure,' Madeline said and smiled. 'My life will be spent mostly in the country in future. I shall not need the more extravagant ballgowns.'

'No, perhaps not,' he said, 'though you may wish to visit friends sometimes in town.'

'Even so I would prefer something simpler. Lethbridge liked me to wear gowns that…I find immodest.'

'Ah, I see.' Hal nodded, looking at her gravely. 'I do understand that you wish for no reminders of your past life, Madeline— but I hate to think you will be deprived of pretty things.'

'I shall have all that I need,' she told him

and reached for his hand. She wondered whether to tell him of the jewels, but was prevented by Jenny coming up to her.

'I am giving a small dance next week,' she said. 'You are in official mourning, I know, Maddie—but shall you feel able to attend?'

'To attend, yes,' Madeline said. 'Of course I shall not dance, but to sit quietly and watch can harm no one.'

'I had business with Adam today,' Hal said. 'Tomorrow I am at your disposal. If you would like to ride out, I am sure a horse could be found for you.'

'You will come with me?' Madeline found the prospect delightful. In town she'd ridden sometimes with a groom or her husband in attendance, but to take a horse out and gallop across green fields was something she'd not been able to enjoy since her marriage. 'I think I should like that above anything, Hal.'

'Then I will order the horses for eight-thirty if that is not too early for you.'

'It is best to ride early in the morning,' she agreed and smiled at him. 'I can be ready by eight if it is not too early for you.'

Hal laughed, amused and pleased by her enthusiasm. Her eyes had lit in a way he'd not seen since before they parted that never-to-be-forgotten day when she'd broken his heart.

'Then the horses shall be brought at eight sharp,' he replied. He reached for her hand, taking it in his own and kissing it. 'My whole desire is to care for you and make you happy, Madeline. You must tell me what pleases you and what doesn't—and do not fear to displease me. I am not Lethbridge and I vow I shall never willingly hurt you.'

Madeline's hand trembled in his. She gazed up into his eyes in a way that made Hal wonder what lay behind the sadness he could sense inside her. She laughed and made conversation with her host and hostess, and she was always willing to listen to whatever Hal had to say, but he could not help feeling that a part of her was held in reserve—as if she could not quite give her whole self.

She had suffered far more than he could know.

He must not ask too much of her. Hal had discovered much about her wretched husband, but he sensed that there was a great deal that Madeline had not yet told him. He doubted she could bring herself to confide the depths of the wickedness that Lethbridge perpetrated on her, even to another woman.

Sometimes, when he touched her, he felt a slight withdrawal in her, even though she struggled to control it. She did not pull away, but he'd felt her stiffen when he kissed her hand, only slightly, but enough for him to know that she was not yet ready to accept his lovemaking.

When he saw the deep hurt in her eyes, Hal wished Lethbridge were alive so that he could strangle him with his bare hands. He could not bear to think of what she might have suffered and knew that if it took years—or the rest of their lives—he would wait until she was ready to accept his love.

Hal would marry her as soon as it was acceptable in the eyes of the world, but he would not force Maddie to accept him in her bed—and when he thought the time was right, he would assure her that her happiness was his only concern.

He knew that there would be times when he desperately wanted to hold her and touch her, but he sensed that somewhere inside Madeline was a wounded creature that must be coaxed and taught to trust again—like a puppy that has been kicked and beaten. That made him want to weep for her, but she would not wish him to pity her. She was still proud despite all that her evil husband had done to her.

All he wanted was to make her happy and banish that look of sadness from her beautiful eyes.

Once again, an evening spent playing cards, some music and relaxed conversation proved so enjoyable that Madeline had been able to sleep well in her comfortable bed. It was a new experience for her to wake and be able to decide for herself which clothes she should wear, for Lethbridge had often sent her to change if her attire did not please his eye.

She chose a dark-blue riding habit, which she had purchased, but never yet worn, knowing that its sober hue would not please her husband. Her hat was in the military style with a dark-blue curling feather pinned with a small diamond brooch. Her father had given the trinket to her in the days before he had gambled his fortune away and was a favourite, though Lethbridge had scorned it as being unworthy of *his* wife.

She was ready well before the appointed time and went downstairs, pulling on her black leather gloves. As she approached the last stair, the sound of voices reached her and then Hal and Adam came from the front salon into the hall.

'Perhaps you ought to tell h—' Adam was saying, ceasing abruptly as he saw her standing there. 'Good morning, Madeline. You are an early riser today.'

'We are going riding together,' Hal said and his eyes were admiring as they went over her. 'You look charming, Maddie. I like the style of your gown. It is extremely elegant and the colour becomes you.'

'Thank you,' she said, feeling the warmth in her cheeks. 'I have not worn it before and I am pleased you approve.'

'You need no one's approval, but I think it very elegant.'

'My maid has packed a trunk with clothes I shall never wear,' Madeline said, turning to her host. 'She and Thomas will be glad of a place in your wagon, Adam—if there is room?'

'Plenty of room,' he assured her. 'I've left word that they are to be given any assistance they require.' He glanced at Hal. 'Think about what I was saying, Cousin. I wish you both a pleasant ride.'

'I am sure it will be,' Hal replied. 'I shall

give your ideas some consideration—and thank you.'

'You are welcome.' Adam turned away, walking in the direction of the library.

'Shall we go?' Hal said. 'I believe the groom has brought our horses round.'

'Are you certain you have finished your business with Adam?'

'Yes, of course. Adam put a suggestion to me that I think very generous of him, but I am not sure I can accept.'

'You are good friends, I think?'

'Yes, the best. We have been through a great deal together—during the war and when Mark was murdered.'

'That must have forged a bond between you.' Madeline arched one delicate eyebrow. 'Was it another proposal of business?'

'In a manner of speaking,' Hal said. 'If I cared for it, he has a place for an estate manager. I do not know if you are aware of it, but Jenny was a considerable heiress and Adam has a lot of property to manage. If I accepted his offer, he would make a house on one of the estates available to me. It is larger than my own in Cambridgeshire…more suitable for a family, perhaps.'

'Oh.' Madeline frowned. 'Do you wish for such a position?'

'It would be a solution to my problems,' he said. 'But I am not sure…it might depend on several things. Adam's present agent retires in six months so there is time to think it over.'

'Yes, of course,' she said.

Hal was clearly undecided how he felt about his cousin's offer. Adam had made it in a spirit of generosity and it was not unknown for such a position to go to a trusted relative, but she was not sure how she felt about the idea. Jenny and Adam were such generous people and she was already fond of them, but Madeline had thought Hal meant to settle near her friend Hattie in Cambridgeshire.

However, she could have no opinion on a matter that was for Hal to decide. Yet it crossed her mind that if she were to sell most of the jewels in her late husband's box, Hal would have no reason to consider the offer. She imagined the jewels might bring sufficient to pay off his father's debts and allow him to retain his family's estate as well as his own.

Yet how could she offer them to him when he had not yet formally asked her to be his wife—and would he accept if she did?

Madeline still felt a little guilty over the way the box had come into her possession. If there were a claimant to Lethbridge's estate she would be morally obliged to hand back a substantial part of her late husband's wealth. But she shut out these anxieties, determined that nothing should spoil her outing with Hal.

She smiled at him as he handed her up. The mare she'd been given was spirited with a sweet mouth that responded to the merest touch of the reins. It tossed its head, as though to challenge her, but she held the reins in a manner that showed she was in command and the mare responded, quieting at the sound of her soothing voice.

As they trotted out of the courtyard and the horses felt the springy turf beneath their hooves, Madeline let her mount have its head. The sensation of speed as they flew over the ground, the mare hardly seeming to touch it with her hooves, was exhilarating and everything but the joy of the morning was swept from her mind.

Hal's horse was on its mettle to keep up with Madeline and the spirited mare, though he seemed content to race at her side and she thought he would not have left her behind if he could. She turned her head to smile at him and saw the gleam in his eyes that told her he had as much pleasure from their ride as she.

They were well matched and rode for some time, then, as the horses began to show signs of having worked off their restive energy, they slowed to a walk and finally brought them to a halt by a shallow stream. Dismounting, they led the horses to a spot where they could drink and stood admiring the view of green fields as far as the eye could see, dotted here and there with ancient trees that must have stood here for at least two hundred years.

'We are still on the Ravenscar estate?' Madeline asked.

'Yes, these fields are used for pasture at certain times of the year. I dare say my uncle has three thousand acres or more, including the farms he lets to tenants.'

'It is a large estate—and must be a burden for the earl.'

'It would be had he no agents and no son.'

'You said his surviving son was in Italy. Why does he not come home to lift the worry from his father's shoulders?'

'He blames himself for…' Hal shook his head. 'I think Paul feels that he is the usurper here. His brother should have been earl when

Lord Ravenscar dies and Paul cannot yet accept that he has the responsibility that ought to have been Mark's'

'Surely he knows his father needs him?'

'Adam and I told him we would do what we could. Paul needs time away. I imagine he will return soon.'

'Yes, of course,' Madeline said. 'Oh, there are some black swans! I think them so majestic. A pity we have nothing to feed them with.'

'I think the keepers feed them with special food. The earl does not encourage giving them bread.'

'Ah, I see.' Maddie moved away, but Hal took her shoulder and turned her back to face him. She gazed up at him, a question in her eyes. 'Yes, Hal—did you wish to say something to me?'

'You must know I care for you, Maddie.'

'You have been everything that is kind and good to me… Yes, I do believe that you have affection for me.'

'My feelings are stronger than mere affection,' he said, his voice throaty with passion. 'I want you to be my wife as soon as it is possible, Maddie—but you must believe that I understand how you feel. I know you have suffered and I shall never—'

She put her gloved fingers to his lips. 'I want to be your wife, Hal,' she said, her voice little more than a whisper, 'but…I fear I am not worthy of you. Lethbridge despoiled me…I feel unclean…'

A tear slid from the corner of her eye. Hal reached out and wiped it gently away with his bare hand. He stroked her cheek softly. Madeline felt a tingling sensation inside and for a moment her heart raced. Would he kiss her? She longed for it and yet feared it, for if she froze in his arms he might come to despise her and that she could not bear.

'You must never think such a thing,' he said and his eyes darkened with anger. 'I cannot know the extent of your suffering at that monster's hand, Maddie, but I swear you will never suffer at mine. I shall never ask more than you can give. And you are not unworthy no matter what that devil did to you.'

'Hal…I do not deserve such love.'

'You deserve much more,' he vowed and took her hands, kissing them tenderly and then letting her go. 'Remember that I would give my life for you—and I would rather die than hurt you. We should return to the house before they send out a search party.'

His jest brought a tearful smile, but she lifted her head proudly and gave him her hand, letting him assist her into the saddle. Hal understood and he was telling her that he would wed her even if she could never be a proper wife to him—but would she be fair to him if she accepted?

The afternoon was spent pleasantly in conversation. Madeline played the pianoforte for the entertainment of the others and Jenny sang a sweet love song, her eyes seeking Adam's across the room. Lord Ravenscar's old-fashioned courtesy charmed Madeline and insensibly she began to feel at home. It was a comfortable, happy atmosphere and Madeline knew that she was beginning to relax her guard here with these kind people. She laughed several times as Adam teased Jenny and the two ladies linked arms, chatting amiably as they went upstairs to change after tea.

It was beginning to seem that the nightmare of her former life was fading from her memory, though now and then something would be said that reminded her sharply. She gave no thought at all to the attack on her as she walked back to the farm and was inclined to dismiss it as perhaps the work of rogues. Here at this lovely estate she must be perfectly safe, for even if the marquis—if it were he who had sent those rogues to abduct her—discovered where she was, he would not dare to attempt anything while she was surrounded by friends.

Another pleasant evening spent with Hal's family and their guests, invited for dinner and cards, brought laughter to her lips and a sense of peace to her heart. Madeline had forgotten that life could be so sweet. Accustomed to a round of social events that she attended because it suited her husband, the simple pleasures she discovered in this house were a revelation and a joy to her.

Every morning she rose early to ride with Hal. On their return she changed into a morning gown and then drank tea in the parlour or walked in the gardens with Jenny. In the afternoons they took it in turns to entertain one another. Hal had a good, strong, reading voice and the knack of making the characters come to life when he read from a novel. Adam had a pleasant tenor voice and could occasionally be persuaded to sing for them, but often they played cards or a silly childish game like jackstraws. Lord Ravenscar enjoyed a game of chess and one of them indulged him, taking it in turns to pit their skill against his, but it was not often that any of them could worst him.

A week passed so swiftly that the day of Jenny's dance was upon them before they knew it. That morning the house was a hive of activity; the servants had been dusting and polishing for days, removing furniture from the long gallery so that it would be clear for dancing. Flowers from the hothouses had been brought in and arranged in beautiful vases and their scent pervaded the house.

Madeline asked if she could help and was given the task of checking the rooms that would be used for entertaining the guests to see if anything had been left undone. Of course nothing had, for Lord Ravenscar's servants had been with him for years and were accustomed to making ready for any occasion. However, by giving Madeline a task Jenny had made her feel she was useful and that was a kindness, for to be always a guest was not what she had been used to.

On the evening of the dance, Madeline

dressed in a gown of pale-lilac crape with an overskirt of silver tissue. The neckline was modest and the sleeves short and puffed, as was the prevailing fashion, the high waist emphasised with a sash of silver embroidered with glass beads.

She decided against wearing any of the more expensive jewels from her husband's box, preferring the delicate diamond pendant that had been a present from her father and a pair of long delicate earrings with diamond drops.

Satisfied that her appearance was modest and subdued enough for a lady recently widowed, she went downstairs to discover that the family was just gathering in the large drawing room. Jenny was looking a picture in a gown of green silk that could only have been fashioned in Paris. When Madeline complimented her, she confessed that it had been bought on her honeymoon and blushed prettily.

'You are very content in your marriage, are you not?' Madeline asked for she could not fail to see the shining happiness in Jenny's eyes.

'So happy I cannot tell you,' Jenny agreed. 'I knew I was in love long before Adam asked me to marry him and I knew he was the man I wished to marry—but I had no idea how wonderful it would be.'

Madeline would have liked to question her further on the intimate side of her marriage, but the guests had started to arrive. It was a delicate subject and one she was shy to raise, but seeing how happy Jenny was had made her wonder. Having experienced only her husband's brutality in the bedchamber, she had come to believe that all men must be the same. Yet Hal was so gentle and kind to her—and she'd seen the way Jenny looked at Adam, such trust and love in her eyes that she could not believe her friend had ever been subjected to anything remotely unpleasant.

Was it possible that she too could find, if not pleasure, at least acceptance of a man's touch?

Madeline would not have thought it possible a few days previously, but a subtle change had been happening of late. Hal had never once tried to take her in his arms or kiss her, but the touch of his hand as he helped her to mount, a light finger on her cheek and a gentle kiss on her hand aroused only feelings of comfort and even pleasure.

Her thoughts were suspended as the guests

began to move into the series of rooms, which had been opened up to make one long, flowing chamber. The footmen were circulating with trays of crystal glasses filled with the finest champagne. Madeline looked round at all the excited faces and smiled. Many of the guests were young ladies, perhaps attending their first ball, and their eager looks reminded her of herself as a young girl. She must have looked just so when attending her come-out ball, before her father lost everything at the tables.

'Will you dance with me, Maddie?'

She turned at the sound of Hal's voice, her heart suddenly pumping hard, as she knew an urgent desire to feel his hand at her waist and be swept around the floor.

'I wish that I might,' she said and smiled up at him. How handsome he was and how much she wished she were one of those young girls meeting a man she admired for the first time. 'You know I cannot, Hal. It would not be right.'

'No, I suppose not,' he said and looked regretful. 'You will not feel neglected if I dance? I must take my share of the responsibility for entertaining our guests.'

'Of course you must,' she agreed. 'Do not

be concerned for me, Hal. I shall be happy to watch.'

'I wish that I might sit at your side and do the same,' he said, touching her gloved hand. 'But I must do my duty as one of the hosts.'

'Go and enjoy yourself,' she said and gave a slight shake of her head.

He remained with her a few minutes longer, remarking on various guests. Madeline did not know all of them and he pointed out various neighbours and long-standing friends, before leaving her to seek out one of the ladies still sitting on the sidelines.

Madeline found herself a chair by the window, where she could watch the other guests mingling. She could hear the music and see the dancers as they whirled by, but was a little out of the crowd. After a few minutes alone, Lord Ravenscar joined her.

'How pleasant to have someone to talk to who does not dance,' he remarked. 'I fear my health will not sustain it, but I like to see the young people enjoying themselves.'

'Yes, indeed, especially the very young girls,' Madeline replied. 'There is a very pretty girl over there—the one with red hair. She looks so happy and excited.'

'You must mean Patience Harris,' Lord

Ravenscar said. 'Her mother was an exceedingly handsome lady, but she died eighteen months ago. Patience could not attend dances last year and I dare say this may be her first affair of this sort.'

'I thought it might be,' Madeline said. 'I dare say some might think it improper of me to attend this evening, but I do not intend to dance.'

'No, I fear you cannot,' he said and looked at her. 'Hal has told me something of your story, Madeline. You must be assured of a welcome here for as long as you wish and if there is anything I can do to make your life easier…'

Madeline was thanking him for his kindness when her eye was drawn to a party of newcomers. They were a little late and Jenny had left her position at the head of the stairs to join the party, but she went immediately to greet the family. As the last of them entered the room, Madeline's breath caught.

What was Lord Rochdale doing here? Jenny would scarcely have invited him knowing that he was suspected of having tried to abduct her.

A feeling of panic swept through her as she saw his eyes move about the room until they rested on her. Had Lord Ravenscar not been sitting with her she thought she would have left the room at once. However, to do so would occasion surprise—and, after some reflection, she realised that it would appear to the marquis that she was afraid of meeting him. She must accept that they would meet socially sometimes and, until she was certain that it was he who had had tried to abduct her, she must greet him with cool politeness.

He had seen her. She knew it from the narrowing of his eyes, but, thankfully, he did not come to her immediately and she was able to control her feelings of panic. He could do nothing to harm her here.

'I suppose I must circulate a little,' Lord Ravenscar murmured. 'I shall return as soon as I have done my duty.'

She smiled and inclined her head as he stood and walked away to greet and welcome other guests. Undecided as to whether she would be well advised to do the same, Maddie was relieved when two matrons sat down on chairs next to her.

'Well, isn't this pleasant?' one of the ladies remarked. 'I was surprised when we received the invitation for it is hardly seven months since Mark was…killed, but I suppose the young people wish to entertain.'

'Jenny consulted with Lord Ravenscar and he said it would do everyone good to put the sadness of his son's death behind them.'

'Ah, yes, a bride must be allowed her amusements, must she not?' the matron said and looked at Maddie speculatively. 'I believe you have been recently widowed, Lady Lethbridge?'

'Yes, that is true,' Madeline replied. 'I am a guest here and felt I must attend, though of course I do not dance this evening.'

'No, that would certainly be frowned on. I dare say London manners are a little different to ours here in the country—and your husband was some years your senior, I understand.'

Madeline murmured something appropriate. She was being tested and perhaps censured for attending the dance, but she kept a cool smile in place and refused to be drawn on the difference between town manners and those that applied in the country. This woman could have no idea of Madeline's circumstances, or of the pain and humiliation that she'd suffered at her husband's hands. Nor did she intend to enlighten her.

After a while the woman got up and moved away. Another lady came to take her seat and smiled at Madeline.

'I believe I am slightly acquainted with your mama,' she said in a friendly way. 'We knew each other as girls. I have only sons, but I've brought my niece Patience this evening. The poor child has been in mourning for too long and I wanted her to enjoy herself.'

'She is the very pretty girl with red hair, I think,' Madeline said. 'Lord Ravenscar pointed her out to me earlier.'

'Yes, she is a pretty girl,' the lady said. 'I am Lady Eliza Smythe—and I know you are recently widowed. I am glad that you have some good friends. It can be such a lonely time and friends always pick one's spirits up. I am a widow myself, you see. My husband died two years this past Christmas and I still miss him.'

'Yes, for I dare say you were happy?'

'Yes, very.' The lady placed a sympathetic hand on hers. 'I was fortunate. I do not ask your confidence, Lady Lethbridge, but I believe…forgive me. The count was not…but perhaps I speak too frankly. I happen to know he was not the kindest of men.'

Madeline swallowed hard. Lady Eliza

meant to be kind and she could not rebuff her. 'No, he was not, which is why…I am not grieving.'

'I thought not. You will recover all the sooner, my dear.'

Madeline's eyes had strayed to the dancers and what she saw made her cry out. Lady Eliza asked her what was wrong and she nodded in the direction of the dancers.

'Forgive me, ma'am. Your niece is dancing with a gentleman I think she ought not… the Marquis of Rochdale. It is not my affair, but he may not be all he seems and perhaps not suitable company for such a young lady.'

'No, indeed he is not. I know of his reputation. Thank you for bringing it to my attention. She will be warned not to dance with him a second time.'

'He was not invited tonight, but came with friends, I imagine.'

'He does have relatives in the area,' Lady Eliza said and stood up. 'Thank you for the warning. I must make sure Patience removes from his company as soon as possible without giving offence.'

Madeline inclined her head as the lady set out with new purpose. A little shiver went through her as she thought of that pretty child at the mercy of an unscrupulous man like the marquis. Thank goodness her aunt had the good sense to know the man for what he was and not be blinded by his wealth or title.

She knew that she was not the only young girl to be forced into an unhappy marriage, though perhaps her father had had more excuse than many parents for obliging his daughter to marry a man she could never love.

Madeline was alone with her thoughts for a few minutes and then Hal came to sit beside her. He looked at her, a frown creasing his brow.

'Adam begs your forgiveness for inflicting Rochdale's presence on you, Maddie. He had no idea the Harrington-Browns would bring him here this evening. Mr Harrington-Brown is a friend of Lord Ravenscar and it was impossible to repulse him—but you are safe enough here.'

'Yes, I know.' She smiled at him. 'I understand completely, Hal. Besides, Lord Rochdale is accepted everywhere despite whispers about his private behaviour. If I am ever to go into company again, I must accept that we may meet—and there is no proof that he…'

'None. If we had even the smallest proof,

Adam would have turned him out immediately even if it offended his relatives.'

'Do you think he knew I was here?'

'We cannot be sure,' Hal said. 'He knows now, however, and we must be extra vigilant.'

'Yes.' She bit her bottom lip, for the marquis's arrival had cast a shadow over the evening. 'I wish he had not come—but there is nothing we can do.'

'He will not harm you. I shall make certain he cannot come near you.'

'I would retire to my room, but that is the coward's way,' Maddie said. 'No, I shall not let him drive me away. I will enjoy the evening despite him.'

'We shall be going down to supper soon,' Hal said and reached across the divide between them to take her hand. 'You will let me take you down?'

'Yes, of course, thank you.' Maddie smiled. 'Should you not be doing your duty and dancing with the guests?'

'I have danced with three very silly young girls and with two married ladies. I think I have done my duty this evening and shall now devote myself to you, Madeline.'

'You may take me for a little turn on the

terrace before supper if you will,' she said. 'It is very warm and I should like a breath of air.'

'Yes, of course,' he said and offered her his hand. 'You have only to say. I wish always to please you.'

Madeline took his arm. They walked through the crowded rooms to the French windows. Hal opened one of the long glass doors and they stepped outside. The night air was cool, but not cold, and there were strings of lights on the veranda and in bushes and trees at the edge of the lawns.

'This is much better,' Madeline said. 'I must confess that it has not been easy this evening, for I am an object of curiosity and the ladies are discussing my situation. Some pity me and others condemn me for not observing strict mourning.'

'You must not mind them, dearest,' Hal said and reached for her hand. He carried it to his lips and kissed it briefly. 'You have done nothing wrong. It is acceptable for a widow to attend an evening of this nature providing she takes no part in the dancing.'

'I must show some respect or lose my reputation—but I have wanted to dance with you, Hal.'

'Not as much as I would wish to have you

dance with me,' he murmured and laughed softly. 'I should like to take you in my arms and hold you close as we waltzed.'

'One day,' she said and smiled up at him. For a moment she thought he would reach for her…would kiss her…but with a sound that might have been a moan of passion or a groan of self-denial, he stepped away from her. 'I have been thinking, Hal. When my affairs are settled I think I should like to go abroad for a few months. In France or Italy I should not be obliged to pretend to be in mourning for a man I disliked intensely.'

'Yes, that might be best,' he agreed. 'We could even make it our honeymoon. When we returned the whole affair would have blown over.'

'But you have things to do here,' Madeline said. 'Your estate, your commission to be resigned…'

'Once I set the estate renovations in hand I shall be entirely at your disposal. As for my commission, it was my intention to journey to London and visit headquarters so the thing may be done in the proper manner, but I shall wait until we are certain Rochdale has left the district.'

'Oh, Hal, you make me feel so much better…so protected and cared for,' she said and reached out to touch his hand. Just at that moment they heard the strains of the supper waltz and impulsively she took his hand. 'Dance with me here,' she whispered. 'No one will see us.'

'Maddie, my love.'

Hal placed a hand at her waist and took her right hand, drawing her close. They swayed to the music, dancing in the shadows of the night, lost in the sweetness of the moment, their unspoken feelings in tune as the world and its censure was forgot. Madeline felt herself swept away by a kind of magic as the years melted away and she was once again a young girl, dancing with a young man she had fallen in love with at her very first ball. All of the hurt and pain of the last few years had somehow melted away and she wanted to be held in his arms for the rest of her life.

After the music died away, Hal stood with his arms about her still and she looked up into his face, her heart beating frantically. He lowered his head, kissing her so softly that it was like the touch of a flower petal, as soft as gossamer and so brief that she hardly knew it had happened. Almost at once he released her.

'Forgive me, I forgot myself,' he said. 'It was the magic of the music…'

'No, no, do not beg my pardon,' she whispered. 'I liked it…you know that I—'

The sound of a slow clapping of hands interrupted her and they both turned to see that they had been observed. A man stood in the shadows of the garden, but as they stood as if turned to stone, he walked towards them. Madeline drew her breath sharply as she saw him clearly in the light of the lanterns.

'How touching,' Lord Rochdale said, a malicious leer on his face. 'The grieving widow and her lover…and Lethbridge hardly dead a month.'

'Madeline does not need to answer to you or anyone,' Hal said coldly. 'It is none of your business, but since you take an interest, we are to be married as soon as it is possible.'

'Romance lives,' the marquis sneered. 'I had no love for Lethbridge. He was a cheat and worse. But perhaps he was right to believe that his wife had a lover.'

'No! That is a lie!' Madeline cried.

'Spread such lies and you will answer to me,' Hal said furiously. 'Come near her again, Rochdale, and I'll kill you.'

'As you did her husband?'

'It was not I that killed him—but an assassin.'

'Paid by someone, presumably. And who had the most reason to see him dead?'

'You are mistaken, sir. I might have killed the count in a duel, but I am no murderer.'

'Have I said you were?'

'If I were you, I should leave a house where you are not welcome. And my warning stands. Come near Madeline again and I shall kill you.'

'You are welcome to the lady. I have other interests,' Rochdale said. 'However, I demand payment of the debt your husband owed me, madam—twenty-five thousand pounds. I shall give you one month to pay or I foreclose on the estate and shall tell what I saw this evening. If you wish to keep your secret, make arrangements to pay me.' He inclined his head. 'May I be the first to felicitate you on your engagement.'

They watched as he walked past and into the ballroom, which was now empty because everyone had gone down to supper.

'Hal…' Madeline said, her hand trembling as she placed it on his arm. 'Do you think he is telling the truth? Did Lethbridge truly owe him so much? I do not know, but I think his whole estate can be worth no more than fifty thousand pounds at the most, and if there are other debts... It may be impossible to pay such a sum.'

'I was told that Lethbridge had lost a large amount at the tables to Rochdale,' Hal said looking grave. 'A gambling debt is normally a debt of honour, but you can only pay what the estate will fetch.'

'And what if he demands more—and supposing I am not the heir?' She looked up at him anxiously. 'He may try to ruin us, Hal. I can bear it for myself, but I do not wish to bring shame on you or your friends.'

'You must send for your husband's lawyers,' Hal said. 'Rochdale must be obliged to show the notes Lethbridge gave him...and then you can pay what is available. You cannot do more. No court in the land would expect it.'

Madeline gripped his hand. The marquis had destroyed the magic of their dance and that sweet kiss, making her remember the last dark days of her marriage.

'I do not care for the estate. My settlement should be safe and that is all I need. If the estate is mine, I will arrange for him to be paid—but if there is another claimant...'

'Then it will be his decision whether or not to pay.'

'If he is not paid, he will make everyone believe that we were lovers. He might spread a rumour that it was you that had my husband murdered.'

'He could never prove it, for it is a lie,' Hal said grimly. 'I have witnesses that I did not even fire when it was my right to do so had I chosen. You must not let Rochdale distress you, Madeline. He cannot harm us if we stand firm.'

'He can and will ruin both our reputations,' she said. 'He is welcome to what he is owed but...' Tears trembled on her lashes. 'I am a curse on those who love me. Forgive me, Hal. I have brought so much trouble on you.'

'Do you think I fear his threats?' Hal said. 'I meant what I said to him, Maddie—if he comes near you again I shall kill him. As for the money, I have no personal desire or wish for you to inherit it, but it would have made you independent.'

'I do not need a fortune to be happy,' she said. 'Truly, all I want is to be your wife, Hal.'

'I had thought we might make our home at my estate in Cambridgeshire,' he said, 'and perhaps we shall one day. But...' He paused and shook his head. 'It might be best if we went abroad soon, Maddie. If there is a scandal, we can live quietly somewhere we are not known until talk has died down.'

'Oh, why did he have to see us?'

'It does not matter. Let him do his worst,' Hal said and took her hands, holding them firmly. 'We shall be married quietly here and then go away. Our friends will not believe his lies—and the others do not matter.'

'I must contact the lawyers as soon as possible,' Madeline said. 'I do not wish to tear you away from your family and friends if a scandal can be averted. Perhaps enough money may be raised.'

'I shall go to London in the morning,' Hal said. 'You must promise me not to go anywhere alone and to be very careful while I am away.'

'Yes, I shall remain in the gardens near the house or the house itself,' Madeline promised. 'You must go to London and see your business done, Hal—and ask my husband's lawyers what my situation is regarding Lethbridge's debts.'

Hal smiled at her. 'Have courage, my love. Even if he does his worst, words cannot truly harm us. If need be, I shall sell all my property in England and we shall make a new life abroad.'

'Yes.' Madeline smothered the sob rising in her throat.

How could she let Hal sacrifice everything for her?

Chapter Ten

Somehow Madeline managed to control the tumult of her feelings as she allowed Hal to take her back into the ballroom. She declined supper, excusing herself by saying that she needed to tidy her gown, smiled, touched his hand, and then went upstairs to her bedchamber.

What was she going to do? Her mind was tumbling with doubts and anxiety. The marquis was a spiteful man and would delight in taking his revenge on them. Lethbridge had promised to give Madeline to him and he'd been thwarted not once but twice, perhaps even three times if it was his men who had tried to abduct her—and she did not believe that he would be satisfied with spreading malicious lies.

She could scarcely believe that Lethbridge had lost so much money to the marquis. Madeline had always believed her husband to be a rich man—but twenty-five thousand pounds…could the estate in Hampshire and the London house together be worth so much? She did not know for sure, but she suspected that there might be a mortgage on the country estate for she'd once heard a few words of it when Lethbridge was speaking to his lawyer.

Of course there was also the strongbox that Thomas had smuggled out of the house and brought here to her. Nothing that remained in the box meant anything to her. She would give the jewels to the marquis gladly in part settlement, yet somehow she did not believe that even if she could pay every penny of the debt he would leave them in peace.

Having splashed her face in cool water and tidied her gown, she looked at herself in the elegant dressing mirror. She was very pale, but her face showed no sign of the tears she'd shed as she prepared to go down again. A knock at the door made her start and freeze with fear, but then Jenny's voice asked if she were all right.

'Yes, I am just coming down,' she said and opened the door.

Jenny looked at her in concern.

'Are you well? I was anxious because Hal said it had upset you seeing the Marquis of Rochdale here. I wanted to tell you that he has gone. You may come down now without fear of being forced to speak to him.'

'Thank you,' Madeline said. 'I am sorry to have cast a shadow over your dance, Jenny.'

'You have not done so. I can see very well why you distrust that man. I should have liked to refuse to receive him, but could not. However, he left before supper and I was relieved to see him go. Are you sure you wish to come down, dearest?'

'Yes, I shall come,' Madeline said and smiled at her. 'Please, do not be anxious for my sake. This is your dance and you should enjoy it.'

'Well, I shall now that that awful man is not here to distress you.'

Madeline linked arms with her and they went back down to the ballroom. Jenny stayed with her for a few minutes and then Adam claimed her for a dance. Madeline decided to circulate the rooms and spent an hour and a half talking to the other guests as if she had not a care in the world, but when the company began to disperse, she said goodnight to Jenny and Lord Ravenscar, then went in search of Hal. Both he and Adam had left the ballroom half an hour earlier and she wanted to say goodnight.

She decided to investigate the library, which was one of their favourite haunts. Approaching, she saw that the door was partially open and, as she hesitated, she heard their voices.

'What else can I do?' Hal was asking. 'Madeline is in danger, Adam. I must take her somewhere she will be safe. If that means going abroad, then so be it.'

'You will give up everything—your family and friends—for her? She is beautiful, and Jenny likes her, but she seems cold to me. Have you forgot that she broke your heart by marrying Lethbridge? I have never once seen her look at you with love, Hal. Are you certain this marriage is what you want?'

'Yes, of course. I love her. I always have. Damn it, Adam, I don't want to leave England, but I do not see that I have a choice.'

Madeline backed away, feeling sick. Hal was ready to give up everything for her, but Adam thought he was wrong. He did not wish to see his friend sacrifice his life for her sake, and who could blame him?

He was right that she had never allowed her feelings for Hal to show. Indeed, until he kissed her in the garden after their dance, she'd not been sure that she could bear to wed him, even though she loved him. His kiss had been so sweet and gentle that her fears had fled and she'd wanted him to go on and on kissing her. In that moment she would have given herself to him—and then the marquis had destroyed the spell that held them.

Tears stung her eyes as she fled back the way she had come, nearly tripping over the stairs as she ran up them, hardly able to hold back the sobs until she was inside her room. Sally was waiting for her. She looked at her as the tears cascaded down her cheeks.

'What is wrong, my lady?' she asked. 'Is it that man?'

Madeline shook her head, brushing her tears away with the back of her hand. 'It is mere foolishness on my part,' she said. 'Please unfasten my gown and then leave me.'

'Will you not tell me what has so distressed you?'

'It is nothing, a mere irritation of the nerves. I have a headache,' Madeline lied as

Sally unfastened the hooks at the back of her bodice. 'I wish to sleep.'

'I shall bring you a tisane. It will help you,' Sally said.

'Thank you,' Madeline said, 'but I think I shall sleep if I am left alone in peace.'

She saw the hurt in her maid's eyes, but all she wanted was to be alone so that she could weep as her heart broke into tiny pieces. How could she let Hal give up everything that he cared for to marry her? She was not worthy of him. Lethbridge had soiled her, made her unfit to be the wife of a decent man.

Hal was going to London. She would give him a letter to her husband's lawyers, instructing them to pay the marquis what was owed and then...then she must go away.

Madeline sat on the edge of her bed as Sally left her, closing the door softly behind her. An icy coldness settled about her heart as she realised that she had no choice.

She must take the opportunity to leave this house while Hal was gone. She would ask Sally and Thomas to accompany her as far as Dover. There she would purchase a passage for France, and they could go with her or leave her and buy the inn Thomas wanted.

Because of the contents of Lethbridge's

box she had enough to make a new start somewhere abroad. The jewels might not belong to her, but she would take them in lieu of the settlement owed to her. The Marquis of Rochdale might have all that was left of the estate for all she cared. She needed only sufficient to start her new life. Indeed, she would not take all the jewels, but only enough to make her secure until she could find work. In truth, she wanted nothing that had been her husband's, but she must have something or she would starve. The clothes Sally had sold for her had brought her but one hundred guineas, far less than they had cost when new. It was enough to take her to France, but in time she would need to sell some of the jewels from the box.

It might be better to dismiss Sally and Thomas when they reached Dover. She could not expect them to give up their hopes and dreams for her—did not wish them to do so. Sally was very loyal to her so she would need to find a valid reason to stop Sally accompanying her to France.

In the morning she would sign a letter asking her husband's lawyer to settle the marquis's claim. She would smile as Hal left and wish him a safe journey, but when he returned to Ravenscar she would no longer be here.

Her decision made, Madeline dried her eyes. Weeping would do her no good at all. She must learn to be strong and to stand on her own. In her haste to flee from her husband she'd accepted Sally's help and she'd gone to Hattie seeking a safe refuge, and then Hal had brought her here—but she must learn to fend for herself. Everyone had been kind to her, but it was time that she learned to manage her own life.

Getting up from the bed, she began to pack a few things into a bag and a satchel. The jewels she was taking with her she would secrete inside her clothes. She had no intention of letting her hosts know what she intended for they would try to stop her, but she would write a letter to Jenny, because she had been her friend. It would be hard to explain why she'd left them after their kindness, but she would try.

It would not be easy to leave secretly. They must walk as far as the posting inn in the village and from there hire a chaise that would take them as far as Dover. Madeline shivered as the ice slid down her back and she knew a cold enveloping fear at the future that lay before her. Her heart would break because she truly loved Hal and believed she could learn to be a proper wife to him if he were patient—but she must not accept his sacrifice. It was selfish of her to think of all she would lose. Hal would never abandon her so she must leave him.

It was the only way to save Hal from himself. If she allowed him to sacrifice everything for her, he would begin to regret that he had ever known her. She could not bear to see the look of love in his eyes turn to resentment.

No, it would be much better to give him up now and let him find someone who would be able to give him all the love he deserved. He would not understand. Perhaps he would hate her for once again destroying his hopes, but it was better than seeing the joy die from his eyes because he had been forced into a life he could not like.

Her decision made, Madeline slipped into an uneasy sleep but her dreams would not let her rest and she woke several times.

Awake again at seven in the morning, she rose and dressed herself and went downstairs.

Hal was in the breakfast room. He rose to his feet as she entered with a cry of concern.

'Did you come down just to see me off?' he asked. 'I thought to be gone long before you rose and I had written you a note.' He moved towards her, taking her hands in his and gazing down into her face. 'You are pale, Maddie. I hope you did not let that devil's threats keep you awake. Do not give him another thought. I assure you I am not bothered by his malice. We shall find a way to silence him, believe me.'

'I have a letter you must give to Lethbridge's lawyers, Hal. The marquis must be paid and I care nothing for the money. There is a box in my room containing jewels the count allowed me to wear; they were not mine, but I do not know if they are heirlooms. If I am heir to my late husband's possessions, they may be sold to help pay his debts. All I wanted was my settlement—but if that is needed to settle the debt then so be it.'

'Your settlement cannot be touched in law,' Hal said. 'No court would take that to pay his debt—but the jewels may be requested. We have yet to ascertain whether you are the heir—but I shall attend to it immediately I reach London and send word as soon as I can.'

'Thank you…' Madeline reached up to kiss his cheek, but he turned his head so that their lips met. Once again his kiss was so soft and sweet that it made her feel weak with longing. If only she could return to the day she'd sent him away…when she was innocent and unsoiled. 'You have done so much for me, Hal. I am grateful and I love you—please never doubt it.'

'You are so lovely, my darling,' Hal told her. 'I regret that I must leave you, but these things must be attended. I shall waste no time in returning to you. Keep safe until I do— that is all I ask of you.'

Madeline smiled, but the tears she could not shed stung her eyes and her throat was tight with emotion. She clung to him for another moment, then forced herself to stand away and smile at him.

'Forgive me, I know you must go.'

'Yes, I must, but I shall return soon. We shall marry quietly and leave England before any rumours can start. In time the gossips will forget us and then we may return if we wish.'

Hal smiled at her, but made no further attempt to touch her. Madeline inclined her head, then turned and walked from the room, her head high. He must not guess what she meant to do for he would prevent her running away if he could.

When she entered her bedchamber she discovered Sally tidying the bed and looking at the bags she had packed the previous night. Sally turned to greet her, looking puzzled.

'Are we going somewhere, my lady?'

'I cannot stay here,' Madeline told her. 'Last night…the marquis saw me with Hal. He threatened to ruin us both if a debt my husband owed was not paid. I have arranged to pay what he owes, if the estate belongs to me, but I fear that even if the debt is paid in full he will not leave us be. He is a vengeful man and I think he may ruin Hal just for the pleasure it gives him. But if I am not here, if I do not marry Hal, people will not believe his lies. Hal can stay here and he will not lose everything he cares for.'

'He would lose you,' Sally said. 'I think he cares for you more than all the rest. It would break his heart if you ran away, my lady— besides, where will you go?'

'I intend to go to France,' Madeline said. 'I

have but one talent and that is sewing, and I speak French well enough to find work there. I should like it if you and Thomas would accompany me as far as Dover, where I should be able to buy a passage on a ship bound for France, but then we shall part company. Thomas can buy the inn he wants—and you shall have a gift as a wedding present. I can only take a change of clothing with me and some of my jewels, but the clothes that remain here can be sold. I will give you a letter releasing them to you and you may sell them.'

'No, my lady, I shall not accept them,' Sally said, her mouth set determinedly. 'I must tell you that I think you wrong to leave the protection of this house. You have good friends here who will care for you until Major Ravenscar returns. He loves you. You are making a great mistake to throw away a love like that. Forgive me for speaking out, but it is the truth.'

'Yes, perhaps it is,' Madeline said and her chest was tight with pain. 'I know that you care for me and I am not angry that you spoke as you feel—but I cannot let Hal ruin himself for me. I love him too much to see him lose all that is dear to him.'

'I cannot agree with you, my lady, but I see

there is no changing your mind. If you are determined to leave, I shall come with you.'

'Ask Thomas to prepare. We must slip away quietly and take a chaise from the posting house in the village.' She picked up her purse and took some gold coins from it, giving them to Sally. 'He may go on ahead of us and hire the chaise. Go to him now and tell him, then pack your things. I must write some letters—and I shall meet you in the rose arbour in one hour. If something should delay me, wait until I come for I shall not fail.'

'If you are sure, my lady?'

'Perfectly sure,' Madeline said. 'Please, do not try to dissuade me. It is hard enough as it is.'

Sally looked grave, but went out of the room, shaking her head over it. Madeline knew her maid would not be easily persuaded to leave her at Dover, but once there she could find a ship for herself and find a way to slip away. She must not let Sally and Thomas give up their dream for her sake. It was time that she learned to look after herself.

Sitting down at the pretty writing desk near the window, Maddie took some notepaper from the drawer and began to write the letters she would leave for Hal and Jenny.

They were the hardest she'd ever penned in her life and she screwed up her first attempts.

It was easier to write to Jenny than to Hal. She wrote of her pleasure in her visit to Ravenscar and in the friendship she'd formed with Jenny, assuring her that she regretted leaving and hoped she would be forgiven.

I do not leave lightly, but I cannot bring disgrace and trouble on such good friends. Rochdale intends to ruin us and I fear he will not be satisfied even if every penny of the debt Lethbridge owed him is paid—so I hope to avert scandal by leaving your house. I know that some gossip may still circulate, but it should not fall on you if I am gone. I believe Hal may weather the storm if I am not there to bring further shame on him— and I would not have him lose everything he cares for, for my sake. Please forgive this selfish wretch for bringing trouble to you. I am so grateful and for ever your friend,
Madeline.

It was so much harder to write to Hal. If she gave him hope he might search for her so

she could not write of undying love. She must
not hurt him more than absolutely necessary
and she could not give him a clue where she
intended to go for he would come after her.
She must, however, convince him that she did
not wish to marry. She wrote at last,

*My very dear Hal, I hardly know how to
write this for I know, whatever I say, I
must inflict pain and that is far from my
wish. You have been all that is good and
honourable and I know you would give
up your very life for me, but I am not
worthy of you, my love. I have thought
about the future and I believe that what
Lethbridge did to me has scarred me for
life. Although I love and honour you, I
fear I can never be the wife you want.
You cannot even begin to imagine the
humiliation I suffered or to understand
the disgust for the physical side of love
he instilled in me. I believe I shall never
marry again and therefore I am setting
you free. I shall always think you the
kindest man I know and I wish with all
my heart that you will forget me and
find a new love.*

With me gone, Rochdale will not

bother you again. You may be free of
the shadows I brought to your life and
find happiness.
Madeline

The tears trickled down her cheek as she
sanded her letter and then folded it, sealing it
with wax. She would leave the letters on the
dressing table, where they would be found
when Jenny came in search of her.

Picking up her bags, she strapped the
satchel over her body and then covered it
with a warm velvet cloak. She could hide
the larger bag under the voluminous cloak
until she was out of the house. Jenny would
not rise for another two hours for she would
sleep late after the dance the previous evening. Adam might be about, but if she slipped
out by a side door she might avoid being seen
as she left the house.

Luck was with her, and other than one
maid and a footman in the hall, she met no
one as she went downstairs. They looked at
her in surprise for it was early and she was
dressed in a thick cloak, which was unusual
for a mild morning, but they took little notice. She was a guest in the house and it was
not their business to enquire where she went

or what she did. The footman did notice that she was carrying a bag, but he was on his way to breakfast in the servants' hall and gave it no more than a passing thought at the time.

Having escaped the house without challenge, Madeline walked swiftly to the rose arbour, where she found Sally waiting for her. The girl had a satchel over her shoulder and carried two bags, which probably contained all her things. Clearly, she did not intend returning to claim the clothes and possessions Madeline had left behind. She would have to give them something else instead. Perhaps one day when she was settled she could ask Jenny to sell the things that remained and send the money to her. She would need to wait for some months or more to give Hal time to get over the shock of her departure.

'What did Thomas say?' Madeline asked. 'Has he gone to secure the chaise for us?'

'Yes, my lady. I told him what you said about leaving you at Dover and he says he can open a tavern in France as easily as here.'

'You are both so good to me,' Madeline said in a voice choked with emotion. She doubted that Thomas knew more than two words of French and would find it very much harder to run an inn in France. However, she

knew better than to argue, for her friends
would protect her as best they could even if
she tried to send them away. The only thing
she could do would be to slip away to a ship
when they reached the port.

The Marquis of Rochdale scowled as he
was compelled to stop at the blacksmith to
have one of his horses shod. Having outstayed
his welcome at his cousin's house, he'd been
forced to leave sooner than he would have
wished. His henchmen had followed Madeline from the farm to the Earl of Ravenscar's
house, which, being close enough to his cousin's estate, had made it easy for him to attend
various social events in the district. Madeline
had not ventured far from Ravenscar, but he'd
managed to wangle an invitation to Jenny
Miller's dance, which had brought him face
to face with his quarry.

Seeing her in Hallam Ravenscar's arms
had made him furious. His threats had been
vicious and made in anger. Lethbridge owed
him fifteen thousand pounds, which was a
debt of honour and would probably be settled by whoever had inherited the estate if
it were possible, though he knew that Lethbridge was badly dipped and his estate al-

ready mortgaged. A man with so much to lose would never have taken to cheating at the tables if he'd not had good reason.

Be damned to the money! Rochdale was rich enough despite his predilection to high stakes at the tables and a temporary setback in his finances. It was *revenge* he wanted— revenge on that proud beauty who had dared to lead him on and then defied him in the gardens, making him look a fool. Her lover had rescued her then and Rochdale was not a man to forgive humiliation. She had become an obsession with him and the longing she aroused in him was beyond his control. Yet if he could have her and the money so much the better. Before leaving London, he'd made certain enquiries. Lethbridge had had a cousin on his mother's side, but the man had died the previous year without issue. His title would now be defunct and his fortune would pass to his only surviving relative—and that was his beautiful wife.

Even if the estate was mortgaged there must be something left…jewels, horses, but most importantly Madeline Lethbridge. It was her Rochdale wanted above all else. He had always been attracted to pretty innocents, but something about Madeline made him want to subdue and own her, to teach her to obey him.

At the ball he'd danced with a pretty young innocent who had been flattered by his compliments. Had Rochdale not been obsessed with Madeline, he might have seduced the chit for she was ready enough and ripe for the picking. She would not be the first innocent he had forcibly seduced. Only once had his iniquity been discovered and he'd fought a duel, which led to the death of Sir William Mardle and the decline of his daughter. Miss Ellen Mardle had retired from public life and, although her name had not been besmirched, there had been rumours about the reason her father had called Rochdale out.

A smile touched his mouth. The honourable fool had insulted him over some trifling incident and, when he responded by sneering in his face, had called him out and chosen pistols. Mardle had never stood a chance for Rochdale was a crack shot as well as being a master with the foils. He had fought half-a-dozen duels and three times killed his man, wounding the other three severely. Since on each occasion he'd been the one called out, he had received no more than a stern warning from the magistrate. Despite his reputation, he still had some influential friends—friends about whom he knew devastating secrets, just as he'd known about Lethbridge's cheating at the tables.

If the fool had been able to control his wife, this business might have been over, for he seldom found a woman of interest once he'd had her a few times, but Lethbridge had reneged on his bargain and he'd paid the price. A ball in the back when he was engaged in a duel with Ravenscar had been a masterly stroke, but because Ravenscar had held his fire it had miscarried. Had he shot no one would have known that it was Rochdale's ball that killed Lethbridge. An observant doctor might have discovered two wounds, but ten to one Ravenscar would have missed. It took a steady nerve to kill a man in cold blood. As it was, Rochdale had had to run in order to escape detection and that did not suit his pride.

His grievances against Hallam Ravenscar were mounting. To discover that Madeline loved him—had given him her kiss willingly and planned to wed him—had infuriated Rochdale. In his anger he'd lied about the amount owed him, but it was an easy matter to forge the other notes for he had a talent that had come in useful on more than one occasion. He'd forged his uncle's signature on a will that made him the heir and disinherited his more deserving cousin. A few gambling debts was nothing…yet the money was scarcely compensation for what he truly wanted.

Money would not satisfy this hunger inside him. Revenge was necessary to him if he were ever to forget his humiliation at her and Ravenscar's hands.

Irked by the length of time the blacksmith had taken to shoe his horse, he told his groom to fetch him when it was ready and strolled over to the inn. He was just in time to see three people getting into a chaise. For a moment he could not believe what he was seeing—what on earth was Madeline Lethbridge doing sharing a post chaise with her maid while the former footman rode behind them on his horse?

Where was Hallam Ravenscar or the Ravenscar grooms?

Perhaps, more importantly, where was she going?

A smile spread over his face and he laughed inwardly. Was the stupid little fool running away again? Hallam Ravenscar would never have allowed her to undertake a journey with only one man for protection—so the chances were that he did not know.

It would be most interesting to discover where she was headed. Rochdale had nothing more important to do with his life and he could feel the excitement mounting inside him. There was now every chance that he could have the prize that had eluded him for weeks—and once he'd used her and brought her to his knees, in a few months, he would invite Ravenscar to come and fetch her. That way he would have his revenge on both of them. If Ravenscar challenged him to a duel, he would kill him.

It was all so simple and easy that he was laughing as he went into the inn and ordered some ale. A few coins in the hand would buy him their destination and then he could follow and bide his time.

She had made it easy for him.

Chapter Eleven

'Madeline...are you still asleep?' Jenny asked, peeping round the door. 'Oh...you're not here.' She walked into the room, thinking that it was unusually untidy. Madeline's maid always kept everything just so, but there was a glove dropped on the floor, some writing paper lying on the desk and a night-chemise thrown over a chair. It was most unlike Sally to leave things like this and it made Jenny wonder. Then she saw the letters lying on the dressing table and walked across to investigate. Seeing that one was addressed to her, she picked it up and broke the seal. 'Oh, no,' she cried as she read the few lines. 'How foolish...'

Snatching up the other letter that she now

saw was addressed to Hal, she went swiftly from the room in search of her husband. Adam was in the library, sitting at a desk littered with ledgers when she entered and did not at first look up from his books.

'Adam, please forgive me for interrupting your work, but I must speak to you on a serious matter.'

He glanced up with a smile. 'If you've overspent your allowance, I quite understand, my love. Just have the accounts sent to me.'

'No, it isn't that,' Jenny said. 'It is Madeline…she has run away because she fears to bring shame on us all.'

'What?' Adam cried, looking stunned. 'No, how could she be such a fool? Does she have no sense in that beautiful head of hers? She may be abducted and goodness knows what…and Hal will never forgive me.'

'She thinks he will be better off without her,' Jenny said, close to tears, 'and that we shall not be exposed to scandal if she leaves now. How can she think that we would care for that? Or that it would much affect us whatever that wicked man tried to do?'

'As to that I dare say it might be unpleasant for a while, but we should come about. Hal was of the same mind. Last night he was convinced that he must take Madeline abroad once they were wed to avoid the scandal. He fears that she would be ostracised and he did not wish to bring shame on our family. We argued for an hour or more. In the end I believe I convinced him that a few months abroad on his wedding trip would be sufficient for the gossip to die down—and he was considering keeping the estate his mother left to him and returning to it when they came home. He would not take the position I offered him. I fear he is too damned proud.'

'She left a letter for me—and one for Hal,' Jenny said and offered it to her husband. He took it, hesitated, and then broke the seal, exclaiming in exasperation.

'Damn it! She must have heard me...'

'What do you mean?' Jenny was puzzled.

'I questioned her feelings for him,' Adam said. 'I thought she was cold and did not love him as she ought. But the foolish woman has run away rather than let him ruin his life for her sake and that shows that I was wrong. She does care for him.'

'Should you have read Hal's letter?'

'It is as well I did for if he read this...' Adam shook his head. 'She makes some excuse about not being worthy of him, but I am certain this is my fault. I caused this, Jenny—and it is up to me to do something about it.'

Jenny watched as her husband walked to the fireplace and tossed Madeline's letter to Hal into the flames.

'Adam! That was not yours to dispose of.'

'Hal must not see that for it would destroy him,' Adam said. 'If he returns while I'm gone, you will show him yours, but say nothing of a letter for him.'

'Are you sure? He may be angry if he thinks she went with no word for him…and where are you going?'

'I must go after her,' Adam said. 'Ask the servants if they've seen anything of her maid or the footman she brought with her. Someone may know how long a start they have on me. I must put up a change of clothing and hope to pick up their trail. I dare say they hired a chaise from the Swan Inn. Unless they've taken something from our coach house.'

'Madeline would not do that,' Jenny said. 'She told me they borrowed a chaise from Thomas's brother to escape from London and he was sent to return it at once. I believe she would have hired something locally if she could.'

Adam crossed the room to her, bending down to kiss her lips. 'Forgive me for leaving you, Jenny. Please have one of the grooms go after Hal and tell him that Madeline has run away again—I'll go after her and try to bring her back safely.'

'Will you take one of the grooms with you?'

'I have my pistols, but, yes, I shall take George with me. He is handy with a pistol. If Rochdale knows nothing of her flight, we shall be home again before you hardly know we're gone. But if he is on her trail we may need the pistols if we are to rescue her.'

Jenny felt her stomach tighten with nerves. 'You will be careful, please?'

'Of course, but I must find her for alone she is in danger. It is most unlikely that Rochdale is aware she has left our house, but she might fall prey to any number of rogues. Do not worry, Jenny. I shall find her and pray that I may persuade her to return.'

The post boys had advised them to change horses at the White Eagle, a superior inn on the London road. It was some distance from Dover still, but had such a pleasant parlour that Madeline had decided they would par-

take of luncheon there. She enquired of the
landlord where it would be best to stay for
they could not hope to reach Dover itself before nightfall. He had told her that the Hare
and Hounds Inn situated at the edge of a
small village some ten miles from Dover
was an excellent hostelry where they could
be certain of clean sheets and a good dinner.
It was but a short drive from Dover and they
could easily reach the port the next morning.

They reached the inn by seven that evening and, since Thomas had ridden on ahead
to warn the landlord, were fortunate enough
to secure a room for the night, which Madeline would share with Sally. Thomas would
make do with a bed in a communal room
over the stables that grooms and post boys
often shared.

Madeline bespoke dinner for them all and
was given a table in the parlour, which she
had only to share with one other lady—a governess travelling to her employer's home to
take up a new post. She was a woman of some
thirty-odd years, dressed in a sober gown of
grey and accustomed to being ignored by
fine ladies, and showed a little surprise when
Madeline asked her where she was going.

'I am to take up a position with Lady

Margaret Marlborough,' she said. 'She has two young sons and the last governess left in some distress for she could not bear their pranks another moment.'

'I dare say it is often difficult to control young boys?'

'Indeed, it can be, ma'am,' she replied. 'My name is Anne Somersham and I am accustomed to dealing with spirited children. I do not foresee any problem.'

After listening to Miss Somersham's account of various pupils she had been obliged to deal with during her years as a governess, Madeline mentally crossed off the possibility of applying for such a post herself. She did not think she would be able to make high-spirited boys mind her and the idea of being at the beck and call of an elderly lady held no appeal. No, she thought her first notion of becoming a seamstress was still the most likely way for her to succeed. She might even set up a small establishment of her own once she'd learned her trade.

A little later, Miss Somersham said goodnight and left the room to go up to her bedchamber. Madeline had finished her dinner and was thinking of retiring to her room. She was just about to ask Sally if she were ready when the landlord entered and asked if they would mind sharing the parlour with a gentleman.

'Captain Mardle is a very distinguished, respectable gentleman,' he said in an apologetic tone. 'He had bespoke my parlour for this evening, but I wasn't sure when to expect him for he said he might be late.'

'We shall be going up to our chamber when we've finished our wine,' Madeline said and inclined her head. 'Please request Captain Mardle to come in. We are the intruders here and will give up the parlour to him in a very few minutes, sir.'

The landlord returned a moment later with a gentleman dressed in the uniform of a cavalry officer. He moved towards Madeline as she rose to her feet and bowed politely.

'Please do not feel obliged to leave, ma'am. I am not averse to sharing the parlour.'

'You are kind, sir, but we have finished our supper. The host was not expecting us until we sent word late this afternoon and was kind enough to allow us to eat our dinner in privacy—and now we shall accord you the same privilege.'

'You are gracious, ma'am,' he said and moved towards the fire, but swayed and

seemed unsteady for a moment. Unthinkingly, Madeline put out a hand to steady him.
'Thank you…'

'Are you ill, sir?'

'I have been for many months,' Captain Mardle replied. 'I am recovered now and it was but a momentary faintness, which still troubles me now and then.'

'If there is anything we can do…'

'Nothing at all, though I thank you for the offer.'

Madeline smiled and inclined her head. Murmuring to Sally that they must leave, she led the way from the room.

'I dare say the gentleman was injured in the war,' Sally said. 'He did look a bit pale, didn't he?'

'Yes, a little,' Madeline agreed. 'There was something about him…something in his eyes that spoke of suffering.'

'Yes, my lady. I noticed that too.'

'We shall be in Dover in the morning,' Madeline said as they went up to their room. 'I want you to think seriously about your decision to accompany me to France, Sally. I have no right to ask you or Thomas to come with me. I intend to seek work as a seamstress and I cannot afford to employ you both.

Thomas will have to seek work for himself. Would you rather not stay here and purchase the inn he desires?'

'No, my lady. Thomas says he will go where I go and I shall follow you. If we set up house together, three wages will be more comfortable than one.'

'As always, you are determined to do everything for me,' Madeline said. 'We shall speak of it again when we reach Dover.'

Once the door was closed and locked, Madeline undressed, refusing Sally's offer of help. She had chosen to wear a carriage gown that had a separate bodice and skirt, which fastened in front with tiny pearl buttons and was easy to take off. In future she must make certain that she could dress herself for she was determined to make no more demands on her friends. Indeed, her meeting with Miss Somersham had made her more determined to stand alone. All her life she had been cosseted and waited on and she believed it was time to fend for herself. If Sally would not listen to reason, she must find a way to slip away from her friends and take passage on a ship for France.

It would be very selfish of her to allow them to sacrifice their lives for her.

* * *

Jake Mardle sat over the dinner he had hardly touched, staring into his wineglass. Something about the beautiful young woman who had tried to help him when he was dizzy had reminded him of Ellie. There was a certain innocence or fragility that had drawn him to her.

Ellie, his sweet sister, who was now a shadow of her former self, living the life of a recluse with his Aunt Medina. Ellie had been so beautiful and so sweet when Jake left his home to join the army. She ought by now to have been happily married to a good man who would love her and give her a home and children, but instead she sat all day in her room and stared at the wall. Even the return of her brother now recovered from a long illness had hardly raised a smile. She had allowed him to kiss her cheek, but then she had moved away, a little shudder going through her.

It was a while before he'd coaxed the story of her shame and his father's death from Aunt Medina. She had not wanted to tell him and begged Jake not to let his sister know that he was aware of her shame.

'It is not Ellie's shame,' Jake raged, 'but that devil who seduced and abandoned her to her fate. He ruined her and killed my father—and for that he shall die.'

'I beg you not to throw your life away as your father did,' his aunt said. 'If I'd thought you would be so foolish, I should not have told you. What will become of us if anything should happen to you?'

'It will not,' he promised her. 'I am not my father, Aunt. I am a soldier hardened to battle—and I shall kill him.'

'And hang for it,' his aunt said. 'Think about us, Jake—your sister has enough to bear as it is. If you die, she will never forgive herself.'

'I intend to bring that wretch to his knees,' Jake replied. 'Do not distress yourself, Aunt. I shall take revenge for Ellie and my father— and then I will return and we shall all go abroad to live. In a warm climate away from people who know of her shame my sister will recover.'

Jake shook his head. He was woolgathering. The young woman he'd seen in the parlour earlier could have nothing in common with Jake's sister—and their paths would never cross again. He must allow nothing to detract him from the business in hand.

He was going to find and kill the Marquis of Rochdale.

Hal was at dinner in the parlour of the inn he had chosen to stay at for the night. He'd ridden hard all day and hoped there would be a soft bed in his chamber. It was impossible to reach London in one day and he would need to spend most of the following day in the saddle if he were to get there by nightfall. He wanted to complete his journey in as short a time as possible, because he had sensed Madeline's unease when he'd said goodbye to her. The marquis's threats had distressed her far more than they had him. He cared little for any gossip the man might spread and his only concern was for Madeline herself. She might suffer some loss of reputation, but, as Adam had convinced him, it would be short term. Once she was his wife, people would merely smile and forget that they had been lovers before their marriage.

If only the gossips knew the truth. Hal had done no more than kiss her, though his body burned for her and he longed to make her his wife. His concern for her feelings and the abuse she'd suffered at her husband's hands had made him hold back. He could never force her into a situation that was unpleasant to her...though his instincts told him that she loved him. He had felt increasingly anxious as he rode further from Ravenscar, though he did not know why. When he saw the Ravenscar groom walk into the inn parlour, he jumped to his feet, instinctively knowing that something must be wrong.

'Major,' the man said, coming swiftly to meet him. 'I'm glad to have caught you. Captain Miller sent me to tell you. Lady Lethbridge has gone missing, sir.'

'Missing? How can this be? Has she been abducted?'

'I don't rightly know, sir,' the groom said apologetically. 'I was sent to ask you to return.'

'Yes, I shall do so at once,' Hal said. His business in London could wait. If Madeline was in danger...yet he could not understand how anyone could get close enough to her to abduct her. 'How did it happen? Did she go out walking alone?'

'I think she left a letter for Mrs Miller,' he said, causing Hal to frown. 'But that is all I was told, sir—just to let you know you was needed back at Ravenscar.'

'A letter for Jenny…' Hal frowned. There was more to this than met the eye. He fixed the groom with a hard stare for the man had not disclosed everything.

'You have no idea where she has gone?'

'None, sir—but Captain Miller went after her as soon as he knew she'd slipped off with her maid and that footman.'

Hal stared at him in disbelief. 'You're sure she took her maid with her?'

'Yes, Major. I heard the lads talking in the stables. They was seen leaving and they was carrying bags with them. Went off in a havey-cavey style they did, though Thomas took his horse.'

Hal felt sick to his stomach and then angry. How could Madeline have run off as soon as his back was turned? Where had she gone? Back to her friend's farm or somewhere else?

Most importantly, why had she left? She must know how dangerous it was for her to leave the safety of Ravenscar. What had driven her to such a desperate act?

He could not understand why she would cause so much anxiety and distress to everyone. He'd believed she was content to marry him, to go abroad with him until the gossip had died down and then return to England.

She must know how much he loved her. Did he mean so little to her that she had not thought it necessary to tell him of her intention?

'My horse needs rest,' Hal said. 'I shall hire a chaise and drive myself back to Ravenscar, but you must stay here and bring the horses back tomorrow by easy stages.'

'I ought to go with you, sir. It's a long way to drive—and you must be tired.'

'I'll drive as far as I can tonight and then sleep,' Hal said. 'Now I must pay my shot—you may have the room I bespoke for the night. I shall pay the landlord myself now.'

Leaving the groom to bespeak a meal for himself, Hal went to the speak to the landlord and then to the stables, where he was able to hire a chaise and pair. He needed speed and for the payment of a few extra guineas secured some sweet goers that would have him back at Ravenscar by morning.

His mood alternated between anxiety and anger, for he could not decide why Madeline had left without telling anyone what she meant to do.

Had he been wrong about her? He'd believed that she cared for him—that she wanted to be his wife—but now he did not know what to think.

If Madeline loved and trusted him, why would she run away?

Having been told there were no rooms available at the Hare and Hounds, Rochdale sent one of his servants to wait and watch while he drove on through the night to an inn nearer Dover.

'When the wench leaves the inn follow her,' he told his man. 'I believe her to be travelling to Dover, but if she should go in another direction come and tell me immediately. I shall put up at the Green Man in Dover and you will find me there.'

Rochdale was content to bide his time. He knew it would be more trouble than it was worth to try to abduct Madeline from a public place with her servants in attendance. Sooner or later she would be alone and he would grab her before anyone knew what was happening.

Madeline had not slept well. Her thoughts were of Hal and the pain her letter must cause him when he read it. She was torn by doubt for her resolution had begun to waver during a long night listening to the sounds of the inn.

Coaches coming and going at all hours, loud voices and what sounded like a fight in the yard had all combined to give her a restless night.

Sally had told her to wait while she fetched a can of warm water and asked the landlord if they could have breakfast in their rooms, but Madeline could not sit still. The doubts had begun to crowd in on her and she did not know what she ought to do.

Was she wrong to have let the marquis win? Her determination to save Hal from ruin was still strong, but she felt tired and close to tears, unsure of what she wanted to do.

If Sally insisted on coming to France with her she might not be able to evade her—and that would ruin the dreams Thomas harboured of having his own inn, for he could not hope to make a success in France when he did not speak the language.

Oh, why could things not be simpler? Feeling uncertain and in some distress, Madeline used the cold water left over from the night before to wash, dressed in the simple gown she'd worn on her journey here and went downstairs. She needed to walk in the fresh air for a while before she came to her final decision.

She paused for a moment to listen to a noisy dispute in the taproom, then went out into the yard. It was a cold crisp morning, but the sun was shining and she felt better away from the stale odours of the inn.

Was her life to be spent in inns or lodgings that could be no better than this, because she could not afford a higher rent? Was she making a terrible mistake? Perhaps she'd let a few careless words upset her too much. Did she really need to run away to France?

Was she such a spineless coward? Remembering the brave governess who was forced to stand on her own feet, Madeline was shamed. She would truly be a coward if she allowed Rochdale to ruin her life.

Suddenly, she found that she was no longer afraid. The marquis might try to ruin her, but what did it truly matter? She did not care what people thought of her—but she would not have Hal ruined. Her mind sought for a solution to her problems and the idea came to her slowly. She need not go to France; instead she would return to her late husband's house in London, but she could not return to Ravenscar for she did not wish to bring shame on Jenny and Adam. She would discover the truth of her situation from the lawyers and, if she were the heir, she would arrange for the marquis to be paid. Then, if she had no other choice, she would go home to her father. Sally would no longer feel it necessary to remain with her and could follow her heart. As for Hal…perhaps in time he would forgive her, though it would be best if he forgot her and found a new life without her.

Madeline was not sure what might happen to her in the future, if she could bear to marry again, whether she would be penniless or left with a competence. She only knew that she must find the courage to face whatever came to her by returning to her old life.

It was the best solution for her friends and preferable to a life spent looking over her shoulder. She must stop running and face her enemy.

Lifting her head proudly, Madeline walked back to the inn. It *was* time she took charge of her own life—but as the lady she was rather than a seamstress. If Rochdale required to be paid, he must produce evidence and the lawyers would attend to it. Surely enough would be left from her husband's estate to enable her to live independently, but if not she would seek help from her family.

'Oh, I am glad you have given up the idea of becoming a seamstress, my lady,' Sally said when Madeline returned to their room. 'I would have come with you wherever you chose to go, but I must confess that Thomas was not truly happy about it, though for my sake he would follow you anywhere.'

'Once I am settled, you must make your own plans for the future,' Madeline told her. 'I want my friends to be happy and I shall make you both a handsome present when you leave me.'

'We do not need anything, my lady,' Sally said. 'Thomas has money enough to set up his inn—but I shall not leave you until you are comfortable.'

'Your loyalty has been more than I could ever have expected,' Madeline said. 'If you will accept nothing more, I shall give you a wedding gift.'

'I could not refuse that,' Sally said, looking pleased. 'Will you not have some breakfast? There are fresh rolls, butter and honey and I could send down for more tea, for I think this must have gone cold.'

'I shall have honey and rolls and the fruit juice you brought,' Madeline said. 'Pray tell Thomas the news and ask him to engage us a chaise for London rather than Dover.'

'Yes, my lady, at once.'

Sally went off with a new spring in her step, unable to hide her pleasure at Madeline's change of plan. It was a sensible one and Madeline wondered why she had not thought of it at once. Until the lawyers had sorted out the business of the estate, Lethbridge's property was at her disposal. It was likely that she would have some claim to the dower house at his country estate if nothing more…but there was little point in thinking too far ahead. Another day of travelling would bring them to London and the lawyers would soon give her the information she needed.

She felt better for having taken her life into her own hands. Rochdale would do his worst for the only person's reputation to suffer would be her own and she cared nothing for it. Her friends would not bear the shame of her making—and Sally's happiness was worth whatever it cost her. In London, Madeline would make plans for the future according to her situation.

She had finished her breakfast and was ready to go down when Sally returned to fetch the bags and tell her that the chaise was ready and waiting. Madeline carried her own bag, as she had when they arrived here. She did not intend to let her maid wait on her as she had in the old days. In future her life would be different for she would live more simply and not as the wife of a lord. Wherever she went and whatever she did, she had changed. For years she'd lived in fear of her husband and then the shadow of the marquis's threats had overwhelmed her, but something had changed. She would not run away again, but face whatever the future brought with fresh courage.

As she left the inn, she saw that Thomas was speaking with the gentleman she'd seen in the inn the previous night. He saw her, shook hands with Captain Mardle and came to take her bags from her.

'I hope you will not dislike it, my lady,' Thomas said, 'but Captain Mardle is riding to London and asked if you would care for his escort. I said that I thought you could not object… There have been tales of highwaymen on the Heath as you approach London. Two pistols are better than one.'

'I have no objection to the gentleman's company,' Madeline said. 'It was kind of him to offer—please thank him for me.'

'Yes, my lady. I was sure you could not object for he is a respectable gentleman.'

Madeline smiled and nodded toward the obliging gentleman and he swept off his hat to her. Thomas helped her into the chaise and the order to move off was given. Thomas and Captain Mardle followed, riding together. She looked at Sally as she settled back against the squabs.

'Was Thomas pleased?'

'Oh, yes, my lady. He says he shall buy his inn in London for his brother knows of one by the river and no more than five miles from his own. It is exactly what Thomas wanted, though he would have changed his plans to please me.'

'Well, now you may please yourselves,' Madeline said. 'We must have a pretty gown made for your wedding and I shall think of something nice to give you.'

'I should like something in ivory, I think,' Sally said 'and a velvet bonnet trimmed with silk roses to wear with it.'

'Oh, yes, that would be charming,' Madeline said. 'We shall go shopping together, Sally. You must let me buy your bride clothes for I owe you so much.'

Sally blushed and demurred, but did not refuse and they spent some happy minutes speaking of various things that a young bride needed when she married. Thomas had not spoken of taking his bride on a wedding trip and it was unlikely that she would need many smart gowns, but simple dresses for everyday, underclothes and linens for her home were essential.

Madeline was determined to make her a present of cloth and linen that she would find useful in her married life and also to give her various bits and pieces for her house, beside the coin she'd already decided on. It was wonderful to have a wedding to plan and Madeline managed to put all thought of the marquis from her mind.

Now and then thoughts of Hal made her heart ache, for she ought to have been planning her own wedding soon, but she must be brave. Her letter had made her feelings clear and she doubted that Hal would pursue her. He would be hurt, but he would realise that their parting was for the best…although Madeline was no longer sure that it was. But he would receive her letter and then he would despise her for being a coward.

Hal cursed as he ran his hand over the horse's left hind leg. It had gone lame and there was no way he could push on further now. He must lead the poor beast to the nearest inn and leave the chaise there—but perhaps he had pushed himself too hard. He was so tired that he hardly knew how to go on. His mind cast for the best solution and he recalled a posting inn he'd passed in the early light of the morning. It was perhaps half an hour behind him. Better to go back to a decent inn than go on not knowing how far he must lead the horse or what he would find there. He could breakfast there and rest for an hour before continuing his journey. It had been foolish to travel without a groom, for he could not leave the other horse and the chaise here in the road. Perhaps he could find help at the farm just ahead, for if he could leave the chaise and horses with a respectable man, he might arrange to borrow a hack and continue his journey.

Hal was debating what to do next when he saw a man riding towards him and shouted, hoping that the stranger might know of someone who could help him. Turning back to the lame horse, Hal began to release it from the traces as the man came up to him.

'Thank God,' a voice he knew said and

he spun round to find himself facing Adam. 'I thought you might be in London by now.'

'Adam!' Hal cried. 'Your man found me and told me that Maddie has run off—whatever possessed her to do it?'

'I fear she may have overheard us in the library. You remember I questioned your intentions...she must have thought I was against her for she left rather than bring shame on us.'

Hal swore loudly. 'I was on my way back to Ravenscar,' he said. 'I thought you were searching for Madeline—what brought you this way?'

'She hired a chaise to take her to Dover. I have asked at all the posting inns and this morning I discovered that she put up at the Hare and Hounds last night.'

'Dover?' Hal was puzzled. 'Why on earth would she go there? She cannot be thinking of leaving England?'

'I think she must have done it to put anyone off her scent,' Adam said, 'for I was told at the inn that the lady had left but had hired a chaise not for Dover but London.'

'She deliberately tried to deceive us?' Hal's mouth set hard for this was deceitful. 'I do not understand this, Adam. Something is not right. What can she intend?'

'I think she is confused and distressed,' Adam said. 'Her letter to Jenny made it clear that she was leaving for our sakes.'

'I must find her, Adam. She is in danger whether or not she realises it—and I must know why she has run away from me.'

'Yes, of course. What has happened to your rig?'

'The poor beast has gone lame. I must lead it to a posting house where it can be looked after until I can have it returned to its owner.'

'Let me lead the lamed horse while you harness mine to the chaise and go on, Hal. I can arrange for this horse to be cared for and eventually returned to its owner—hire another horse at the posting house and leave my horse for me. I shall rest for a while and then return to Jenny, because I know she must be anxious.'

'Are you sure?' Hal looked doubtful for his cousin's horse was a fine animal and unused to being between the shafts of a chaise.

'Horace is well trained and will obey you, but treat him gently. Here, I'll give you a hand.'

'How far behind her were you?' Hal asked as the cousins re-harnessed the horses. 'I saw a chaise heading towards London some time back. Now I think about it, there were two men riding behind on horses, but I did not look at their faces for I was in too much hurry.'

'It could not have been them for she took only her maid and Thomas.'

'No, I dare say you are right,' Hal said. 'I shall return to the post house that I passed some time back. I think I shall hire a groom to drive me this time, for otherwise I may fall asleep. You should rest there before you return home, Adam.' He clasped his cousin's hand. 'I am sorry Madeline has caused distress. I think she did not mean to upset anyone.'

'I blame myself, Hal. If she heard what I said to you, she may have felt I did not welcome her in my house. I should have been kinder, but I could not forget the pain she had caused you in the past. Now I realise I was wrong to doubt her. Do not think ill of her for what she has done—go after her and tell her you care for her. It is all she needs to know, surely?'

Hal thanked him and they parted, Adam preparing to lead the horse as Hal set off at a more measured pace than before. At least he knew where Madeline was headed now.

Before, he had been uncertain what had happened, but now it seemed that she meant to return to London—perhaps to her late husband's home? She had every right to do so, of course, but she had told him she wanted nothing more than her settlement so that she could find a home of her own.

Why had she decided to return there? Hal could make nothing of her flight for it appeared to contradict all he'd believed. Adam seemed to imagine that Madeline was uncertain of Hal's feelings, but she could not have thought he cared a jot for the marquis's spite—could she?

He was torn between hope and anger. His cousins had taken her in and given her a comfortable place to live while she sorted out her life—why could she not have accepted their kindness instead of causing distress? Why had she chosen to run away as soon as Hal's back was turned?

Was it possible that she cared nothing for him—that she preferred to return to her old life as Lethbridge's widow?

Madeline must know that Hal loved her more than his life. How could she have done this knowing what distress it must cause?

Adam had reminded him that she had

chosen to marry the count when she knew it would break Hal's heart. He had dismissed the warning, excusing her and telling himself that she'd had no choice. But supposing he was wrong?

Supposing she was a cold-hearted selfish woman who thought only of herself?

No, she could not be. She was tender and warm and loving. But then why had she run away when she must know it would break his heart to lose her all over again?

Hal shook his head, feeling relieved as he saw the posting house just ahead of him. He would discover the answers to his questions only when he caught up with Madeline, but he could drive no further without resting. He would pause at the inn, change horses and eat something, and he would hire a groom to drive him so that he could sleep for a while.

He could not be that far behind Madeline if she had come from the Hare and Hounds. Half an hour to change the horses and eat, then they would be off again. With luck they could not be much more than an hour or so behind.

'What? Damn you, Joseph. Are you certain?' Rochdale looked at his servant hard.

'You are sure she was bound for London and not for Dover?'

'Quite certain, my lord. I heard her servant tell the post boys of a change of plans. They are headed for London—and for a house in Grosvenor Square—and she has a gentleman's escort as well as her servants. He looked a military man to me.'

'She is returning to her husband's house?' Rochdale cursed beneath his breath. He'd thought her alone apart from the servants and therefore defenceless. But if she had an escort, Ravenscar must have joined them on the road, which meant she was now well defended. They must have decided to dismiss his threats as worthless, and indeed, though he might cause them some trouble, there was very little he could really do other than strip them of as much of Lethbridge's wealth as he dared. If he dropped hints that she was no better than a whore, a few eyebrows would be raised, but with Lethbridge's reputation most ladies would simply titter behind their fans and think that in Madeline's place they might have done the same.

It seemed he'd missed his chance to snatch her. Unless he could somehow pass them— and lie in wait for their chaise on the road.

He was driving a sporting curricle and could make better speed than a hired chaise. If he could dispose of Ravenscar and the footman, he would have her at his mercy. Rochdale had heard the rumours of highwaymen on the Heath. Madeline was certain to stop for nuncheon to break her journey. If he drove at all speed he could pass them and then... A smile touched his lips. Masked, he could take advantage of the rumours and kill both Ravenscar and the footman. Their deaths would be laid at the door of the highwayman. Madeline would be truly alone then and he would have her.

'Put my horses to,' Rochdale ordered. 'I shall be on my way as soon as I've paid my shot here.'

'What would you wish me to do, my lord?'

'You are going to assist me in holding up a chaise and capturing its passenger. I've had enough of chasing after the wench. I'll take what I want and she shall learn to know her master.'

Joseph blenched, but did not dare to answer back. He'd known that his master was a wicked man, for he knew all the marquis's secrets—but never before had he been asked to take part in such a desperate act. His throat felt tight with fear, for he could end at the hangman's noose for such work as this—but if he refused his master might kill him in a rage.

There was nothing he could do but do as he was told, but he would leave the marquis's employ and seek another master as soon as he could.

Chapter Twelve

Madeline smiled at her companion. It was late in the afternoon and they had made good time, stopping for only half an hour to eat their nuncheon while the horses were changed. Dusk was falling as they began to cross the Heath at Hampstead, but it was not yet dark and she did not think they needed to fear the highwayman who was said to haunt this place. When the shots rang out and the chaise was brought to a shuddering halt it took her so much by surprise that she was flung across the carriage into Sally's arms.

'Oh, my lady,' Sally said as Madeline apologised her and they righted themselves. 'Is it the highwayman?' She was obviously shocked and distressed and before Madeline could stop her, she had opened the window to look out. 'There are two of them. And—oh! I think Thomas is hurt!'

Madeline was powerless to stop her as she scrambled out of the carriage and ran to where Thomas was lying on the ground. The sound of her maid's screaming made her follow her from the chaise. She could see two masked men, each with pistols. One of them seemed to have covered the coachman and the post boy, who accompanied him, the other man had his pistol trained on Captain Mardle.

'Stay in the carriage, ma'am,' Captain Mardle warned, but it was already too late. Madeline was out and making her way to Sally's side.

'Is he alive?' she asked in a whisper and Sally nodded, her face very white as she replied,

'Yes, but hurt.'

Turning towards the masked men, Madeline said. 'We have some money and I have a few jewels. I will give them to you, but please allow us to go on our way. My companion is badly injured and needs a doctor.'

'Your companions may go where they please when I have what I want,' the man covering Captain Mardle with his pistol snarled. 'Bring your jewel box and come here to me.'

'As you wish,' Madeline said and returned to the carriage. She reached inside and picked up her velvet muff and the box that contained her valuables, holding it by the handle at the end. Inside her muff was a small pistol with silver chasing on the butt. If she had the chance, she would shoot. Her stomach was churning as she walked towards the masked man and offered the box to him.

'Bring the groom's horse and mount it. I want you and the gold—the others will be free to go if you come with me. Any bother and I'll kill them all.'

'There will be no trouble,' Madeline replied in a calm voice, though she was far from calm inside. She was actually seething with anger for, though he had tried to disguise his voice, she knew him. This was the man who had attempted to seduce her and, when he failed in his aim, had sent his rogues to abduct her. She turned and looked at Captain Mardle. 'Will you help me to mount, sir, for I cannot alone.'

Captain Mardle hesitated for a moment and then dismounted, caught the bridle of Thomas's horse and began to lead it towards her. He had almost reached her when the sound of horses being driven at speed made everyone looked towards the newcomer. In that instant, the masked man made a mistake for he turned to glance at the oncoming vehicle and, as he did so, a shot rang out. Madeline was aware that the shot had come from Captain Mardle. He was standing so close to her that she felt the breeze as the ball passed her cheek. It hit the highwayman full in the chest and he gave a cry of disbelief, then pitched sideways and fell from his horse at Madeline's feet. She moved back, a startled cry of warning leaving her lips as the second man swung round to point his pistol at them. He seemed to hesitate, but then as someone jumped down from the newly arrived chaise and fired in his direction, he turned his horse and fled across the Heath towards a stand of trees.

Captain Mardle dropped to his knees and pulled the mask from the face of the man he'd shot. He gave a cry of astonishment and looked up at Madeline.

'This is the Marquis of Rochdale,' he said. 'I thought him a common highwayman...'

'He wanted to abduct me,' Madeline said. 'I must thank you for saving me, sir. This is not the first time he has attempted to harm me.'

'I knew him for a rogue, but this…'

'Is he dead?' The newcomer had arrived. He glanced down at the marquis with contempt and then at Madeline, before addressing Captain Mardle. 'It was fortunate that you were here, sir. This man was a vile seducer and has threatened this lady too many times.'

'Indeed, I know what an evil man he was for he harmed a lady who was dear to me,' Captain Mardle said. 'It was my intention to demand satisfaction for it—but I never intended this.' His face was very pale. 'But I shall admit my fault and take the consequences.'

'I pray you, sir, do not speak of fault,' Madeline said. 'All of us here will bear witness that you shot in defence of me. You will speak for Captain Mardle, will you not, Hal?'

'Indeed I shall, sir. I am glad to meet you. In my opinion you have acted just as you ought and I am eternally grateful, as we all must be.' He shook Captain Mardle warmly by the hand. 'I might have arrived too late had you not acted so bravely.'

'It was your arrival that gave me the chance

for he looked to see who had come upon us and in that instant I fired.'

'Then I am glad to have been of some use.'

There was a note in his voice that made Madeline look at him and what she saw caused her to feel as if she wanted to weep.

'Excuse me, I must help Sally,' Madeline said. 'I see that Thomas has recovered consciousness. I must help her get him into the carriage for he needs a doctor.'

'Allow me to assist him,' Captain Mardle murmured and moved away.

Madeline stood immobile, gazing up at Hal. He looked angry, his eyes cold, his mouth set in a hard line. She hardly knew how to speak but knew that she must apologise.

'This is all my fault,' she whispered. 'I should not—'

'No,' Hal said harshly, 'you should not. Why did you run away like that? Without a word to me?'

'You did not receive my letter?'

He looked at her hard. 'Adam spoke of a letter to Jenny, but made no mention of a letter to me.'

'Oh…' Madeline shook her head. She could not know why Adam had not told him, but she was for the moment relieved. 'I—I did not wish to bring shame on your friends or—or to ruin you.'

'Was that all?' he asked. 'Surely you must have known what could happen? Did you not think of the risk you ran? I have been out of my mind with worry.'

'Forgive me,' she begged, and now there were tears on her cheeks. 'I never meant to hurt or distress you or your friends.'

The stern line of his mouth softened a little. 'That is what I told Adam. He blamed himself for he thought you must have overheard us talking in the library the previous night.'

Madeline turned away. 'Yes, I did,' she admitted. 'I did not wish you to give up everything you cared for me when…when I am not certain I could welcome you as a wife ought.'

Hal's hands were on her shoulders. He turned her to face him.

'What are you saying? Do you not wish to marry me?'

'I love you,' Madeline whispered. 'I am…'

'My lady, we are waiting,' Captain Mardle's cry broke her thoughts. 'Your servant needs urgent attention for he is bleeding and once more unconscious.'

'I must go,' Madeline said. 'I cannot desert Sally when Thomas is hurt. They have both been so good to me.'

'Yes, you must go with them. You go to your London house?'

'Yes. We sent a messenger yesterday and they will be expecting us.'

'Very well, I shall follow you, as soon as this unpleasant business has been reported to the proper authorities.'

'Please…we must talk again?'

'I shall come to your house, Madeline. This must be settled between us.'

'Yes, I know,' she whispered. 'Forgive me.'

Leaving him to return to his own vehicle, she walked over to her chaise and was helped in by Captain Mardle, who then returned to Hal.

'I must report this business to the nearest magistrate, sir.'

'I shall come with you,' Hal told him. 'My groom will place the body in the chaise and I'll ride Thomas's horse. I would not have you suffer from what you did this night, sir. You saved a lady I care for from great harm. I understand that you, too, had reason to wish this devil dead—perhaps you would honour me with your confidence as we ride?'

'He caused a lady I love to suffer shame and much distress—and he murdered a good man,' Captain Mardle said. 'I would have called him out, but the rogue who died this night deserved no better than he received.'

'I perfectly agree with you,' Hal said and smiled. 'And that is exactly what I shall tell the magistrate.'

He mounted his horse and together they followed the chaise as it was driven back to town.

Madeline knocked and then entered the room where Thomas was lying in bed attended by Sally, who had so far refused to leave him. Madeline had changed her gown and drunk a dish of tea, though she could eat none of the cold chicken and thin bread and butter the chef had sent up to try to tempt her appetite.

Arriving at the house, she had been surprised at the warmth of her reception. Having sent a messenger on ahead, her servants were apprised of her coming. The butler and housekeeper were waiting in the hall with a full array of servants to greet her as their rightful mistress. Madeline had expected they would obey her, but had not expected to receive such warm care for her comfort. It seemed that they bore no malice for the loss of their former master and were eager to serve her.

Now, she approached the bed softly. In the light of the candles, she could see Thomas was sleeping as Sally sat beside the bed to watch over him.

'My lady...' Sally began.

'No, do not get up,' Madeline said and smiled at her. 'I just came to see how he was and to ask if you needed anything. Why do you not let one of the maids attend him while you rest for a while?'

'I cannot leave him yet, my lady,' Sally said, her voice caught with tears. 'At first I thought he was dead; then he seemed to rally but, as you know, he fainted again. Doctor Broome said it was from loss of blood. His wound was not deep for the ball merely scraped his shoulder, but we could not stop the bleeding for an age.'

'I know,' Madeline said and handed her a clean kerchief. 'But Dr Broome removed the ball and said he would recover. It is merely the fever we have to watch for. I could watch over him while you have a rest—if you wished?'

'You are kind to offer, my lady,' Sally

said, 'but I shall not leave him until I know he is safe.'

'Of course. I understand. You love him so very much, do you not?'

'Very much,' Sally said and wiped away a tear. 'He has asked me to marry him so many times and I've begged him to wait—but if he lives I shall marry him as soon as it may be arranged.'

'I am glad for you,' Madeline said. 'Do not lose hope, my very good friend. I believe Thomas will recover. He is a strong man and he has you. Why should he give in when he has so much to live for?'

'Thank you.' Sally smiled at her, and then, at a slight sound from the bed, she turned back to her patient. 'Thomas…are you awake?'

'Sally?'

Madeline heard his voice and touched Sally's hand. 'Go to him. I shall see you later. Ask for anything you need.'

She went out of the bedroom and walked along the landing to the room she'd asked her maids to prepare for her. Her old room had too many unhappy memories and she preferred what had been the best guest chamber. Once she knew that this house belonged to her she would sell it and find a new house.

The marquis had claimed that Lethbridge owed him a huge sum of money, but he was dead. If he had an heir, that heir would no doubt claim what was owed in time. Madeline would pay what was asked if she could… but these things were for the future. All she wanted now was to see Hal, to speak to him…to explain what had driven her to run away from him.

She was not sure that he would forgive her, but perhaps he might understand why she was afraid that she could never be the wife he deserved.

She had hoped he might come to her that night, but it was now early in the morning and she was sure he would not visit at this hour for he would imagine her to have sought her bed long ago. She must rest and then tomorrow…she would see what the morning would bring.

As she entered her room one of the maids was waiting to attend her.

'Good evening, Maria. I am sorry to have kept you up so late.'

'I know you were concerned for Thomas and Sally,' the girl said. 'How is he, my lady?'

'A little better I think,' Madeline said and sighed. 'I see you have put out my nightgown.

Thank you, I can mange if you unfasten the hooks at the back of my gown.'

She stood as the girl attended her, then told her to go to bed. Sitting in the light of the candles, she brushed her hair and gazed into the mirror.

What would she do with her life now that she was free? If Hal no longer cared for her... She had run away from him and he must think her a tiresome creature. She'd seen how angry he was when he came upon them on the Heath. At first he'd looked at her as if he hated her, though he had softened to her at the last—but had she killed his love for her?

Madeline shook her head. It was no use in chastising herself. She was tired. She would go to bed and think about this in the morning.

A maid drawing back the curtains and letting the light flood into the room startled Madeline. She blinked for she had been sleeping and it was unlike Sally to draw her curtains before she rang. Pushing herself up against the pillows, she looked at the girl.

'Why have you woken me like this?'

'Mr Henry told me to wake you, my lady. He says it is important—there's a person asking to see you.'

'A person—what kind of person?'

'Mr Henry thought him impertinent, my lady, for he demanded to see you immediately—and at this hour.'

Madeline glanced at the clock on her dressing chest and saw it was almost ten. She frowned for she was unused to being demanded at such an early hour, especially by persons unknown to her.

'I shall dress and come down,' Madeline said. 'Leave my breakfast for I shall eat in the breakfast parlour when my business is finished and then return to my room to change.'

With the help of the maid, she slipped on a simple morning gown, brushed her hair and curled it up under a fetching lace cap. Leaving the girl to set out the gown she wished to wear later, she went downstairs to the front parlour where the visitor was waiting. A man dressed in a shabby black coat and grey breeches was standing by the empty fireplace. He looked round as she entered the room.

'Lady Lethbridge,' he said. 'John Hedges at your service, clerk to Sir Anthony Ironbridge, Magistrate and Justice of the Peace. I must apologise for disturbing you at this early hour, but the gentlemen were most insistent that you would wish it once you knew the purpose of my visit.'

'Of whom are you speaking?'

He referred to a small notebook. 'I am given their names as Major Ravenscar and Captain Mardle—do you know these gentlemen, my lady—and were you there on the Heath when a shooting took place last evening?'

'Yes, of course,' she said. 'Has it not been explained to you what happened? An attempt to rob and kidnap me was made. The rogue had his pistol trained on us, as did his accomplice. I was ordered to ride the horse that my footman had been riding; he lay bleeding on the ground, shot by the highwayman. Captain Mardle was ordered to get down to assist me, but it was only when Major Ravenscar arrived on the scene unexpectedly that he had the chance to shoot at the highwayman. He saved my life and I am very grateful.'

'Yet the man killed was the Marquis of Rochdale. Your account matches that of the gentlemen, my lady—but why would a man of such social standing attempt to abduct a lady such as yourself?'

'I have no idea,' Madeline said coldly. 'He had shown an unpleasant interest in me, which I rebuffed. I believe if you enquire into his reputation you may find that he is not all you might think. He shot my footman who was riding with us and the poor man lies in bed in this house. He is lucky to be alive for he lost a great deal of blood.'

'May I speak with this man?'

'Thomas may be sleeping, but if he is awake and has no objection…' Madeline raised her eyebrows, giving him an imperious look. 'Do you doubt my word, sir? This is not the first time this man has tried to abduct me. Have you questioned the post boys and driver of my hired chaise?'

'They had already left town. It was your testimony Sir Anthony required. No, I do not doubt you, my lady,' he said. 'I shall return to my master and give him your account of the incident and I am sure he will arrange to have the gentlemen set at liberty.'

'What? Have they spent the night in the cells? This is outrageous! They rescued my maid and injured footman, and me from a vile rogue—and their reward is to be locked up for coming to report the incident? Such injustice is to be deplored. I shall certainly speak to the Prince Regent, who has been a friend to me, about this matter.'

'Oh, no, my lady. I am sure it will not be necessary,' Mr Hedges said, his neck brick red. 'I shall assure my master that everything is in order—and I do beg your pardon for disturbing you.'

'I trust that my friends will be released immediately.' She was at her haughtiest and Mr Hedges bowed low as he left her.

Torn between anger and laughter, Madeline went into the breakfast room and served herself from the silver chafing dishes with a little kedgeree and soft rolls. She drank a dish of coffee with cream and sugar and then left the parlour. On her way to her own chamber, she knocked at Thomas's door and was pleased to hear his voice answer.

Entering, she saw that he was now fully conscious and sitting propped up against a pile of pillows.

'My lady,' he said and pulled the covers over his bare chest. 'Forgive me, I did not imagine that you… I thought it was Sally or one of the maids.'

Madeline smiled. 'Do not feel awkward, Thomas. I have much to thank you and Sally for and I am sorry that you should have been injured because of me.'

'Yours was not the blame,' Thomas said.

'Sally told me that Captain Mardle killed the marquis. It was well done of him for it sets you free of his threats, my lady—but I hope he will not find himself on the wrong side of the law.'

'You may be asked to testify for him when you are well again,' Madeline said. 'I've had a visit from the magistrate's clerk this morning and I gave him my account of the affair. I hope that Major Ravenscar and Captain Mardle will be exonerated of all blame and free to continue their lives very soon.'

'I shall be very willing to tell anyone who wishes to know, my lady. That devil cared not whether he killed in cold blood and if he were not dead, I should wish to see him hang for his crimes.'

'I came just to see how you went on,' Madeline said. 'I shall leave you to rest and I'm sure Sally will be here soon.'

'I made her seek some rest,' Thomas said, 'for she sat with me all night and I told her she would be ill if she did not lie down for a while.'

'She was worried for you, but she is relieved of her duties and free to nurse you, Thomas—and I hope we shall soon have a wedding to cheer us all. I mean to give you a handsome present and I hope you will invite me.'

'Sally wouldn't dream of anything else,' he said. 'We'll be living in London, my lady, and you will always be welcome in our house.'

Madeline thanked him and went away. She returned to her own room where she found warm water in a can.

Some half an hour later, having washed and dressed in a fresh morning gown of grey silk trimmed with pink braid, she was on her way downstairs when Mr Henry informed her that a gentleman was waiting in the parlour to see her.

'Not Mr Hedges again I hope?'

'No, my lady. Mr Symonds is—or was, I might say—the count's lawyer. He asked if we would let him know as soon as we heard from you. I took the liberty of letting him know you were home and he called round in the hope of seeing you—but he says if it is not convenient he can call again whenever you choose.'

'I shall see him now,' Madeline said. 'Thank you for letting him know. It was my intention to send for him this morning.'

The butler nodded and preceded her to the

parlour, where he flung open the door and announced her.

Madeline entered to see a gentleman very correctly dressed in a grey morning coat and breeches with a pristine white shirt and a black cravat held by a modest gold pin. He was an elderly man with greying hair, but his eyes were a piercing blue. He had been seated in a solid mahogany elbow chair, but stood up at once and bowed to her.

'Countess. A pleasure to see you. I trust my visit does not inconvenience you, ma'am?'

'No, not at all, sir. It was my intention to contact you this morning and ask you to call. My husband's unfortunate demise has left me in something of a dilemma. I am not certain of my situation.'

'On that I can put your mind at rest immediately,' Mr Symonds said. 'Your settlement is intact for that could not be touched. Your late husband's estate in the country is heavily mortgaged and I have received a foreclosure from the bank. Unfortunately, there will be nothing left after the estate is sold. This house is free of debt, but there are some small tradesmen's bills to be paid. I have received a claim for five thousand pounds for a gambling debt. There are insufficient funds in the count's bank to pay this, but you may know of some further funds—or you may choose not to pay it.'

'If the debt has been proven you should pay it,' Madeline said. 'I am not sure what my settlement was—perhaps you could enlighten me?'

'You have capital of ten thousand pounds, which is invested in the ten per cents, ma'am. Your income for the past several years was hardly touched and has accrued to another four thousand pounds, which is in a separate bank account in your name.'

'So I am not penniless.' Madeline nodded. She had expected the news to be something of this nature and was not dismayed. 'My servants must be paid what they are owed and I should like to make sure they are given another six months' wages when I close the house. They will, of course, have references. I have thought of selling this house and purchasing a smaller establishment in the country and shall take some of them with me if they wish to come. Do you know what I might expect to receive for a property like this?'

'I imagine it might fetch ten or possibly twelve thousand pounds—the contents perhaps upwards of ten thousand, my lady. Some of the pictures and heirlooms may be worth more, but would need to be valued before they were sold.'

'Yes, I imagine so.' Madeline frowned for the marquis had claimed that he was owed twenty-five-thousand pounds. 'Are there any other debts?'

'None that have come to my hand as yet.' He frowned, hesitating for a moment, then, 'Are you sure you wish to settle the gambling debt? Such debts are sometimes written off when the debtor dies.'

'Once the house and contents are sold, I shall pay all those debts I can,' Madeline said. 'There are some jewels that might be sold if need be—may I rely on you to handle that for me?'

'Certainly, but do not include anything that was given to you personally, my lady. Your jewels are your own, though heirlooms are of course part of the estate…but I can see no reason why you should need to sell unless you wish. I have advertised in the newssheets and no one else has come forward to make a claim.'

'Perhaps they will not,' Madeline said and smiled. 'It seems you have done just as you ought while I was away. I thank you for your care of my affairs, sir.'

'I am honoured to serve you, ma'am.' He hesitated, then, 'I wished to make your settlement available to you on your marriage, but was told it was not necessary. I suppose the income accrued will be of some use now. I am sorry I cannot give you better news of your husband's affairs.' He cleared his throat. 'I've heard unfortunate rumours of the count's gambling, but have squashed them wherever possible.'

'You have done just as you ought,' Madeline said and smiled at him. 'Please make certain that there are sufficient funds to pay your own account. I shall give you certain heirlooms that I have no use for so that we have funds available for any unforeseen debt.'

'Why not wait and see what is needed?'

'No, if the jewels are mine I shall sell them for I do not intend to live the kind of life that will require the more elaborate pieces. I have some with me—and if you will wait I shall bring them down to you. The remainder are elsewhere.'

'I am at your service, my lady.'

'I shall not be a moment.'

Madeline left him and went up to her room.

She unlocked her travelling box and removed a set of sapphires that she had thought she might sell if she'd followed her intention of setting up as a seamstress. Taking them back downstairs, she discovered that Mr Symonds was no longer alone. Her heart caught when she saw Hal, but he was frowning and she kept the rush of gladness that surged through her to herself, merely inclining her head to him.

'Hal…Major Ravenscar, I trust you are feeling better now,' she said in a cool manner that gave no hint of her feeling. 'This is the set I would have you sell for me, Mr Symonds. Please place whatever it may fetch in the bank and…' She had opened the box for him to see and was surprised at his reaction. 'Is something wrong?'

'I fear I have more bad news for you,' her lawyer said, looking grave. 'The count asked me to sell that particular parure and some others a year or so back. He had copies made…and I fear these are merely paste. They are excellent copies but worth very little, perhaps a few pounds.'

'I see…' Madeline was shocked. 'Did my husband sell many of the family heirlooms?'

'He sold an emerald-and-diamond tiara,

this set and, I believe a valuable ruby necklace. Those are the only things I was asked to have copied and then sell—though he might have sold others elsewhere.'

'I see.' Madeline laughed. 'I was never allowed to keep the jewels in my rooms. I thought my husband feared they would be stolen, but perhaps he feared I would discover they were worthless.'

'I shall take my leave now.' Mr Symonds bowed his head to her and then to Hal. 'I am glad to have met you, sir. If you will excuse me…'

He left the room and silence fell for some seconds, then Madeline said, 'I am sorry you should have spent an uncomfortable night.'

'I've spent worse when with the army,' he said, his tone matching hers in coolness. 'Thank you for seeing the magistrate's clerk at such an early hour, Madeline. I am sorry to have disturbed you, but we needed your help.'

'I believe Sir Anthony may have found it difficult to believe that Lord Rochdale had held up my carriage in the guise of a highwayman. I suppose it might be thought unusual for a man of his standing to do such a reckless thing.'

'He might be a marquis, but that does not

make him a gentleman,' Hal said harshly. 'I wanted to let you know for I thought you might be concerned. When Sir Anthony heard our story himself, and his man agreed you had confirmed it, he apologised for the way we had been inconvenienced.'

'As he should,' Madeline said. 'I thought it outrageous that you and Captain Mardle should have been treated so ill when all you did was save me from an evil rogue.'

'Well, you are finally free of the marquis and your husband.' Hal's mouth was set in a hard line as he studied her. 'May I ask what you intend to do now?'

'I shall need to sell this house and most of the contents for there are debts to pay. Rochdale claimed he was owed twenty-five thousand, which I fear I could not pay.'

'Nor should you,' Hal said. 'It is likely that he cheated Rochdale at the tables—and even if he did not, he is dead. Let the debt die with him.'

'I want nothing that belonged to Lethbridge,' Madeline said. 'My grandfather's settlement is intact and will suffice for my needs. I shall leave the sale of what remains to Mr Symonds and retire to a small house in the country. He may deal with any claims that come on the estate. My servants must be recompensed when the house is closed and after that.' She shrugged. 'I do not care what becomes of the rest of it.'

'And what of me…of us?' Hal asked, a nerve twitching in his throat. 'I thought you loved me, Maddie. But now I am not sure. You ran away from me without a word…why did you do that if you cared for me?'

'I did not wish to drag you down with me. Rochdale would have ruined us both if he could.'

Hal seized her by the arms, gazing down into her face. She saw anger and hurt in his eyes and her throat tightened with emotion.

'I'm sorry, Hal. I never meant to hurt you.'

'I thought I should die of the wound you inflicted when you wed him,' he said. 'For a time I hoped I should be killed in battle. It was my cousins who brought me through.'

'Forgive me…' Tears were burning behind her eyes. 'I believed I had no choice. I have regretted it so many times.'

'If you heard Adam question me that night, it was because he knew that I had suffered the first time and he feared it might destroy me if you hurt me again. Is that why you left me, Maddie? Tell me, I beg you, for I have been in agony since I learned you'd gone. If you do not care for me, tell me now and let us be done.'

'Oh, Hal,' Madeline said and the tears began to trickle down her cheeks. 'I have always loved you b—'

She got no further for he crushed her against him, bending his head to kiss her fiercely on the lips. His kiss was filled with a desperate need and hunger that she could not help but know for desire. Yet she found herself pressing her body closer, felt the heat rising from within her and knew that she wanted him to go on kissing her. She wanted to be held for ever in just this way. She had feared that she would freeze and shrink away when he demanded intimacy of her, but suddenly she knew that she could never feel revulsion for anything Hal did to her. It was Lethbridge's coarse, brutal treatment of her that had made her shrink away, but even in the midst of his passion, Hal was tender and his love caressed and coaxed rather than took. She slipped her arms up about his neck and kissed him back, her lips parting as his tongue explored and flicked at hers in a way that made her tingle and want to melt into his body.

'Oh, Hal, I was afraid…' she said and now she was laughing and crying at the same time. 'But you have been so sweet to me, so loving that you have banished what he did… the shame he made me feel…'

'You should never feel shame,' Hal murmured and stroked her hair as she buried her face in his shoulder. 'You were innocent and sweet when he forced marriage on you. I vow that I will never force or hurt you, my love. You have only to ask me to stop and I would let you go.'

The tears were trickling down her cheeks so that she tasted their salt. 'I feared I could not be a proper wife to you and I did not want you to give up everything you cared for, for my sake. I thought you would become bitter and hate me if I could not…but I can,' she said and gulped back her tears as he wiped them from her cheeks with his fingertips. 'I love you, Hal. I do want to be your wife so very much.'

'Then we shall be married as soon as I can arrange it,' he said and smiled. 'Be damned to the gossips and those who censure us may do so. We shall have friends who accept us and I dare say we shall not often come to town, for my estate is small and I fear we must live the life of a country gentleman and his wife.'

'It is all I want,' Madeline told him, smiling through the tears. 'I shall let Mr Symonds save what he can from Lethbridge's estate and it shall be put aside for our children. If amongst the jewels I left at Ravenscar there are any worth selling, they may be sold for I shall need only the pearls that came from my grandmother.'

'I have some pieces that my grandmother left to me,' Hal told her. 'All I have is yours and I own I would rather not keep anything that belonged to your husband.'

'We shall not,' Madeline promised. 'Our children may inherit what there is, but we shall do very well on your estate. To be your wife is all that I care for, my love.'

'If I have you, I am richer than any man deserves to be,' Hal said and bent his head to kiss her once more. 'I can hardly wait for our wedding day, my love.'

Afterword

'It was so good of you to give us the reception here,' Madeline said as Jenny entered the bedchamber where she was dressing for her wedding. 'I do not think I deserve it after I ran away and caused you all so much distress.'

'Adam told me it was his fault. You heard him question Hal's wisdom in giving up his estate to go abroad, and he should not have doubted you—as I soon told him. You are my friend, Maddie, and I am glad that everything has turned out well for you after all.'

'I never thought I could be so happy. Lethbridge was not a kind man. I believed I could never give myself to anyone, not even Hal— but I saw how happy you were, Jenny, and

Hal was so tender and gentle. I did not know it, but my stay here helped me to recover my pride and forget my shame, and now I cannot wait to be Hal's wife.'

'There can be no shame where love is,' Jenny said and smiled. 'To love and be loved is more pleasure than I could ever describe in mere words. Trust Hal for he is a good man and would never willingly hurt you—and if you fear anything tell him.'

'Yes, I shall, though I do not think I shall fear anything in his arms. We have not stopped at kisses.' She blushed as her friend laughed. 'I did not wish to wait for I wanted to be sure that I was not a shrinking violet on my wedding night, though we have not… lain together. Yet from his touch and the way I felt, I know now that there is much happiness to be found with the man you love.'

'Yes, there is. You look beautiful,' Jenny said. 'Hal will think himself lucky to have you, Maddie. I hope you will both visit us whenever you can spare the time.'

'We shall, you may depend on it—and you must come to us.'

Sally entered the room then, bearing Madeline's bouquet of lilies and roses dressed with lace and ribbons. Her wedding to Thomas had been a simple one before they left London, but although she would return to her husband's inn after the wedding reception, she had wanted to dress her former mistress one last time. She was to be a maid of honour and carry the train of Madeline's shimmering ivory gown.

'You do look lovely, my lady,' Sally said and handed her the flowers. 'I am so glad I have seen you—you look so happy.'

'I am. Thank you both for helping me. I am ready and we should go down now, because I do not wish to keep Hal waiting.'

Hal turned his head to watch as his bride approached down the long nave of the ancient church. She looked so regal and beautiful in her gown of satin and lace and he caught his breath. Was she truly here or was it just another of the dreams that had haunted him for years?

She came to stand by his side, then turned her head to smile at him. His breath caught and he felt a surge of love and joy. Her bonnet of blue satin was trimmed with ribbons of ivory with silk roses stitched under the brim, the colour of the satin setting off the greener shade of her eyes. She looked pale and he wondered, but then she smiled up at him and his heart sang, because he saw the joy in her eyes. She had longed for this day as much as he had and she had overcome her fears, trusting in him to love her and cherish her for the rest of their lives. He smiled at her, feeling the love flow between them. She was truly his at last and he knew that happiness awaited them.

As the vicar began to intone the marriage ceremony, Hal reached for his bride's hand and held it firmly. She was his and he would care for her and protect her for the rest of his life.

The sun was shining through a high window, sending showers of colour through the stained glass on to the flagstones. A surge of happiness went through Hal as he glanced sideways at his bride. He wanted her, desired her, but most of all he wanted to make her happy.

Lord Ravenscar had made the dower house available to them for their first night together. Everywhere had been polished, fires lit and vases of flowers placed in every room. The chef at Ravenscar had sent down some delicious food for them and it was laid out in the small breakfast parlour, the candles arranged to give an intimate atmosphere. Maddie's new maid had fussed around her, arranging her skirts in the carriage so that they would not crease and making sure that she had all she needed. She was even now upstairs in the bedchamber they would share, laying out her nightgown and making sure it was perfect.

Hal smiled at Maddie as she touched the silver horseshoes tied with ribbons, the small gifts that awaited them and the pretty flower arrangements on the table that held the tempting buffet.

'Is everything as you would wish, my love?'

She turned to him, lifting her eyes to his with a shy smile. 'Everyone has done so much. This is perfect, Hal—but I should not have cared if it had been a modest room in an inn. I have you and that is all I want.'

'Will you have some wine, my love?'

'I believe I've had enough,' she murmured and moved towards him, lifting her face for his kiss. 'I am ready to go up, Hal. I want to be completely alone with you—sure that no one will intrude.'

'Go up, then, and send your maid away when you are ready. I shall come to you as soon as I've seen that the house is locked for the night.'

'Yes…' She gave a little gurgle of laughter. 'That sounds as if we have been married for ever.'

'Do not imagine I am not as impatient as you,' he said and the fire leaped in his eyes. 'But I want to give you time to be ready.'

Maddie nodded, leaned forwards and kissed him lightly on the mouth, then turned and left the room. She went slowly up the stairs, her mind reviewing the reception with her friends; more of them had come to wish her well than she would ever have expected. So many lovely gifts had been sent to them that Madeline thought it would take her many days to reply and thank them all. She seemed almost to float on air and could not help humming a little tune as she entered her bedroom.

'I have laid out the lace nightgown, my lady,' Maria said. 'I hope this is the one you meant?'

'Yes, it is,' she said and smiled at the girl. 'If you will help me to undress and then leave me, please.'

'Yes, my lady. At what time would you like me to dress you in the morning?'

'I shall ring when I need you.'

Maddie stepped out of her gown and then stood as the girl unlaced her bodice. A lovely filmy white nightgown was slipped over her head, and the pins taken from her hair, but when Maria offered to brush her hair she shook her head.

'I can manage now, thank you,' she said. 'You may go to bed. I shall not need you again tonight.'

Maria curtsied, wished her happiness and went from the room, a little smile on her lips as she turned away.

Madeline began to brush her hair as the door closed behind the maid. It was a little strange not to have Sally waiting on her, but she would get used to it in time. She enjoyed the feel of the brush on her hair and had stroked it several times when the door opened and Hal entered. He was wearing a long dressing robe of dark-blue velvet and his feet were bare. As he approached she caught the smell of soap and knew that he had washed his face and shaved before coming to her.

'I am not too soon?' he asked hesitantly. 'You know that I am prepared to wait until...'

'There is nothing more to wait for,' she said and moved towards him. She slipped her arms about his waist, lifting her gaze to his. 'I love you, Hal. You are not Lethbridge. I love you and I trust you. Please make love to me. It is what I want—to be yours, to be your wife and to love you forever.'

Madeline woke slowly to a feeling of well being. She smiled as the memories of Hal kissing her, of his lips lingering in the most intimate places, came filtering back into her mind like sunbeams of pleasure. She had never known that she could feel this way... never known that her body could sing and cry out for more. She had been swept away on a wave of desire and sensual pleasure, reaching such heights as they loved that she'd cried out, her nails scoring his shoulder as she shuddered and moaned with need. All the love she'd shut away inside her for years poured out, welcoming this man who had taught her to feel again. She clung to him and wept when the storm of passion had settled and then laughed at his anxious face as he wiped away her tears, reassuring him that they were tears of happiness and not pain.

'You are awake,' Hal said and leaned up on his arm to gaze down into her face. 'You looked so lovely as you slept that I did not want to wake you.'

'Yes, I am awake.' She glanced towards the window and saw that sunshine was peeping through the crack. 'What time is it?'

'About eleven, I think,' he said and bent down to kiss the end of her nose. 'I kept you awake most of the night, Maddie...but you tempted me so much I could not leave you alone. I have wanted you for so long.'

'I hope you will always want me as much as you did last night,' she said and reached up to kiss him at the corner of his mouth. 'You made me so happy, Hal. I knew that I loved you, but I did not know I could feel that way...so content and secure in your arms.'

'It is the way I always want you to feel,' he murmured and bent his head to kiss the little hollow at the base of her throat. He kissed the valley between her breasts and then licked delicately at her nipples. 'You taste so good that I want to gobble you up.'

Madeline laughed, because she had never known what it was to be teased like this or to luxuriate in the warmth of a man's adoration and tender love. She trembled as his hand explored and stroked her body, feeling little flickers of desire shoot through her once more. She could feel the heat between her thighs and the moisture as her body welcomed him to her again, lifting her hips to allow him to ease into her, his smooth hardness filling her in a way that brought no pain, but only aching delight and pleasure that grew and grew until it exploded inside her.

Afterwards, they lay in each other's arm, talking and laughing, remembering that time when they were young and forgetting the hurt that had kept them apart so long.

And when at last they rose and Madeline rang for her maid, while Hal went away to wash and shave, she knew the true meaning of happiness at last. After eating a light nuncheon they would leave for Hal's estate in Cambridgeshire, for Madeline had wanted to begin her new life at once.

'I have clothes enough,' she told Hal when he'd asked where she would like to go for her honeymoon. 'Why should I need a trip to Paris to buy more? I would rather spend the money on curtains and things for our home—and then perhaps another year, if we can afford it, we shall go on a little trip somewhere. If not to Paris, to Scotland or even to the coast of Cornwall, which I hear is very wild but beautiful in summer.'

'We could have a wedding trip if you wished,' Hal told her. 'My mother's brother has written to me. He tells me that I am to be his heir, because his son died in an accident, and asked that I should bring you to meet him in a few weeks. It is like to be some years before we inherit, but I am content to be a country gentleman, if you are content to be the wife of a gentleman farmer?'

'Quite content, my love,' she said, 'but I should like to meet your uncle for he must be lonely having lost his family—and I should like to share a little of our happiness.'

'And we shall have plenty to share,' he said and kissed her again.

* * * * *

Special Offers

Every month we put together collections and longer reads written by your favourite authors.

Here are some of next month's highlights— and don't miss our fabulous discount online!

On sale 7th February   On sale 17th January   On sale 7th February

Save 20%
on all Special Releases

The Regency Ballroom Collection

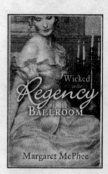